HAUNTED SOU

HAUNTED SOUL

THE CURSE OF THE BLACK SKULL

DR. LOUIS BERNARD ANTOINE

HAUNTED SOUL: The Curse of The Black Skull

1846 E Innovation Park Dr STE 100 Oro Valley, AZ 85755
1-855-674-2878 | info@stonehengeliterary.com

Stonehenge Literary and Media is committed to excellence in the publishing industry.

Published in the United States of America

ISBN: 978-1-0882-1433-6
eISBN: 978-1-0882-1439-8

O quanta sunt, quod nescitis!

(Oh, how much there still is which you do not know!)

(Hermetic ABC of the Philosopher's Stone)

I love him who liveth in order to know, and seeketh to know in order that the Superman may hereafter live.

(Thus spake Zarathustra., Nietzsche, Friedrich)

Dedicated to the memory of those that our mortal eyes can no longer see!

To my father whom I hardly knew!

To my mother who waited until the job was done, days after my postgraduate training was completed to be" promoted first assistant to God!"

And to you Lizette, my sister and soulmate! The world will never be the same without you. You took the final trip to the Great Beyond without saying goodbye.

But, somewhere in the heavens amongst the twinkle of the stars, we feel your presence!

Dedicated to the living!

All of those whose love and affection we share, especially my wife Ivy and my children: Ti Ben, Donnell, and Renee.

To my brothers Michelet and Georges-Yvon, and my sisters Andrea, and Gladys on whom I could always count for words of encouragement.

ACKNOWLEDGMENTS

Special thanks to Marie-Yves Collins for her technical advice about the Voodoo ceremonies.

Scripture quotations are taken from the Holy Bible, New Living Translation, copyright 1996. Used by permission of Tyndale House Publishers, Inc. Wheaton, Illinois 60189.

INTRODUCTION

"I've studied now Philosophy

And Jurisprudence, Medicine,

And even, alas! Theology

All through and through with ardour keen!

Here now I stand, poor fool, and see

I'm just as wise as formerly. "

Faust by Goethe,

It has been over forty years since I came to this country, an immigrant from Haiti. My training in Western bio-medicine both as a pediatrician and a psychiatrist has granted me the privilege to touch many lives. Some of my younger patients have become adults and achieved their dreams as young fathers, young mothers, college students, and established professionals Others have returned to their re-arranged families as fathers or stepfathers, mothers or stepmothers, or to professions they love...as lawyers, nurses, interior decorators, storekeepers, social workers, bankers, CEO's and housewives. They have shared their world with me. As a result, my worldview has been immensely enriched. They have left my office as changed individuals with a new take on life, full of hope that they too, can achieve their goals. Some, alas, were willing or able to give up demons they knew for the ones they did not know. They have represented all the different cultures and sub-cultures, all the races, ethnic groups, and sexual or political orientations that make our community rich and strong. The therapeutic relationships we have forged have been very rewarding. Through them, I have become familiar with the many facets of the American culture. I am grateful. Any one of my patients could be the hero of this fictional novel. But I will not write about them. I will leave it up to my Anglo-American colleagues to tell their stories. Instead, I have chosen to write Jacques' story. Like my patients, Jacques had to confront his demons, his phantasms that wanted to keep him from achieving his lifetime goals. Like my patients, Jacques started with a very heavy burden on his shoulder, a seemingly insurmountable challenge, a curse. His problems mimicked those of my patients who expose their broken dreams, their fear, their losses, and the sequela of sexual trauma... Jacques comes with a recurring heartbreaking and tormenting dream together with a history of incurable seizure disorder leading to a life of underachievement, sexual dissatisfaction, and frustration. Unlike my patients, Jacques, with my help, is being allowed to tell his story as seen through his own eyes.

Why is he so lucky? Why? ...

Because like me, Jacques is Haitian-American...

Ladies and gentlemen, meet Jacques Gaetan!

PART I

TORMENTED SOUL,

SHATTERED MIND...

Pass, wretched band! Well for the wakeful one, if, riotously miserable, a fiercer tribe does not surround him, the devils of a guilty heart that holds its hell within itself...

Haunted Mind, Nathaniel Hawthorne

Chapter 1

"In visions of the dark night

I have dreamed of joy departed-

But a waking dream of life and light

Hath left me broken-hearted..."

(A Dream by Edgar Allan Poe)

Jacques Gaetan is 44-year-old. His hair has started to turn grey. After all, he comes from a family where the male members turn grey and bald at a very young age. He has developed a protuberant belly very quickly, and no longer looks like the svelte and athletic young man with an unstoppable left shot when he used to play in the junior soccer league back home. He was born in Roche-a-Bateau, a small coastal town of twenty-five hundred inhabitants of the Southern peninsula of Haiti. His great-grandfather was Giraud Gaetan who was by far the most famous member of the family. This man with an affable demeanor worked as a custom agent for decades. He then became a judge. He was on his way to become the mayor of the town when he suddenly died. He had his eyes on the mayoral seat. Almost every month, Jacques was told, Grandpa Giraud would don his Dacron grey suit, his well-starched white shirt, and his oversized silk tie to make the three-hundred-mile trip to the capital city. Upon his return, everyone would come around and listen to his embellished tales about the notables that he had met. Grandpa Giraud had political ambition.

His lifelong rise was about to be rewarded when he suddenly died. Rumors have it that Giraud died of a supernatural cause because of a judicial decision he had rendered. Peasants do not forgive when they feel their land has been taken away unjustly. His zombie, legend has it, still roams the corn fields and the roads of the neighboring towns at night. Some late travelers even claimed to have occasionally heard a strange mixture of sounds that were neither human nor animal disturbing the still of the night.

"Clack! Clack! Giraud Gaetan! The sound of the whip
Mwin fout di-ou Mache pi vit."

"Clack! Clack! Giraud Gaetan! Giraud Gaetan! I bid you to move faster", would yell in a threatening voice attributed to a zombie handler.

The repeated cracking of a goat skin whip would continue.

Clack! Clack! Di tout moun ki es ou ye!!" (Tell everyone who you are!), the zombie handler would order with his stern voice.

"Clack! Clack! Clack."

Then a reedy whisper that sends a quiver down any listener's spine:

"Giraud Gaetan, min map passe! ("Giraud Gaetan. Passing through)

Giraud Gaetan min map passe! (Giraud Gaetan. Passing through! ")

The voice would change into a moaning sound that could frighten even a highly trained Special Forces officer.

After all, like cows, Zombies are supposed to be peaceable, docile, and submissive. They stand somewhere between an animal and a human being. They are kept in check with a combination of timely whipping and a salt-free diet. Salt is that one ingredient that should be kept away from them at all costs, lest you want them to become human again. The reporter explained that Giraud the zombie was being hurried from one assignment to the next on different banana coves. How could Giraud Gaetan, a respectable civil servant have possibly ended up in the nether world of the zombies? What golden rules did he transgress? What powerful man or woman had he dared to take on? I guess no one will ever know.

Jacques was very much aware of his position in the family as Jacques was the oldest of 6 siblings: Raymond, Jean-Paul, Georges, Martine, and Josephine. They all now live in various parts of the world, including Canada, Switzerland, and New York. They communicate over the phone mostly on birthdays and holidays. Madam Maurice, the matriarch of the family is about sixty-two years old and lives not too far from Georges in Brooklyn, New York. Madam Maurice will not admit it but had always shown preferential treatment towards Georges, the youngest of the family. Therefore, it was not surprising that the mother decided to settle in New York.

The family had great expectations when Jacques, the firstborn of Maurice and Marie Gaetan came to the world. The Gaetan family were mostly farmers. They wake up in the wee hours of the morning, spend the day on the farm, supervising dozens of workers and get back home late in the afternoon. They own a vast swath of tillable land extending hundreds of acres in the Southern part of Haiti. They would have made a small fortune cultivating coffee and vetiver, were not for the instability of the market. At least, that is what they were told by the large exporters of crops who would come into town and get their products for next to nothing.

Jacques' future was very promising. He was always the head of his class and for sure, as his teachers used to say, he will be the pride of the family. He will be the first one to get a diploma from the State University of Haiti. His parents were encouraged by these words and did not hesitate to invest in his education. They first sent him to Les Cayes, the third city in the country, to attend private Catholic school. By the time Jacques reached adolescence, he was already contemplating the next phase of his education. He would move to Port-au-Prince, the capital to attend secondary school and the university. Jacques's head was full of dreams. He would imagine himself wearing the white coat while in medical school and becoming a neurosurgeon.

Jacques was quite gifted. He was an avid reader. At the age of twelve, he had already read most of the classic works like Les Misérables de Victor Hugo, Les Freres Karamazov de Fyodor Dostoevsky, or Gouverneurs de La Rosée de Jacques Stephen Alexis. Was young Jacques able to grasp the basic thesis of these masterpieces? Did he even understand that at birth man was entrusted with the poisoned pill of free will as argued in Dostoevsky, that believing or not believing in God was a choice as is the choice between good and evil? Was he able to catch the symbolism of the idea of getting the people of the village together to bring water to the area facing a drought after the death of the main character Manuel, killed by the very people he wanted to save? Jacques did probably get all of this. Not giving him that much would be underestimating the intelligence of this young man, precocious at best, a born philosopher who would not hesitate to engage much older adult in sophisticated debate.

One is reminded of Jesus taking on the high priests in the temple at age 12. It was not just about world literature. Jacques was a very motivated youngster who showed interest in Greek mythology and Mathematics. He was fascinated with stories about the pantheon of ancient gods that instilled fear in most children. He imagined himself navigating amongst giant animals and plants with supernatural powers. Even though Jacques was born and raised in a devout Catholic family, Jacques soon adopted a pantheistic view of the world, more in keeping with the beliefs of the original inhabitants of the lands, the Tainos, who saw gods everywhere. They prayed to the large mountains, the falls, the animals, and the sun.

If any member of the family were to be successful or become a scientist, or a scholar, it would be Jacques. He was quite inquisitive and dabbled into every aspect of science, asking questions, and spending hours on the internet, looking for answers. He was a typical nerd, a bookworm, a sort of living encyclopedia. The comments about Jacques were not always flattering. He was often the object of derision, causing him to withdraw or on occasion go into outbursts of anger. Managing his emotions was not his forte. He was called names. "Cet age est sans pitie"(This age has no mercy) wrote French fabulist Jean de La Fontaine dans "Les Deux Pigeons".

Jacques would become so nervous at times that he would start avoiding all interactions with his peers. Even though he was very bright, Jacques did not do well on tests. It took Jacques three trials before he could pass the official examination, marking the end of his secondary school. He was ready to go to the university. However, he felt exhausted and wanted to take a break. Much to the chagrin of his widowed mother. It seemed that all his grandiose plans were coming to a screeching halt. "Adieu veau, vache, cochon, couvee! " (La laitiere et le Pot au Lait, Jean de La Fontaine) What deception! What disillusion! Jacques's-confidence was shaken at its core. There was a bit of hope when his application to migrate to the United States was finally approved. There was hope, he figured, that he would pursue his studies and get treatment for his seizure. Maybe, he could still pursue his dream of going to medical school and becoming a neurosurgeon. America, after all, was the land of opportunities.

He was apprehensive about leaving his native land, but with documents in his hands, he boarded an American Airlines flight *en route* to Kennedy Airport, New York.

Things, however, were not going to be easy. He was greeted by a nasty winter. Snow was everywhere. To venture outside, he had to wear layers of clothing. How was it possible that some people were seemingly enjoying skiing and other winter sports? Jacques felt cold just looking at these revelers. Jacques's second shock was his difficulty mastering the English language. Often, he tried to conceal it, but his French accent always gave him away. Americans are not known for their patience and their tolerance for anything foreign. The deceptions in his encounter with the American culture were many. It still causes him great pain to even think about it. The dwellings were so different. Your next-door neighbors could be living a few feet away from you and you never get to talk to them. When spring came, they discovered that there was a vibrant Haitian community in Brooklyn along the Church Avenue, Flatbush, and Nostrand Ave axis. It was not like the Haitian neighborhood back home, but it was something. Loud Haitian Kompa music could be heard from the loudspeakers coming from the Haitian businesses. Displays of produce including mangoes Francique directly imported from Haiti farms were there for your delectation.

But something was just not right. An essential ingredient was missing. A "je ne sais quoi" was amiss. Jacques could not describe what he was feeling. It was like a sense of emptiness, a sense of foreboding as if his life was being put on hold. How long would Jacques be able to endure this bitter cold and the high pace life of New York and especially the feelings that he was experiencing? One winter morning, only a few days after what was described as one of the worst blizzards that ever hit New York, Jacques' decision was clear. He would move to Miami.

He heard that Miami was like a tropical paradise. He would not have to worry about the cold. Hurricane season can be deadly, but Haiti was not any different. Leaving behind his younger brother Georges and his loving mother Madam Maurice would be his only regret. Little did he know that he would be in for a rude awakening. A community is not just about the beautiful sunshine and the seemingly easy lifestyle. It is also about access to health care, social services, and a support network. Miami was still a community in flux and offers no comparison to an urban city like New York, known for its network of hospitals, its mental health system, and its support for its citizens. Jacques might live to regret this hasty decision. Call it maternal instinct or feminine intuition, Madam Maurice was not in agreement with this move. She made it clear to her older son that it did not make sense to move to a place where you hardly know anyone and where Jacques would have to start over securing doctors for the care that he needed. Madam Maurice also knew that Jacques could be very stubborn and that when he has his mind set on doing something, no one could convince him otherwise. I guess, Madam Maurice was thinking, my son would have to find out for himself. After hours of discussions with Jacques trying to dissuade him, Madam Maurice gave up and wished him well.

"Son, she said, if you have any problems, call me!

Deep in her heart, Madam Maurice knew that she would probably have to follow her son to Miami. After all, Georges seemed to have adapted well to life in New York. He was working to support his young family and they were expecting a baby in a few months.

Chapter 2

In Miami, it was a different story. The Haitian Community had just started to move out of an enclave baptized Little Haiti where the population was trying to resist being engulfed in the "American culture:" The vestiges of yesteryears America where access to certain beaches or neighborhoods were restricted, were still noticeable. Racial profiling was alive and well. Promises of economic and cultural development made in grand fanfare during campaign seasons were not kept. Haitians were getting it from all ends. Black Americans often saw Haitians as intruders. Jacques realized that the majority of African Americans were not aware of the prowess of the Haitian ancestors and how they had made the black race proud bringing their ideal of Liberty all over the world to places as far as Greece, Israel, and next door in Latin America. However, they were not to blame. He always looked different. It is not that Jacques necessarily wanted to adopt every fashion that came along. He just wanted to fit in. For some reason, he felt that people were always focusing on what was different about him. It took Jacques many winters to realize that his out-of-season worn-out leather jacket was a dead giveaway. Years after Jacques migrated to the US, he still could not understand the fascination of North Americans for Winter sports and the grief over Christmas without snowfall. And then, there was the language. For some time, Jacques felt locked out. He felt that he had so much to say, yet he could not communicate. It was as if he had turned one more time into a baby and had to babble. When he tried to express his opinion, he was often ignored. Whatever he had to say did not count, because he did not have the right intonation, the right accent. He thought he could conceal it sometimes; his French accent always gave him away. Gosh, people were so impatient! Such history was never taught in the classroom. America kept silent about the history of Haiti until after the civil rights movement of the sixties. Jacques could recite by heart, the words of the famous and immortal French fabulist, Jean de La Fontaine, describing a calamity of his time in "Les Animaux malades de la Peste." (Plague-Stricken Animals) That famous fable captured very well social behavior in situations of crisis. While the powerful members of society (the lions in the story) inevitably got exonerated from their crimes, the weakest member of society is condemned for a minute infraction. In that fable, the donkey got the blame - In America, the downtrodden Haitian got blamed for the AIDS epidemic. As the fabulist wrote "Suivant que vous soyez puissant ou miserable, les jugements de cour vous rendront Blanc ou noir." (According to whether you are powerful or lowly, the judgments of the royal court will paint you white or black). This is the stigma Jacques and all the Haitians living in America and around the globe have been carrying for the past few decades. Some social scientists will go as far as saying that the Haitians were made to pay for daring to challenge and vanquish Napoleon's army. Haiti probably representing the victorious army instead of being acclaimed with laurels and ticker tape parades, was made to pay a ransom to the loser over more than half a century, thus condemning the black nation to a life of poverty. Jacques lived with the pain and the anguish every single day of his life. Should the lovers, sons, and daughters of the victims be denied an explanation? This was a perfect example of the dangers of racism. It would be a losing battle for Jacques to try to hold on. Faust, the Goethe character, knew it all too well:

> The magic air that breathes around your shapes
> Wakes old emotions from my mouth, old shapes. . .
> All that brave company is scattered now,
> Their loud voices have long ceased echoing. . ."

Jacques' past was getting further behind him and would never come back. He often lamented about not having pursued his studies. Maybe that is why Jacques has grown to be a very bitter man. One could occasionally catch him smiling, but not for long. Jacques felt most comfortable when he was away from the crowd when he did not have to bow to the pressures of social conformity. It is not that he was disconnected from his world.

Jacques was a thinker who often ponders both the

mysteries and the problems of the world.

Jacques had to deal with his emotional issues but also with the stigma of being a "Frenchy" or belonging to a group that was blamed for propagating the AIDS epidemic. Jacques had always been taught that he should walk with his head high and bow to no one. He felt that he was being depicted in the media as a pariah, a nobody, someone that was unwanted. Jacques watched his fellow Haitians being held like cattle in immigration detention camps when everyone else seemed welcome. Jacques resented the fact that other foreigners were welcome and treated like kings, while Haitians were treated like expandable aliens.

Jacques had flashbacks about the pictures of Haitians' bodies washing off the beautiful Miami beaches and of Haitian chained on a ship while waiting to be processed by immigration officials. That was just too much to bear. Jacques grew into a very unhappy and mistrustful man. Jacques was a man haunted by his past, overwhelmed by his present, and uncertain about his future. Jacques like the mythological figure Atlas was carrying the globe on his shoulder. Jacques seemed to be always on the move. First, he left his birthplace of Roche-a-Bateau to move to Les Cayes, then to Port-au-Prince. He was then on to the US in New York, and then Miami. Where could he go now? With each move, his old wounds were reopening, ever so painful. Each time, he would seem to lose a bit of himself, a feeling of paradise lost would set in. Never would the happy days of his youth when he felt on top of the world would come back. Bitterness and rancor were taking over his soul.

One could catch Jacques smiling for a fleeting moment to be quickly replaced by a rictus, a grin that hardly masked the bitterness he carried in his heart. His isolation was now total. He no longer felt obliged to social conformity. No longer had he felt the need to smile when his heart felt otherwise. More and more he became disconnected from reality. He would rather seek refuge among the mythical figures that he used to be so fond of. Dragons spitting fires, and large cats with glowing eyes were always a nightmare away. The man with a sharp and analytical mind was crashing down into the unreal. No longer, Jacques seemed interested in seeking the meaning of things. He has lost his luster. Everything seemed mechanical. Jacques was quickly descending to the point of no return.

There was one person, however, that Jacques could call a friend, dating back from elementary school. His name was Pierre Boutin. Jacques ran into him fortuitously in a liquor store.
Pierre! Exclaims Jacques. Is that you? My old friend Pierre

Jacques had not exhibited such a display of joy in a long time. It was genuine.

"Yes Jacques, It's me!" Responded Pierre, surprised to see his old friend.

"I heard that you were in Miami, continued Jacques. I did

not know how to contact you. "

"I have been living here for 5 years. I could not take the cold in Chicago", Pierre said.

Jacques could not catch his breath. He would have a lot to tell his old pal about his own experience in New York.

Are you working? Inquired Pierre.

"Oh! Nothing special", Jacques said. Manual labor, that's all that is available around here. You know I was never very good with my hands."

I know, Pierre said, Jacques the intellectual"

Pierre paused and continued:

"What are you doing in a liquor store anyway?" Are you going to have a party? Pierre asked jokingly.

Jacques was caught off guard. Did not answer. He could not tell his old friend that for the past few weeks, he had picked up drinking. His favorite drink was rum and coke. Just about any rum. He has tried Appleton, Meyer's dark rum, or Havana Club. Call him a bit biased. His favorite was "Rhum Barbancourt" which over the years has collected several international awards and is considered one of the best rum in the world for over one hundred and fifty years. Jacques will not tell his friend that he has slowly but surely transformed himself into an alcoholic. Was it that he wanted at all costs to remain connected to the mementos of his homeland? Or was it that he wanted to drink himself into oblivion, and his increasing feeling of emptiness with it? What have I done? Jacques will often wonder in a rare moment of sobriety. He would often go into moments of self-pity when nothing seems to matter. Look at me! He would say looking in the mirror. A total failure! Maybe being drunk was better than being depressed. Or so he thought. Deep inside, however, he knew that sooner or later, his body would pay the consequences. He has read enough health magazines to know that denial can be your worst enemy.

Why would he want to burden his old friend Pierre with his problems?

"I must admit Pierre continued, it has not been easy" Most of the jobs seem to be in landscaping or the tourist industry.

Jacques once held a night job in a foundry where they were manufacturing auto parts. He was to throw some powder over the melting metal to keep the smoke down. Jacques needed to be on his guard. He needed to keep the smoke out of his eyes.

He also needed to fight off sleep. The job was repetitive and boring. A moment of inattention could be catastrophic. He was fired after the second paycheck. Thank God! Jacques was too much of an intellectual for this kind of job. Jacques felt that it was beneath him. He knew though, that his passion for reading and his discussions about literature and philosophy would not put food on the table or pay the bill. Was there a place in this world for this man? He tried his hands at many jobs, working in a warehouse as a stock keeper in a food distribution chain. His heart was not in it. Jacques felt misunderstood. He grew more and more resentful that his talents were not being recognized.

He started to project his sense of failure on the people around him. What do they know anyway? Ignoramus! That is what they are. He had so much knowledge and wisdom to share. He had no audience. A warehouse was no place to find the kind of followers he was looking for. His earlier interest in the medical field took a different turn. He became an information freak. He would read every published article in free medical journals and health magazines. He would inquire about the latest treatment for ailments like cancer or AIDS. He wanted to stay on the edge of the information explosion. Even though, he seems to be in over his head. No one would dare tell him so.

Pierre told him about openings at the Taxicab company where Pierre was working.

"On a good day, Pierre enticed him, you could go home with good money" If you are lucky to get a few airport runs, your day is made."

"Not bad, Jacques thought, it sounds much better than what he has had so far. Let me buy you a cup of coffee, Jacques said, leading the way towards the corner Cuban cafeteria.

Two cortaditos, please! Jacques ordered.

To old times, Salud!

They exchanged telephone numbers, agreed to meet with

the Taxicab company owner the next day at 10 am, and separated.

"See you tomorrow!" They said in unison.

The next day, they met at the agreed place. The owner, a burly man with an unkempt mustache, was waiting for them, the interview was not complicated. He went over some safety rules, and the procedures to retrieve and return the car at the end of the day. The cars were inspected at the end of the shift for any damages or irregularities'. Any incidents, like traffic tickets, lost items, and unruly passengers, were to be reported at once. They agreed on a route and the procedures for clients' assignments. Jacques received some orientation about the dispatch system. That was it. He was officially hired. No specific time was decided on when the taxicab would be picked up, but Jacques was to report at the end of the day and discuss problems that he might have encountered, Jacques quickly established his daily routine.

Jacques was very good with directions. You know what, Pierre, I think it could work, Jacques offered. Yes! It could work.

Jacques would learn the shortcuts and back streets of Miami very quickly.

He was a natural. His geographical area included the Miami Airport, the South Dade Coral Gables, and up to North Miami Beach, including Little Haiti. He soon started to make a decent living, clearing over nine hundred dollars a week after expenses. Jacques started to enjoy his job a lot. He could engage in small talks with some of his clients about just anything.

Some of his encounters were quite interesting. Jacques became aware of all the different perspectives and theories about the origin of AIDs. His fellow Haitians quickly bought into the widely held belief that the establishment had conspired to exterminate black people, the same way crack cocaine was introduced in the ghettoes. He also had his ideas about why the response to the epidemics seemed so slow. He remembered how some groups including Black people were used to study the natural course of certain illnesses like Syphilis. It was like music to the ears of his compadres who see most illnesses or negative events in conspirational terms. No one could convince Jacques and his fellow Haitians otherwise. He went as far as calling a few radio shows to express his views on the matter. Jacques felt at ease talking to an imaginary audience. It was like a professor lecturing a class of avid listeners. He even participated rather loudly in some marches protesting the injustice inflicted on Haitians on such matters as immigration policies and interference in internal Haitian politics. One could see Jacques involved in some heated arguments in front of stores in Little Haiti. He would make a large gesture like a preacher delivering a sermon to his flock. At least for now, Jacques had overcome his isolation. He would leave home around 4 a.m. and reach his studio apartment at dinnertime. He had discovered a few Haitian restaurants where he could grab some dinner on his way home.

He alternated between Jamaican cuisine and Haitian cuisine. His favorite dishes are Legumes over rice and beans or Jerk pork and fried plantains. He was away from the advice of his mother who often reminded him that he should watch what he eats.

No one was waiting for him at home. No wife. No children. Jacques was pretty much alone in this hostile town. At least he could enjoy some foods that reminded him of home.

This honeymoon period did not last long. One morning, Jacques woke up and smell the all too familiar rancid smell of vomit in his bed. The bed was still moist. Jacques also tasted blood on his lower lip which felt a bit sore, Jacques knew right away that he was in trouble. The seizures had come back. The episodes were often very dramatic. He had always known that there was a strong possibility that the seizures would return. He was just keeping his fingers crossed. He was strongly advised to continue his medications and to have regular checkups. He was in total denial. Not only did he stop taking the pills, but his drinking had increased significantly. Jacques decided to live his life as he pleased and wanted to believe that the seizures were a thing of the past. The seizures, he thought, would never come back. It was very convenient for Jacques to think this way.

Out of sight, out of mind!

No symptoms, No illness!

A concept engrained in Haitian culture.

All it took was a short period without a seizure for Jacques to take the leap. Jacques wanted so much to be cured that he acted against his best judgment.

Big mistake!

Two years since the last seizure episode. That was remarkable. How long now since has been off the medications? Maybe a year or a little more? One of the medications Dilantin used to make his gum bleed and leave a metallic after-taste in his mouth,

What were his options now? He could continue to deny the problems and run the risk of death with respiratory complications. Or he could start over. He had some idea that treatment options might have improved and that new medications were now available. He chose to look the other way. I must call Dr. David Coleman, Jacques tried to convince himself. Dr. David Coleman is a clinical professor of Neurology at the University of Miami with many peer-reviewed publications to his credit. He has been involved in research about Epilepsy for more than 20 years, there was no doubt, that it was the right decision to make. Jacques however remained apprehensive. What would Dr. Coleman say? Jacques dreaded the moment when he would be walking once again in the hallway of that office. He started to imagine all kinds of scenarios. What if I had a brain tumor or an aneurysm? Jacques was thinking aloud. He started to doze off and suddenly stood up.

Overcome by fear. "I must do this call, he said to himself.

By now, he was in full panic mode. His heart was racing. Things could only get worse. For a moment, he thought about going to the Emergency Room." No! He finally decided. I'll wait for tomorrow".

Jacques changed his mind. He decided to call right away.

He lifted the phone and dialed Dr. Coleman's number.

"Hello! Is that Dr. Coleman's office?"

Yes! This is Gwen. How can I help you?"

"My name is Jacques Gaetan. I am a patient of Dr. Coleman, and I would like to make an appointment."

"Is it an emergency?"

"I have been having three to four seizures a day..."

Dr. Coleman's assistant sounded worried." Would you hold on for a minute?" Less than a minute later, she came back to the phone.

"Dr. Coleman feels that you should be seen today."

It has happened before. Jacques knew that it was serious. He dreaded the emergency room chaos. He knew that no matter how skilled the personnel was, death always loomed around. Gwen was still talking, but her voice was suddenly very distant.

"It would be better if you go to the ED immediately."

"We will send an ambulance to transport you to the Emergency Room. Dr. Coleman will see you there." Gwen's voice was full of resolve. It was useless to argue.

"Okay, I will be waiting. "Jacques said sheepishly.

Chapter 3

The approaching noise of the sirens indicated that the ambulance had arrived.

The EMS workers checked the vital signs and went to work immediately. They were in constant communication with the ED. The lead worker was shaking his head in agreement with the physician at the other end of the line.

"Ok Doc, we are starting an IV line, and we will give him an IV push of Valium as you instructed."

He was hooked up to a monitor. Everything was happening in rapid sequences. Jacques was vaguely aware of the presence of the workers standing over him. It was like a dream.

When Jacques woke up. He was in the hospital. A circular curtain separated him from another section from where he could hear the moaning of an old lady who seemed in a lot of pain.

A nurse in a flowery top was standing over him and giving him a cursory examination. An IV apparatus with digital reading was attached to him.

"Mr. Jacques my name is Tamara. I'll be your nurse tonight. We will continue to monitor your condition. We already notified Dr. Coleman that you are here. He soon will be here to examine you."

Before Jacques could say a word, she was out of the room.

Off to the next patient.

The emergency Room can be a very impersonal and a very scary place. One never knows when death will come and knock on someone's door. There were moanings and there were sighs, and there were tears. There was also the continuous chatting and unrelated conversations of the nursing personnel that at times seemed oblivious to the life dramas that were taking place around them. They could go from a young patient with an open gunshot room struggling for his life to an old man with a heart attack worrying about leaving his lifetime partner alone. And there is always the fear that Emergency Room workers might contract some contagious disease from unsuspected patients. One never knows when the next epidemic will start.

Medical and nursing staff have mastered the art of compartmentalization as a defense mechanism that allows them to mentally separate conflicting thoughts, emotions, and the gory scenes that they come across throughout the day. They will not allow such scenes to take over their lives and keep them from functioning. They seem impassible and avoid the discomfort brought on by the chaos around them.

Jacques received a full workup. He was sent for several laboratory tests. The faces of the Emergency Room staff were new. Not much had changed about the setup. The smell of blood and commercial disinfectant was enough to make anyone sick.

Dr. Coleman came. He did not seem too worried. The test results came back normal. After a few hours, the situation was brought under control. He felt that Jacques was stable enough after a few hours of continuous drip. For some reason, he decided to release Jacques and asked him to come back the next day to the office.

Jacques could not quite understand why he was being released, but he was quite happy to leave that place where death was always roaming around.

I'll see you at 3 pm tomorrow Dr. Coleman said.

Yes, doctor!

Still groggy from the effects of the medications, Jacques got into a taxi and went home. He slept well that night. For the first time in many nights, he did not have the horrific dream.

The next day, he reported to Dr. Coleman's office on time. He was eager to know the results of the remaining studies.

"The doctor will see you now. Said Josette. I believe that was her name.

Jacques was taken to the imaging department for another CT scan of the brain. The one done in the ED the previous day was without a contract. They wanted to inject Jacques with a dye to have a better delineation of the brain structures. That was good enough, for now, Dr. Coleman indicated to his assistant. The studies could reveal the presence of a space-occupying lesion if any.

Jacques was examined by a group of residents under the watchful eyes of their mentor Dr. Coleman. Then the residents went into a lengthy presentation, discussing the different diagnostic possibilities. How scary? Jacques on the one hand wanted to hear every detail of what they had to say. On the other hand, he would rather not know. An electroencephalogram (EEG) was to be scheduled later.

The staff at Dr. Coleman's office had not changed much. Lisa, the registered nurse was still there. She was clearly in charge, giving orders and making sure everything was running smoothly.

Then came a young lady in her mid-twenties. The phlebotomist, a five feet eight inches beauty, was all dressed in dark blue scrubs and wearing gloves. You would think, she is ready for a major operation.

She had brown eyes with a scrutinizing and intimidating look and a perfectly shaped body. A real beauty! The kind of girl that one could easily fall in love with at first sight. The kind of girl that would make men fall off their feet.

Under normal circumstances, Jacques would make some flirtatious comments. Not now! The circumstances were anything but normal. Jacques was fretful about what was coming.

Ms. Carol, that was her name, broke the ice, stating: Relax! She continued; I am not going to hurt you."

"I am here to draw your blood, Carol said in a soft and reassuring voice.

At first, despite her beautiful appearance, she was a bit scary and behaved as if Jacques had some deadly disease. In this setting, paranoia always runs high. Was it an after-effect of the treatment Jacques has received in the past?

I am not going to hurt you" she repeated.

Are you sure? I believe the vampires always say the same", Jacques said sheepishly with a porcelain smile on his face, trying to disguise his fear.

Jacques found an escape and let his mind go into a wild and unlikely fantasy about this pretty woman that stood a mere foot away from him. He could easily imagine befriending her and having her fall in love at his feet. The mind is a powerful thing.

Falling in love? Nah! Jacques finally resigns himself that is impossible.

Wake up, Jacques! It is not going to happen.

Impossible!

The moment seems too grave for Jacques to entertain such crazy thoughts.

No matter how many times Carol would ask Jacques to relax, it was not going to happen. No one, but no one, could do anything to allay Jacques' fear. It was not just about the needle. It was not about the barely perceptible pinch he would feel when the needle entered his skin. It was all about the baggage that Jacques has been carrying with him, God knows for how long.

What if I had some deadly disease like a brain tumor or an aneurysm?

What if these seizures were just the warning signs of impending death?

Maybe Carol did not get the humor in Jacques's statement about vampires. It was a line she has heard many times anyway. It was a kind of stale. She did not even smile. Now, she was all business. In no time, causing very minimal discomfort, Jacques's blood gushed into the tubes. With dexterity, Carol changed from lavender top-colored tube to red, to green, and finally to grey. Carol had once again skillfully completed her duty.

Another patient! Another victim for the day!

Dr. Coleman walked into the examining room with his entourage. University professors hardly ever walk without an entourage, how have you been, Jacques?

Okay, I guess, Jacques responded. Dr. Coleman went on to ask a series of questions, his residents glued to the attending physician's every word. Did Dr. Coleman still want him as a patient?

Nothing that the good doctor had asked Jacques before.

But this time, it was different. The seizures had been more frequent and would last longer. Often, Jacques would go back into consciousness with the tell-tale signs that an event had taken place. Dr. Coleman was an excellent clinician. He has always been very kind and seemed genuine. He inspired confidence. Yet

Jacques was still apprehensive. Dr. Coleman told Jacques that he needed to stay overnight for more testing and closer observation. Jacques' alarm went off. His anxiety had reached its paroxysm. Something must be wrong for Dr. Coleman to make that decision. What could Dr. Coleman be looking for? Jacques was placed in an enclosed area with glass observation windows all around with nurses in attendance at all times watching both the patient and the monitors. He could barely hear any sounds except for the instructions given through a small speaker by the bed. It was like something out of a fiction movie. Everything was snow white. A camera barely visible was recording Jacques' every move.

At the end of the twenty-four hours, Dr. Coleman came in with the same group of residents and revealed that the seizure activities had taken a turn for the worse. He had all the data collected in the past 24 hours to support his view. And that as indicated by The EEG strip printouts, showing the patterns of electrical activities in various areas of the brain were very telling.

Why did they have to put through this? Jacques wondered. I could have told them as much. I know that I am not well.

There lies the difference between the clinician and the patient. The physician could have an impression but will not commit to a diagnosis until he has some conclusive data to sustain it.

This is awful! Jacques thought.

What does all that mean, Doc?

"Simply that it is going to be more difficult to treat your condition. We'll have to be more aggressive. We'll use newer medications, and we'll need your full cooperation. The good news is, the condition can improve, Dr Coleman said matter-of-factly.

Jacques was still not reassured. For a while, Dr. Coleman seemed uneasy.

He came closer to the bed and said in a whisper:

Mr. Gaetan...he started...

To Jacques, for the doctor to address him by his last name, could only spell trouble. Something was wrong. He anticipated the worst.

"Mr. Gaetan, Dr. Coleman continued, the continuous drip of Dilantin and the Valium you have received has not given us the results we were expecting. We will need to add another medication because you are still seizing. You are in Status Epilepticus which simply means a state of continuous seizure.

All the knowledge that Jacques supposedly had accumulated about medical issues was gone by the wayside.

"I have what... Doc?" Jacques asked, still unable to process what he had just heard.

Your seizure has not responded to the usual treatment. If you permit us, we would like to start newer drugs that have recently been approved by the FDA for situations like yours. One might say it is still experimental.

Experimental? Does that mean I am going to be part of some studies?

Yes and no! The neurologist responded. Adding more confusion. Yes, because we will study your response and compare it to that of other patients. No, because you will only become part of a small group of patients treated with this drug.

Before we continue, is there a family member who would like to notify you about your condition?

Just at that moment, it dons on Jacques that he has been very secretive about his deteriorating condition. Sometimes, withholding vital information from someone is equivalent to lying. He has not kept his mother abreast of his deteriorating condition since he left New York almost a year ago. He rarely communicated with his mother, as he tried to avoid the probing questions from his mother. He started to feel guilty. What if something were to happen to him? It would be devastating to his mother. It was unfair to his mother and the rest of the family. He had to garner his courage and make that call.

He hesitated for a moment and then said to Dr Coleman:

In fact, yes, I would like to notify my mother. She lives in New York. I do not want to alarm her unnecessarily. But I trust that you will do a better job explaining what is going on than I can anyway.

The phone number is in my wallet."

The nurse dialed the number and handed him the phone. His mother came to the phone right away, worried.

Jacques, Are you okay?

I am in the hospital Mom, but I am okay. My seizure came back. Dr. Coleman is here. He wants to start a new treatment. Let him explain it to you. He said that I would be okay, Jacques lied."

"Mrs. Gaetan, Dr. Coleman said, taking on a more serious tone, we are treating your son for his condition. We are about to start some newer medications. So far, they have been safe and have shown good results. Chances are, your son will do well on them. We just wanted to let you know."

Madam Maurice had a lot of questions but did not dare to ask. She did not like to discuss important matters like this over the phone.

"I trust that you will do your best for my son, Doctor, I'll be in Miami in a day or two, as soon as I can book a flight."

The conversation was short. Jacques felt a bit relieved that his mother had been made aware of the situation. It was up to him to seize the opportunity to maintain the line of communication open... The mistrust about university centers had come back in full force. "They are always ready to experiment on people. Like many minority groups, Haitians believe that universities are often too eager to use people as guinea pigs. What would be the risk of this treatment? Jacques still did not know. He was not about to ask either. He was too afraid of the possible consequences.

What would be his options if he were to decide not to go along with the treatment?

Informed consent means that the patient clearly understands the consequences of treatment and non-treatment.

It is doubtful that Jacques fully understood what would happen if he did not accept the suggested treatment.

Sensing Jacques's hesitation, Dr. Coleman offered: "Well! We could keep the same treatment in place for another 24 hours and see what happens.

Jacques jumped on the opportunity: Why don't we do that, doc? Jacques was off the hook at least for now.

Okay then! I'll see you in the morning. If anything, let the nurses know. They will notify me right away.

Good night, Jacques!

Thank you, Doc!

Jacques was somewhat relieved that Dr. Coleman did not force the issue. He did not want to offend the doctor. He did not feel that he could trust the new treatment.

Jacques then closed his eyes and made a prayer to the "Virgin of Miracles".

"Virgin of Miracles, intercede on my behalf. I know that you listen to your children. I promise that I will go back to church and make offerings to the poor if my condition improves. Amen!"

The prayer was simple, but it worked. Jacques

surprisingly did quite well that night. The seizure stopped. Jacques was more optimistic. Dr. Coleman maintained a very cool demeanor and did not seem thrilled at all He remained skeptical about the course of the illness and the prognosis. Not surprising, Jacques thought. Doctors like all scientists are supposed to be cool-headed and not give in to the excitement of the moment. Or maybe, he felt that he had just lost an opportunity to emphasize the importance of compliance with the treatment regimen. Jacques could not possibly see it that way. Maybe Dr. Coleman was a bit upset about losing another subject for his studies.

Jacques was discharged from the hospital the very next day. He was given specific instructions about the medications. His follow-up appointment was scheduled for a week. An MRI would be performed on his next visit. The doctor wanted to rule out some tumor or some degenerative disorder.

The magnetic resonance studies created even more confusion. The tests at first were deemed inconclusive. The specialists went back and forth for a couple of days and after further consultation with specialists as far as Singapore via the Internet, they concluded that the finding that seemed to disturb them so much was an artifact. What it all meant was that the test was negative. Meanwhile, Jacques went days without sleeping worrying that maybe he had a tumor. They had even suggested consultation with a neurosurgeon.

However, such beliefs lie in sharp contradiction with Jacques's initial dream of becoming a neurosurgeon himself. How would Jacques reconcile such opposite views? What a contradiction! What a turn of fate! Jacques whose dream was to become a neurosurgeon could not see himself benefiting from the knowledge and the skills of one. In Jacques's view, the contradiction lies somewhere else. In his culture, seizure disorder, "mal caduque" as it is called, is not necessarily a bad thing. People with this disorder are supposed to be endowed with some special gift of divination if properly channeled.

Jacques has not explored it and did not necessarily believe it. If he did, the magnetic resonance studies created even more confusion. The tests at first were deemed inconclusive. The specialists went back and forth for a couple of days and after further consultation with a radiologist, they concluded that the finding that seemed to disturb them so much was an artifact. What it all meant was that the test was negative. Meanwhile, Jacques went days without sleeping worrying that maybe he had a tumor. They had even suggested consultation with a neurosurgeon.

No, no, and no! Absolutely not!

Jacques never consented. Surgery on his brain?

To Jacques, it would be an unforgivable, undue interference in an intrusion in his soul's journey towards ultimate liberation. Such interference, undoubtedly with the "covering of

Karma over his soul would condemn him forever in a dumpster of the universe with other wandering souls that will never know peace.

That would be too disturbing to his karma.

What a contradiction! What a turn of fate! Jacques whose dream was to become a neurosurgeon could not see himself benefiting from the knowledge and the skills of one. In Jacques's view, the contradiction lies somewhere else. In his culture, seizure disorder, "mal caduque" as it is called, is not necessarily a bad thing. People with this disorder are supposed to have some special gift of divination if properly channeled. Jacques never explored it nor necessarily believe it. If he did, he would never admit that he did. Subconsciously, he wanted to interfere with this "gift" as little as possible. Jacques, therefore, remained at great risk of not complying with the prescribed treatment. Why did I bother to come back to this place? He wondered as he was waiting to see the doctor for a follow-up treatment. Dr. Coleman looked unusually solemn that day. The suspense was unbearable. He started with this typical monotonous and detached voice so characteristic of university professors:

"How are you doing today, Mr. Gaetan?"

For some reason, Jacques felt that Dr. Coleman was always expecting the worst. How could Jacques feel comfortable, when his doctor did not seem to have any confidence that Jacques could get better? Jacques could remember the time when it was a pleasure going to his family doctor for a check-up. Jacques did not feel he was on the same page with his doctor. Jacques felt that there was not much to be gained from the doctor-patient relationship. From now on, he was just going through the motion. He continued to go to his follow-up appointment, although he hated it.

Dr. Coleman did a good job keeping Jacques informed of every new medication on the market, including Felbatol, a medication that is supposed to work for intractable seizures.

It seems to be very promising and has shown excellent results with intractable seizures, Dr. Coleman said, let me suggest that you try it!

How much will it cost and what are the side effects, Doc? Not that Jacques was about to let this good doctor use him for experimentation this time around, but he felt compelled to ask. As you know, Jacques never missed an opportunity to have a medical discussion and show his degree of sophistication. After all, this information would be very good when he is ready for his next round of discussion with the guys at the taxi station.

"The drugs are free and so are the tests that will be done to monitor your progress, while you are taking the medicine. As I told you, your condition has steadily deteriorated, and it would be a good time to start something new. Jacques was feeling under pressure to give a straight answer to the doctor. He believes that Dr. Coleman is a very good doctor, but he never could trust him fully. What if, Dr. Coleman was not telling him the whole story? There was a long moment of silence.

"Well, Dr. Coleman, I will have to think about it. Is that Okay?"

Fine, Mr. Gaetan, let me know soon what your decision is! If you agree, I would like to start you with the next group...

So that was what this was all about, thought Jacques, Dr. Coleman had not given up on trying to use me as one of his subjects, Jacques thought. Those damned academicians! Against all odds, Jacques decided to try the new drug. In the final analysis, Jacques knew that Dr. Coleman was a concerned physician, but he could not admit it to himself. He was ambivalent about giving all his trust to a physician that has dedicated his life to helping suffering people and a Western scientist who makes no effort to accommodate other people's worldviews. For over thirty years now, Jacques has been dealing with this awful and shameful illness. He could feel the despair setting in. Things were going so well. He was able to save a few thousand dollars and was thinking about buying a house in Haiti. What is going to happen, now?

The drug study did not go well. Jacques had decided to go on the medication after he had five seizure episodes in less than two weeks. He was hospitalized one more time. His diagnostic label had changed once again. He was now referred to as having ***an intractable seizure***. The study had to be discontinued after some of the subjects started to develop liver and blood complications. Jacques's trust in the ability of his doctor to improve his condition was gone. To make matters worse, Jacques was now sleeping only three hours a night. He started to have panic attacks. His eyes remained wide open throughout the night. He would toss and turn. And when he finally shut his eyes, he would suddenly wake up in cold sweats with a recurring nightmare. He had developed bags under his eyes and felt that the sky was falling on him. As soon as he walked into Dr. Coleman's office, the doctor expressed his concern.

He asked right away:" Jacques, what is wrong? You seem like you have seen a ghost!"

Jacques did not know where to start. He did not know how much to tell his doctor. He was afraid that Dr. Coleman might not understand.

"I do not know what to make of it, Doc. I have been having the same dream, at the same time every night. No matter what I do. I have tried to go to bed at different times. I put my head in different positions on the bed and slept with two pillows instead of one. I have slept without a pillow."

Jacques could not tell his doctor what else he has tried. He has also tried to sleep in red pajamas. He has placed the bible open with Psalm 91 under his pillow.

Jacques was interrupted in his thoughts.

"But Jacques, you have not told me the dream", Dr.

Coleman inquired.

Jacques was still reluctant. He was afraid that Dr. Coleman might laugh at him and dismiss his dreams as plain superstition from another Haitian. Do you know? The "voodoo stuff" as the health care workers always referred to anything that they cannot explain about Haitians. Jacques decided to take his chances.

He stated: "For the past five nights I have been seeing myself in an old house, which looked like a place where I used to live as a child. A black skull keeps on popping out of a wall. He kept on saying these words with laughter that I cannot describe. It has that deep remote echo effect as if it is coming out of a grave. Maudit! Maudit!! I cannot get these words out of my head. I am scared, Doc! I am very scared. I do not know what to do. Please, help me! Jacques's voice was desperate. He was almost begging. He was visibly disturbed. His eyes were full of tears. The secretary must have heard some of the commotions. She rushed in to help. Jacques did not know who she was here to help: Dr. Coleman or himself.

Are you guys okay? She asked.

She was waived away by Dr. Coleman. She apologetically left the room.

The doctor was visibly puzzled. He was unprepared for this mysterious and sudden display of emotions. He remained silent for a long moment. He smiled awkwardly and said almost laughingly:

"A black skull, he repeated over and over, you are not going crazy on me, are you, Mr. Gaetan?"

Jacques regretted immediately having poured his heart out and shared his plight with the doctor.

How can one be so insensitive? I'll concede, thought Jacques, he is no psychiatrist, but he is an educated man. Could he at least hold back and show some humanity? Could he at least accept that there is another world out there that he and many people are not necessarily familiar with?

Jacques was disappointed and felt destroyed by these lightheaded comments. Dr. Coleman did not have any idea, how powerful those words were, they were coming from him. In a way, we only have ourselves to blame to put an aureole on the head of our physicians. Oftentimes, we consider them as superhumans and place them on a pedestal. Jacques had just found out that his good doctor, Dr. Coleman, was no superhuman. He was culturally inept and had much to learn about human behavior. All his degrees and all his training did not amount to a hill of beans. They did not teach him how to mince his words and how to be attuned to the emotional distress of his patients.

Subconsciously, Jacques had already decided.

If Dr. Coleman was a concerned physician, he was not showing it at this very moment. Right now, he had just proven that he was a commoner who could not show a bit of understanding and compassion towards a fellow human being in distress. When he needed it the most, Jacques could not count on Dr. Coleman. For over thirty years now, Jacques has been dealing with this awful and shameful illness. He will have to continue to deal with it alone. Emptiness and despair were setting in.

At this moment of distress, Jacques could only turn to his Creator.

He remembered the verse from Psalm 61:

"Hear my cry, O God Listen to my prayer.

From the ends of the earth, I call to you,

I call as my heart grows faint.

Lead me to the rock that is higher than I. For you have been my refuge, a strong tower against the foe.

I long to dwell in your tent forever, and take refuge in the shelter of your wings…

Things were going so well. He was able to save a few thousand dollars and was thinking about buying a house in Haiti. What is going to happen, now?

He had started to have panic attacks. He was extremely restless. He had developed bags under his eyes and felt that the sky was falling on him.

His experience with Dr. Coleman is not one that he would soon forget. Jacques was thinking. "We have nobody to blame but ourselves. We place an aureole on the head of our physicians. We think of them as superhumans. Dr. Coleman has just proven that he is no superhuman. He has much to learn about being simply human.

To Jacques, his hallucinations, and his recurring dreams had a meaning. It was a gift. Soon, he would have to discover their meaning.

He wanted to interfere with this "gift" as little as possible. If so, getting Jacques to comply with his treatment would be a losing battle. As far as Jacques was concerned, there could not be many benefits in taking "Dr. Coleman medications". Why did I bother to come back to this place? He wondered as he was waiting to see the doctor for a follow-up treatment.

Dr. Coleman looked unusually solemn that day.

The suspense was unbearable. He started with this typical monotonous and detached voice so characteristic of university professors.

Chapter 4

The next morning, as he was being wheeled out of the hospital lobby, his phone rang. His mother had just landed at the Miami Airport. Jacques would not be able to retrieve her and wanted to inform his mother that he was just being discharged. Before he could say anything, his mother said that she was about to hop in a taxi and that she would wait for him in the lobby, if she gets there before him.

Jacques made it to his apartment in no time, as there was little traffic at the end of the morning. His mother, however, was already there sitting in a leather chair in the lobby, courtesy of the superintendent, a middle-aged Cuban lady who was very kind to everyone.

Mom! Exclaimed Jacques. You got here quickly, how was your flight?

It was fine son, it was fine! She said with a worried expression on her face.

How did it go in the hospital?

"As you can see, I am doing better. Otherwise, Dr. Coleman would not have released me" Jacques responded without hesitation.

It was only half the truth. The real story was that his condition was quite serious and that he needed to take care of himself and follow the instructions he received if he were to get better,

Why lie anyway? His mother would just look around the apartment and realize that her son had not been doing well.

Madam Maurice had seen enough to get a sense of the emotional turmoil that her older son had been going through. Jacques needed to get back on track and fast.

Had Jacques known that his mother coming to visit without any planning, maybe he would have tried to make the place more presentable.

Madam Maurice would have to use all her persuasive power to get Jacques to comply with his treatment. Would she be successful? Only time will tell.

First, she wanted to prepare him a good meal. She looked through the cupboard. It was almost empty. She wanted Jacques to take her to the nearby grocery store. She took the opportunity to remind Jacques how important good nutrition was for good health. She did not even talk about the drinking. One thing at a time. Besides, she did not know how fragile her son's condition was. After a good meal, if it is possible, she would sit down with him and come up with a plan.

So far, Jacques had not offered any resistance and seemed to be going along with everything. He did not want to get his mother upset on her first day after a long absence. The load of medications that he received in the hospital was also helping him stay calm. On the menu tonight vegetable stew with pork, a dish called "legumes" over rice with pigeon beans. Delicious! No one beats Madam Maurice at preparing this dish.

The evening ended with some Corosol leaves tea (soursop) known for its calming and soporific effects. Would that be enough to guarantee Jacques a good night of sleep? This time, he took his prescribed medications without prompting.

Madam Maurice settled her sleeping spot on the couch after refusing the bed that was graciously offered by Jacques.

Madam Maurice said her night prayers and went to sleep.

After the death of her husband Maurice Gaetan many years ago, Madam Maurice, as the wife is often called, found herself morphing into the role of both father and mother. The youngest child Georges was still a toddler. She needed to maintain a tight grip on the situation. She tries to instill in the children all the necessary moral values that they would need to earn respect and be successful citizens. Education was not negotiable. Everyone will do their best every single day to meet with success in school," It was like a refrain the children would repeat to themselves until everyone gets it. No slacking off would be tolerated. "If you do not set up goals for yourself, you stand no chance to ever achieve them" was another lesson. If you say you want to be a lawyer or a doctor, do not way until you complete your classes. Start preparing now by developing good study habits. No procrastination allowed. Those were the words of wisdom that the siblings would get from their mother daily.

Such words coming from a lady that did not go beyond some secondary years of education were remarkable. She saw her role primarily as that of a mother who took take care of her children and keep the family together. She was much more than that. She was a matriarch that would receive children from extended families with open arms. It did not matter whose children they were; they were welcome in Madam Maurice's home.

The dynamics of the family started to change a bit when Jacques became ill. Madam Maurice felt that she needed to afford Jacques added support.

When Madam Maurice received that call from Dr. Coleman it was like a call of duty. She knew that like a soldier, her new assignment would be at the side of her eldest son Jacques. Mentally, she had been preparing for this. She knew that something was afoot when Jacques would go weeks without checking in. That was not like him. Jacques can indeed be stubborn and hardheaded sometimes but his relationship with his mother was very tight. She was one of the few people Jacques would yield to in an argument. Madam Maurice needed to thread the waters carefully. Jacques's move to Miami also meant that he was trying to become more independent without the supervision of others. Madam Maurice did not want to appear overly intrusive and overbearing. That would be a challenge. Haitian mothers are not known to take a passive stance. They usually jump right into the situation and try to manage it. They favor a directive stance over inaction. Different options could be discussed later but first, let's use proven paths. Let us do what has worked in the past. As the other children would tune their mother out and do their things, Jacques was more likely to engage in a debate. Madam Maurice would have to pick her battles carefully if she were to successfully help Jacques through this rough patch that Jacques was going through.

The first order of business was to find out exactly what was the health status of her son. By communicating with Dr. Coleman before, consent to continue to communicate was implied. She needed to ask the right questions. What were the chances for the medications to work? What were the possible side effects?

Any possibility that the medications might make the psychiatric condition worse?

The next issue was to find out Jacques's psychiatric status. Are they any new medications that might help control the symptoms better?

Are there any proven strategies to help compliance with treatment?

Madame Maurice found several vials of medications in the bedside drawer, untouched. Jacques has not been taking his prescribed medications. Instead, he has been relying on alcohol to alleviate his anxiety. Madam Maurice also noticed that Jacques has not been bringing new bottles of liquor home. Could it be that Jacques has finally realized that alcohol was only making matters worse? It is doubtful.

Change is never spontaneous. An incident with a family member, a friend, a co-worker, or an encounter with a law enforcement officer might be the trigger that puts the process into motion. The stages to change have been researched. In the pre-contemplation stage, the individual does not even acknowledge that there is a problem. Later, the individual might admit that there is a problem but still questions his readiness or his ability to make the change. At some point, the individual might reach the stage of preparation /determination when he starts getting ready to make the changes. Then the individual jumps into action and displays some willpower. Change is here. The new behavior needs to be maintained. Not everything is well however, the possibility of relapse still looms. The individual needs to identify the triggers. For example, if going to the bar after work always leads to drinking, one might need to avoid the bar altogether.

Each one of the stages requires specific strategies to help with the process. Such strategies are often facilitated by a sponsor or a life coach.

It would be difficult to envision Madam Maurice being able to guide Jacques through this complicated process. All she could do at this point is to encourage Jacques to seek professional help while offering him her unconditional love and support.

With the tender loving care that he received from his mother, Jacques was looking better every day. If he was still having the dreams, at least they were not waking him up every single night. For a while, he seemed more rested in the morning. It has been almost a month since his discharge from the hospital. He had his follow-up appointment. His condition could be described as stable. He is contemplating returning to work gradually. His mother does not agree but it could be negotiated. When a family is dealing with a member who has a mental illness, such a family tends to hang on to every minor sign of progress, maintaining hope that a cure was on the way.

However, Madam Maurice was no fool. She could not lose this opportunity to try to get her son back into treatment.

"I'll tell you what, Jacques. Madam Maurice started, I think that you could go back to work after you see Dr. Dickenson for your follow-up psychiatric appointment. What do you think, son?

It is always better to make such suggestions in the form of a question. The individual feels that he has a choice.

It worked. Jacques has been getting along well with his mother and did not want to disappoint her.

“I believe, my appointment is in a couple of days, Jacques said. Let me see what Dr. Dickenson has to say. “

Madam Maurice felt that she had just scored a point.

Jacques did not say a straight-out no. That was progress.

"I think I should accompany you this time," said Madam Maurice, pushing her luck.

"You want to show to "those people" that you are not alone and that they'd better take good care of you," Madame Maurice continued with a smile, playing on the paranoiac tone she has often detected in Jacques' conversation.

"Okay Mom, you could come". Jacques said, feeling that any resistance would have been futile at this time.

Another score for the worried mother.

Chapter 5

"And Penelope answered,

"Stranger, dreams are very curious and unaccountable things, and they do not by any means invariably come true.

There are two gates through which these unsubstantial fancies proceed; the one is a horn and the other ivory..."

Odyssey, Homer

Jacques went to the psychiatric appointment with some trepidations.

Dr. Dickenson inquired about his general health and wanted to review the reports from the neurologists and the results from all the studies. He expressed some concern about the lack of sleep.

By that time, Jacques had made up his mind. He would tell Dr. Dickenson about the dreams and watch his reaction.

Dr. Dickenson's office was surprisingly very modernly decorated.

William A. Dickenson, M.D., the sign simply read. Absent from the office was the proverbial couch. There were two beige-looking recliners positioned at a comfortable distance from each other, and at the left corner of the room, a massive oak desk with unfinished work spread all over. Books and magazines! There were medical journals all over. The whole right side of the room was occupied by a wide and tall oak bookcase. When does he get the time to read all those books? Jacques was thinking. Dr. Dickenson was a man obsessed with clocks. Jacques could count at least a dozen of them. The collection included digital clocks and analog clocks. Some were art deco style. One was encased in a richly decorated crystal frame. It caught Jacques' attention. It looked like the front of a monument carved out of a massive block of crystal. Two pillars were supporting a triangular-shaped dome, and in between a white round surface with large Roman black numbers. Perhaps, Dr. Dickenson was a philosopher fascinated by the passing of time. Perhaps, he was simply keenly aware that he would inevitably meet his end. Perhaps he was a man obsessed with his destiny. Knowing that by the end of the day, everything had to be done. As the Haitian proverb goes:

"We pa we, anteman pou ka tre," ("Like it or not, the funeral is set: 4 o'clock").

. From the inner circle, rays were like coming out of the sun. No! Dr. Dickenson did not wear a plaid jacket or an eccentric bow tie. His shirt was well tucked into his pleated wool slacks. His Bally's shoes were surprisingly well polished. What is in the appearance of a psychiatrist anyway? If only they could look like regular people. Dr. Dickenson introduced himself and led Jacques to one of the two recliners. He spoke with a New England Bostonian accent.

He tried his best to make Jacques comfortable. Jacques could see the difference between his demeanor and Dr. Coleman's.

"Do you want me to call you Jacques or Mr. Gaetan?" he started.

"Well!" Jacques thought, "I am being given a choice."

"Call me Jacques," he replied.

"You could call me Bill or Dr. Dickenson, whichever you are more comfortable with," the psychiatrist continued.

"Tell me Jacques, how do you feel I can help you?"

Jacques went on to describe his current symptoms. He went on to tell Dr. Dickenson about his anxiety attacks, his lack of sleep, and his preoccupation with the intrusive thoughts. Jacques used a lot of hand gestures. His facial expression changed from one extreme to the next. He raised his voice as he repeated the dreadful words he heard from the black skull:

" Maudit! Maudit!" He demonstrated in a dramatic and loud fashion.

It could not possibly be worse than the mocking laughter he got from Dr. Coleman. He was a psychiatrist after all. He was ready to bet on a more informed and more humane response.

Dr. Dickenson listened to Jacques with attention, taking occasional notes, and then said:

"A recurring dream? Dr. Dickenson said, with a puzzled look on his face. It must probably have a deeper meaning. Something cultural, I suppose I must admit. I have not encountered such a situation before. I certainly will research the matter and get back to you on this. I promised."

"That was very promising." For Jacques that was magnificent. A good physician, Jacques was thinking, is one that he ready to accept his limitation and is ready to tap into the vast amount of knowledge that scientists have at their disposal. What we already know is just scratching the surface of what knowledge is yet to be known. What a difference with Dr. Coleman's dismissive attitude!

Dr. Dickenson had just earned Jacques's respect and confidence. The good doctor now had Jacques's undivided attention. Interestingly, he did not ask too many questions about the details of the dream on that first visit.

"Jacques, do you have any family here?" Dr. Dickenson asked.

Jacques could not see the immediate relevance, but he cooperated.

"No, most of my family is in the Northeast," Jacques replied.

The psychiatrist seemed to take an interest in Jacques's response.

"Where in the Northeast?"

"Brooklyn, New York," Jacques said.

He inquired about Jacques's habits and interests and looked for obsessive traits. He inquired about repetitive behavioral patterns.

"Besides this dream, do you sometimes have thoughts that you cannot seem to get out of your mind?"

"Like what?" Jacques asked.

"Worrying thoughts, preoccupations?"

Jacques did not feel comfortable revealing more about himself. He has been burned before. Not again! At least not yet anyway!

"No, I don't," Jacques replied.

The interview continued and became quite probing and uncomfortable at times.

"Do you get the feeling at times that people out there are out to get you?" The doctor asked.

"What do you mean?" Jacques asked suspiciously.

"Are you talking about how Haitians and Black people are treated in this country, or are you talking about me?"

The psychiatrist seemed uncomfortable with the implications of these clarifying questions. He was not ready to deal with it. He copped out.

"I mean you, personally," Dr. Dickenson said.

Jacques would not let him off.

"Well, as a Haitian living in this white-dominated and hostile world, I feel at times that I am the target of a lot of racism and discrimination. But I do not think I take it very personally. I feel that if people are racists, they have a problem, not me."

There! Jacques was testing his interlocutor.

Jacques had always wanted to make this statement to a white man in a position of power, without having to face recriminations. Dr. Dickenson, the psychiatrist, was a logical choice. Psychiatrists are supposed to be sincere with their patients. They are supposed to have a very strong ego. They are supposed to let pointed remarks from frustrated patients bounce off like nothing.

How is Dr. Dickenson holding out so far? Would he take it like a man, or would he fall apart like some psychiatrists who no matter how many years of psychoanalysis they go through will remain very fragile and will never resolve their basic inner conflicts and inferiority complex? Watch out! These individuals can be very dangerous. They are likely to play adopt an advisory role behind the scenes and support extremist ideology leading to white supremacist views, to unfortunate events like the holocaust, slavery, or apartheid.

Well, if Dr. Dickenson was sincere, he would agree that Jacques was right about inequality and racism in this world. At least, Jacques thought that he should.

If only Jacques could read Dr. Dickenson's notes. Jacques was described as follows:

Forty-four-year-old Haitian man, very agitated, possibly psychotic. He is preoccupied with thoughts about the devil. Seems paranoid about issues of racism and discrimination...He seems to carry a chip on his shoulder.

It was quite a leap that the psychiatrist took, based on the statements from Jacques. Which patient was Dr. Dickenson describing? Was he projecting his uneasiness about being confronted with issues of minority culture, race, and discrimination all at once? Did he understand why Jacques wanted to make it clear from the start that the issue of Jacques' blackness and "Haitianness" would have to be dealt with if Jacques were to get any help from Dr. Dickenson, a white man?

It was obvious from the notes that he missed the whole point. Jacques often wondered why people in America were so uncomfortable discussing the issue of race. Don't all psychiatrists teach their patients that the first step to solving any problem is to realize that you have one? Why couldn't the same model used with drugs and alcohol treatment be applied to eradicating racism? An affirmation: "Yes, we have a problem," would be the very first step out of many. That statement, however, "Yes, I am a racist," can only come out of a feeling of uneasiness about the issue. The question is: Is America uneasy about racism? Jacques seemed ready to tackle the issue, but Dr. Dickenson was not. After all, Jacques was the patient here, not Dr. Dickenson. Since Jacques was having symptoms, it was only natural that he would want to work on this central issue at once. It was not likely to go away, as Dr. Dickenson might find out.

Dr. Dickenson wrote his observation and moved away from the subject altogether. Jacques and Dr. Dickenson were not on equal footing. Dr. Dickenson had the upper hand. He was calling all the shots. Jacques had the option of not responding to any of the next few questions. Since Dr. Dickenson was going to be like that, let him answer his own questions. Jacques was visibly upset, and Dr. Dickenson had no way of knowing why. He inquired about Jacques' past interpersonal relationships.

"Have you ever been married?" He asked.

Wrong question! If Dr. Dickenson was in tune with his

patients, he might have chosen to stop the interview at that point.

"Why does he want to know? Is he trying to determine if I am gay?" Jacques thought angrily. Nothing that Dr. Dickenson was going to say would strike the right cord. The interaction was ruined, and Dr. Dickenson did not even know it. The responses from Jacques would just be pro forma.

After a long silence, Jacques realized that Dr. Dickenson was still awaiting an answer to his last question.

"You asked me if I was ever married. The answer is no. I have never been married. I thought I was in love once; nothing ever came out of it. The relationship abruptly ended, after the girl moved away. I was heartbroken to tell you the truth."

Jacques was kind of surprised at his answer. He never admitted this to himself before. He just blurted it out. The issue of Jacques's relationship with Suzanne has never been resolved. Jacques often wondered why Suzanne suddenly dropped out of sight. Did Suzanne have expectations that Jacques was unable to fulfill? He was never allowed to find out. Jacques retreated. He needed to be more careful. He did not know what else he might say to this stranger. Yes, a stranger that was what Dr. Dickenson was!

He was interested in letting Jacques ventilate.

The doctor took copious notes and was careful not to interrupt Jacques. Maybe, Dr. Dickenson figured that his best piece of information would be collected as Jacques was talking.

Maybe he could catch bits and pieces of information from Jacques's subconscious. Jacques had taken his focus completely away from Dr. Dickenson's reflective, "I-am-not--going-to-get-you" attitude. Jacques was a master at this cat-and-mouse game. He started to count the plaques on Dr. Dickenson's wall. It was time for him to get to know his psychiatrist. Eighteen plaques and awards in all. Jacques found out that his doctor graduated from Boston University. He completed his training at McLean Hospital. He has been around. Jacques' anger was subsiding, but he decided to end the interview. He was not going to walk out, but he would give no more information to Dr. Dickenson for now. Jacques felt relieved talking to him. Probably feeling Jacques' hesitation at times, the doctor offered some encouragement:

"First of all, let me tell you that the fact that you were referred to me does not mean that you are crazy. What I hope to do, is to review the information that you gave me and try to determine how I can best help you, if at all," he continued.

"Was Dr. Dickenson attempting to make peace, to offer the proverbial olive branch? Or was he collecting his strength ready to charge like a bull in the arena?"

Jacques's guard was still up.

"Beware of the enemy who walks into town bearing gifts and making peace offerings! It will be your downfall."

It was like Jacques was holding a piece of material and Dr.

Dickenson was carefully pulling out every single thread to examine it and then weave them all of them back together. At times, the questions did not even seem connected. Well, that was quite a change. Jacques was expecting Dr. Dickenson to read his mind, tell him what was wrong, and tell him what to do to get better. If Jacques knew what was wrong, he figured, he would not have to go to the psychiatrist.

After the interview, Dr. Dickenson discussed a treatment plan. He suggested some sleeping pills and anti-anxiety agents.

"I want you to take some Xanax over the next couple of weeks. I want to see you for weekly sessions so we could continue to explore the problems you started to tell me about."

"I want...I want... At no point did he ask me what I hoped to gain from this treatment." Jacques was thinking. *"It is going to be interesting."*

Dr. Dickenson means that they both could play mind games. The psychiatrist made it clear it would be a very slow process and that he was expecting Jacques to keep his appointments. At the end of the hour, Dr. Dickenson said:

"Mr. Gaetan... Jacques, we will continue this chat in about a week. It was not too bad, was it?"

Jacques did not quite understand what the doctor meant with his last comments. All that Jacques knew is that it was a very exhausting hour. He could not believe that he had survived his first encounter with a bona fide shrink, and he was not immediately certified crazy. Maybe there was hope after all. He felt better talking to this man. He promised himself that he would come back next week.

"Thank you for seeing me, Dr Dickenson, see you next week!" Dr. Dickenson escorted Jacques to the door.

After Jacques left the office, he realized that he did not elaborate on the details of the dreams which had caused him to seek help in the first place. The week had been extremely rough. Jacques was having the dream every single night, sometimes more than once a night. He had completely shut himself off from everyone. He did not even feel like going to the grocery store to pick up bread and milk. Jacques was becoming malnourished. His mother was doing her best to keep him connected and provide him with some nutritious meals, but Jacques had lost his appetite. His mother tried to entice him with his favorite dishes. Jacques simply was not interested. He felt very weak. He was not sleeping at all. He had no energy. He had not even turned his color television on in almost a week. He was quickly disconnecting himself from the world around him. Something was wrong. Usually, Jacques would thrive on the consumption of daily news broadcasts. He would listen religiously to Haitian radio programs bringing him fresh news from back home. Something needed to be done, right away. Jacques seemed to be losing his mind. When Dr. Dickenson saw him, he contemplated psychiatric hospitalization but could not convince Jacques.

Besides, he was not a danger to himself. He just wanted to get well.

Chapter 6

The first individual session was extremely difficult given Jacques's condition. Dr. Dickenson attempted to lay some ground rules. Jacques vaguely remembered the doctor saying something about timeliness and a fifty-minute hour. The psychiatrist had some expectations and he tried to make them as clear as he could. Jacques had his too. The least that he could expect was for Dr. Dickenson to have his undivided attention. He expected Dr. Dickenson to be directive and to make practical suggestions to help him. Jacques did not expect him to sit down and doze off, waiting for the hour to be over. The doctor was a good listener, but he did not seem very comfortable with the vivid contents of the dreams. Jacques explained that he was awakening at night in cold sweats, afraid to go back to sleep. He was even anticipating the start of the dreams and would just let them run their course until they were over. This time Dr. Dickenson asked him detailed questions about the dreams. Jacques went to every single frame as if he was a detective analyzing a crime scene.

Dr. Dickenson continued: "I want to suggest some sleep studies. Your sleep/wake cycle has been disturbed and I want to be able to pinpoint at what stage of your sleep those dreams occur.

"Maybe it is some past life experiences that you dread reliving.

In the meantime, your brain needs to be able to rest in the night. That is the only way, you will have the strength to face the challenges of the day."

As to your depressive symptoms, your mood swings, and your agitation, I would like to prescribe you a medication called Abilify. It seems that this medication does not carry a significant risk of making your seizure worst. We would want you to remain on the anti-seizure medications anyway. I will consult with your neurologist.

It has been two months since Jacques was started on a new drug regimen by the neurologist. His sleep has improved only slightly but he continues to have the recurring dreams. The dreams seem to be more elaborated and richer in details. He now could distinguish the ghostly face of an old man pointing his finger at Jacques while screaming with his cavernous and horrific voice: Maudit! Maudit!

Jacques continued to toss and turn in his bed. One could often hear him having a full conversation with an imaginary person.

"Why won't you leave me alone?"

"Get away from me! "

His mother would wake up, get on her knees and go into lengthy prayer sessions, reading the Psalms, imploring the saints, and asking for protection for her son:

"Almighty God,

I give my precious son to You.

You have journeyed with me, from his birth till now.

Come walk with him, to protect him, keep and help him at this difficult time.

Give me all that I need to love him and support him.

I surrender to you my concerns, worries, and regrets.

Please wipe away my guilt and fill me afresh with new vision and hope.

Bless his life with contentment and joy and may his cup overflow with goodness and love.

I entrust him to you, O Lord

Amen. "

What is there for a mother to do when she feels so powerless? Whom can she turn to when the world around her seems upside down, when her beloved son seems so burdened? What else can she do when her son seems so overwhelmed by life itself?

Madam Maurice would follow with the rosary and the Lord's Prayer: "Our Father who art in heaven, hallowed be thy name, thy kingdom come…"

No one was sleeping well in this house that night. Madam Maurice was afraid that the commotion would wake up the neighbors.

In the morning, Jacques would look exhausted. He had

difficulty waking up. He felt under pressure to maintain his job and to continue to bring home an income. He started to have more frequent mood swings. It became increasingly difficult for Jacques to modulate his emotions.

Maybe he was not taking his medications. The behavior has become more unpredictable. Was Jacques at least taking his medications? Rule number one. Before you start saying that a medication is not working, you must make sure it is being taken properly. Madam Maurice needed to find out. While Jacques was out, she went on a search. Jacques was not taking the medications. He was burying the pills in the soil inside the flowerpot.

Busted! No want should test the perspicacity of Madam Maurice.

Maybe she did not want to confront him, but she knew why Jacques's condition was not improving.

The question now is: What does she do if the condition continues to escalate? Madam Maurice has never felt afraid for her safety around Jacques but the problem is when Jacques seems to have lost control of his senses and to have lost control of reality, one should not trust that Jacques will act appropriately.

Madam Maurice would have to resign herself to the fact that the police might have to become involved. They are the only ones that are trained to deal with such situations. That was a difficult decision to make. Madam Maurice has heard on the news of situations where the police were called for help and it all ended up in a tragedy. Patients who were supposed to be helped ended up being shot to death by multiple officers responding to the scene.

Very scary!

Jacques was on a rampage. After running through the small apartment, yelling profanities, screaming, and gesticulating, he punched a hole in his room door and slammed it shut. The apartment seemed to shake in its foundation. Then a big bang and sounds of shattered glasses.

Get the hell away from me!

Why don't you go and...?

This time, Jacques was totally out of control.

Madam Maurice could not figure out what happened. They had breakfast at the kitchen table earlier in the day. Nothing could predict what was happening now.

Madam Maurice knew that she had to act. Not out of fear for her safety. True or not, she does not think that her son would ever try to hurt her. Jacques was not himself. It was as if some evil force, some demon had taken control of her son.

She overcame her prior hesitation and her misgivings about the police.

She had no choice this time. She decided to make the call.

She went to the phone and dialed 911,

A firm but reassuring female voice responded at the other

end of the line:

What is your emergency? She asked.

"It's about my son? He is totally out of control. He is yelling and screaming and talking to himself."

The words were all jammed up together and Madam Maurice had no idea how much the lady was able to understand.

Madam, Stay calm! Is there any part of the apartment where you feel safe? The lady asked.

Yes madam! I am in the kitchen area. I am ok.

What is your son doing now? Can you ask him if he is ok?

I don't know. He has been quiet for the past minute or so and I am worried.

Maybe Jacques became aware that his mother was on the phone and was trying to listen to the conversation.

Let me confirm your address. You are at ...

Madam Maurice picked up a piece of mail and read over the address.

Ok, madam! Try not to engage him too much! You don't know what might trigger him. Make sure the front door is open.

Thank you, Miss!

A loud and decisive knock on the front door. The police officers were here in less than 10 minutes. All 7 of them with three patrol cars in front of the building. They were already briefed by the 911 dispatcher.

Good afternoon, madam! Where is your son?

"In his room," responded Madam Maurice still frightened.

"Is there any weapon involved?"

"Not to my knowledge."

The officers were on high alert. They had their hand on their side, ready to pull their gun if necessary.

Jacques, I am Officer Jones. What is going on?

Jacques was suddenly quiet and did not offer an answer.

The officer repeated his question.

Are you on any medications?

Yes sir!

When was the last time you took them?

I don't remember. Last night maybe

Where are the medications now?

In this draw said Jacques pointing toward the drawer at the bedside

Would it be okay if your mom gives it to you?

After some hesitation, he nodded affirmatively.

Is that a Yes?

I'll take it.

Stay in the corner over there. I am going to call your mother to help you, okay?

The police officer waved the mother in, asking her to retrieve the medication and administer it to her son.

The police officer was careful not to go into Jacques's

personal belongings because he did not have a warrant to search the house.

Jacques's demeanor had changed. He was now calm and cooperative.

Madam Maurice was expecting something different. She thought they would come and haul away her son to an emergency room.

The officer explained that at the moment because Jacques responded appropriately to all the questions, seemed calm, and cooperated fully with the procedures, there was no reason to take him to the hospital against his will. In other words, he did not meet the criteria for involuntary commitment.

The police officers took turns explaining that the mother needed to initiate an *ex-parte* at the County Clerk of the County office. The document will be signed by a judge and filed with the local police. If something happens again, the police will be able to take him to the nearest Crisis center for psychiatric examination and further care. For now, because your son's behavior did not indicate that he was an imminent danger to himself or others, there is not much more we can do.

It is not clear whether Madam Maurice understood all this mumbo jumbo, the police officers left some information about the court and their business cards and left. The rest of the evening went on without further incident. Jacques, after he took the medication, fell asleep.

It could have been worse. Jacques did not reveal the fact that he had an unregistered gun. They did not search the place. This is Florida where you could carry a gun without a permit.

What happened there?

Was it the impressive display of officers in uniforms and military gear?

Or was it that his temporary episode of psychosis had just vanished?

He was not a happy camper. He could not believe that his mother had called the police on him.

Chapter 7

Miami, Florida circa 2004

"Be merciful unto me, O God: be merciful unto me: for my soul, I trusteth in thee..." chanted the crazed man behind the wheel of his taxicab as he looked at the reflection of his unshaven face in the rearview mirror. For hours passengers from all walks of life have trusted this man to make it on time to their destination. They have placed their safety into the hands of this troubled man. It is quite easy to get duped by this man's easy demeanor. Most passengers are too self-absorbed to pay attention to the cab driver. Even if they did, it is doubtful that they could discern the extent of this man's distress. If the eyes are a vista to the soul, this man's distraught look should easily reveal his internal turmoil. In so many ways Jacques has become a master of disguise. Until now, he has been able to conceal his mercurial character behind an air of *bon enfant*. The twelve-hour shifts behind the wheel of his official yellow Crown Victoria Ford have seemed interminable. Construction projects are popping up every few miles. The huge signs put up by the municipalities easily tell the story. For many years this tropical paradise looked like it would never recover from racial unrest. There had been riots and whole neighborhoods were burned to the ground after what some minority groups perceived as the unjustified shooting of a Black

man by a white police officer. Maybe, it was the price that this splendid city had to pay for wanting to be everything to everyone. On any given day, Miami's population is made of Northern migrants running away from the inclement weather, South Americans and Caribbeans chased by political unrest, not to forget native Blacks who continue to claim partial ownership of this fertile land. A series of man-made disasters and major hurricanes left gaping wounds in many spots of the city. Investors who had run for cover at the first time of trouble are coming back in throve. South Beach has not returned to the glorious days of Al Capone and Frank Sinatra but has witnessed a revival, catering this time to those who refuse to accept the passing of time and are forever chasing the elusive shadow of the fountain of youth. Miami wants to be the magic city of the future and has embarked on huge development projects. Very soon, theater lovers will be able to enjoy a new art district a la Broadway anchored by a brand-new performing art center. Camelot and outdoorsmen from all over the world will come to this maritime mecca to see memorabilia that celebrates the city's unique position at the crossroads of the Americas with countless stories of recovered ships laden with treasures made of bullions and precious stones stolen from the natives in colonial time. It is easy to dream when you are in Miami. Dreaming is not a difficult thing to do when you are in Miami. It is also the city where all the cultures mix, the well-advertised sports events as well as those that occur in the underworld by invitation only. It is not uncommon for a taxi driver to come across a Santeria ritual in the morning, a loud political protest in front of the INS building by midday, a voodoo ceremony by dusk, and to end the day on a cockfighting ranch in some well-guarded park of Hialeah. All in one day!

Meanwhile, navigating through the streets has become an ordeal designed to test the patience and endurance of the most skilled driver. On most days, Jacques could have easily fit into the category of a skilled driver. Not today. Making it through the day has become increasingly difficult for this deranged man. Jacques had the presentiment that something bizarre was about to happen. Not just one of these minor events that could be attributed to chance. Something much more serious, something apocalyptic that had the potential to change Jacques' life forever. He knew it and felt powerless to stop it. Jacques has never felt this way before. They say that some people are endowed with the unique ability to predict catastrophic events. If canines can be granted better olfactory sense than humans, why can some humans have more acute sense than others? Jacques never pretended to anyone that he had any special ability to predict supernatural events. Nor that he cared to find an explanation for the unusual once they happen. This time was different. Jacques was in the middle of it all. Nothing around him seems to matter. Not the splendid Miami skyline. Not the iridescent kaleidoscope of colors of the setting sun. Not the parade of gorgeous beauty queens that zipped by him in their late-model convertibles. Something extraordinary was about to happen and it commanded his full attention. All the signs were there, the flashing lights, the throbbing headache, the pounding behind his eyebrows, and the sudden urge to throw up. Jacques had just entered a danger zone.

"*Be merciful unto me, O God: be merciful unto me: for my soul, I trusteth in thee…*"

These few words have become his mantra at the first sign of trouble. Right about now, Jacques had the visceral knowledge that trouble was about to visit him. He needed every single bit of help that he could get. Images of doom were flashing in front of his eyes at a vertiginous pace.

Car wrecks!

Mingled bodies tossed hundreds of yards away!

Blood-covered faces!

Fighting Roosters!

Explosions!

Racing black cows running away from the fatal dagger of their slayer and succumbing!

Girls laced in silk danced frenetically.

Around an altar where the chosen virgin awaits!

Walking zombies!

The smell of burning incense!

Chanting warriors with spears and daggers!

Unearthed skulls!

An apocalyptic mixture of the ancient with the modern carrying an unmistakable message of foreboding came rushing to Jacques' consciousness. He was now under the control of a force greater than anything imaginable to man. He would have much preferred to avoid the experience altogether, but it was not his choice to make. A sense of inevitability had overtaken his will to resist. Fear and despair were the order of the day. Jacques felt as if a heavy burden was suddenly placed on his shoulder. Without warning, the picture-perfect Miami landscape was replaced by a live and gory fresco painted on a huge canvas of shattered glass. Adding to the fright, were the deafening sounds of drumbeats from faraway lands. How was it possible for the mind to fall for such trickery? The intensity of the moment was too much for anyone to bear. For a while, Jacques was oblivious to his surroundings. Instead, he was drawn into a world of confusion that offered no escape. He could not distinguish between these horrific visions and his reality. He was tempted to immerse himself in the mayhem that had taken over his very essence. Visions and reality were merged into a dysmorphic and beastly mass. Was Jacques supposed to be a mere observer or was he supposed to be the main actor?

Jacques did not know. This sheer moment of uncertainty only added to his torment. Anything was better than this feeling of helplessness. Maybe he could find relief by ramming his vehicle into a passing gas truck. Maybe he could just disintegrate in a fume of silvery smoke. Maybe he could disappear, lock, stock, and barrel into the center of the earth. He might as well because the feeling was unbearable. Anywhere but here! But at this very moment, was there any place in the universe where Jacques could find peace?

"Be merciful unto me, O God: be merciful unto me: for my soul, I trusteth in thee..."

Jacques was sinking quickly into a bottomless pit, a point of no return, a netherworld where evil runs unchallenged. The convulsion that ran through his body ceased. A frozen stare replaced the shuddering of his eyes. Evil was challenged. It was not time. Something, a greater force maybe, pulled him back. Jacques had suddenly been rescued from the untimely encounter with a world where gargoyles and demons plot to create havoc within the universe. His hands held tightly onto the wheel. So tightly that blood oozed from around his fingernails. Jacques looked as if he had just returned from a long journey.

Jacques lets out a mysterious and unintelligible sound, a cavernous sound that seemed thousands of years old.

AAAYEEBOBO!

Was it a war cry? Or was it instead the cry of someone who had just been liberated from the tentacles of a fearsome and inescapable monster? Would this release be temporary? For now, at least, Jacques was summoned back into the real world.

It was over.

This whole episode lasted less than three minutes. It was not unlike the many ones that Jacques has been experiencing lately.

Jacques recovered rather quickly. There was no escaping the essential task of finding his way back to his neighborhood. Jacques turned off the light on the top of his cab, signaling that he was off duty. Until dawn the next morning, hookers and lawyers, doctors and patients, cheating wives and husbands, runaway teenagers, and fleeing criminals would have to find another cab to ferry them to their destination.

Throughout the day, many have attempted to engage Jacques in their daily little dramas. It is not only true that whenever they think they can get away with it, humans will violate every rule. They have an inherent need to portray themselves as heroes, as better than the next person. Everyone wants to be the little train that could. No loser stepped into

Jacques' car that day. At least that is what they would have you believe. In the marathon of life, everyone was a champion that day. Impassible, Jacques has maintained the neutral and taciturn face of a cleric sitting in a confessional. Hardly ever would Jacques allow himself a furtive smile. Jacques has mastered the art of tuning out his interlocutors while maintaining a non-committal grin. After a while, it all became so obvious.

The continuous rambling from these transients was nothing but unintelligible background noises of which the true content Jacques has learned to ignore. He clearly understood that his duty was to transport his clients not to entertain them, to take them safely to the destination of their choice, not to counsel them. In exchange for a hefty fee, of course! His calls have taken him from exclusive gated communities where guards clad in their perfectly pressed uniforms showered visitors and residents with kindness before ushering them to their destination. He has also driven through neighborhoods of Miami so filled with squalor that inhaling the pestilent air would truly be hazardous to anyone's health. The day has not gone well. Twice earlier today, his daily routines have come close to changing into chaos. All day long he had to withhold his disdain for the weird individuals that he had to serve. He could not feel any keenness to the weird characters that would choose to sport outlandish hairdos, artificial nails, and distasteful attires. He could not stand the sight of them, let alone the fact that he had to display a modicum of courtesy since they were his clients. Jacques was not a happy camper. Things got worse. When a tall and anorexic transsexual clad in a tight dress and high heels tried to bargain her way out of paying her taxi fare by offering him some special sexual favors, Jacques could no longer contain himself. He exploded in a long tirade of unintelligible epithets. For a moment, he contemplated pulling his unregistered magnum to terminate the miserable life of this loser. Who would miss this rejection anyway? Jacques held back and moments later started to feel ashamed for harboring such rancor and lack of tolerance. It was not meant to be. A police officer drove by. The strange character dashed out of the cab and disappeared into an apartment project. Years of work as a taxi driver have changed Jacques from a simple and amiable individual into a calculating, mistrusting fellow, filled with bitterness, a man that is yet to be convinced that people do not deserve every bit of pain that is handed out to them. This was not the kind of life that Jacques had contemplated. If the people that he left behind back in his native country only knew! It seems so long ago when Jacques was filled with the better-world ideology of the sixties. He held the belief that the world was guided by the irresistible force of good. This force would lead to revolutionary changes that would sweep across the planet to wipe out all the injustice and inequity around him. His mission as a human was to give in to this force and let it transform everything around him.

The era of social engineering came. Many youths follow the utopic peregrinations of visionary leaders and then everything came to a screeching halt. Like many others, Jacques turned to the large cities of the North to pursue his version of Shangri-la. There, he would not pick gold coins off the streets as the folktales from his homeland would have you believe. He would not find seven virgins waiting to serve him milk and honey. He would at least find the opportunity to work and earn an honorable place in society. He had dreamed of a place where he could escape the daily chaos and despair and find internal bliss. He had dreamed of a place where hope could once again flourish. Almost ten years to the day since he left his hometown, Jacques could not find cause for celebration. It was quite the opposite. Jacques feels that every day he was moving further away from that dream. There he was behind a wheel, barely maintaining his sanity, fighting every instant the impulse to join in the chaos that surrounds him. Indeed, it was everywhere. The daily broadcasts were replete with news of youths maiming peaceable citizens attending to their daily businesses. There were stories about school shootings, stories about senseless drive-by gang killings by drug dealers. Many seniors were living in fear, locked away into an electronically protected perimeter, remotely monitored by watchful guards. It seemed like the very core values of the social fabric were under attack. There had to be more to life than this.

Jacques wished that he could find an outlet from all of this.

One thing is for sure, Jacques' unassuming demeanor was only telling part of his story. There was a much darker side filled with many unanswered questions. Even if Jacques could delve into his unconscious and bring them to the surface, he is not sure that he could reveal them to anyone. Had he revealed to the DMV that he suffers from an intractable seizure, he most likely would have been disqualified for a chauffeur-class driver's license. How could they entrust the life of the public in the hands of someone that could become ill in the middle of traffic in a large metropolitan area? Jacques knew that much. When the questions came up on his application, he did not hesitate a moment. His answers were unequivocal.

Do you suffer from any illness that would prevent you from safely operating a vehicle?

No.

Are you taking any medication that could impair your motor skills?

No.

Jacques had more secrets. Often, he has fantasized about what he would do if violence suddenly showed up at his door.

"Thank God! The day is over. Or almost over!" Jacques thought.

Navigating his way through the interminable lanes of moving headlights was going to be particularly difficult that night. Many times, he has felt on the verge of a convulsive episode. All the familiar signs were there, the flashing lights, the sudden headache, the nauseating feeling. Jacques felt like he was in a trance. Everything seemed on automatic pilot. The mad rush before the long weekend was not helping. Add a throng of tourists driving their rental cars from the beaches to your regular crowd of workers emptying these humongous downtown skyscrapers to get back to their suburban homes. What do you have? An unstable and explosive mixture of travelers filled with road rage. Remarkably, these travelers for the most part behave well. Every so often a crazed driver will have enough and shoot at another car for being shown the finger. These incidents are extremely rare. Of course, Jacques never revealed to the Department of Motor Vehicles that he suffers from intractable epilepsy. He is still holding onto the last prescription that he received at the community clinic. Jacques did not believe that he needed to reveal his matter to some State agency or anyone else for that matter. Jacques hardly confides in anyone. A little bit of information here, a little bit there, and before you know it, your whole life is known to everyone. That could become very damaging to his reputation. Besides, how is he supposed to make a living? Driving a cab is all that he has ever done. When he is behind the wheels of his cab, he is the master of the universe. What a dangerous proposition to operate a vehicle under Jacques's condition. What would happen if he started to have a seizure while in the middle of a traffic jam? So many times,

Jacques has daydreamed about crashing underneath one of the large gas tankers. What a spectacular ball of fire it would create! To get his mind off these morbid thoughts, Jacques has become accustomed to reciting the now familiar verses from the good book "Be merciful unto me, O God: be merciful unto me: for my soul, I trusteth in thee…"

This early evening was not any different from the previous ones. Soon he will be bearing left into the Miami Lakes exit of Highway I-95. He will look with envy at the well-manicured lawn of the expensive estates and find his way to the decrepit enclave that he calls home. As he approaches the driveway, a group of teenagers scrammed as if they have seen a ghost. They know better not to loiter around when Jacques is home. He takes pleasure in scaring them away and has threatened to report them to the police for smoking pot.

Once he enters his apartment, it will be difficult to get him out. He spends most evenings watching reruns of old movies until he falls asleep.

Chapter 8

"No, not again!" Jacques Gaetan exclaimed, almost jumping out of his bed. The wrinkles on the linen bear witness to the struggle that Jacques has waged during the seemingly endless night. Sitting up at the edge of his bed, Jacques seemed terrified. Jacques could not take his eyes off the glowing red numbers of the digital clock laying on top of his 13-inch television set. He wished that the night would just go away. How long would he be able to tolerate this sinking feeling that had suddenly come over him? His heart was going on a one-hundred-meter dash. Jacques was a very frightened man. He has hardly had any sleep. He was afraid to shut his eyes. He looked like a man who had just been handed a death sentence. He was awestruck. Did the Specter of Death, dressed up in his all-too-familiar black tunic, just knock on Jacques' door with his claim check in one hand and his sickle in the other? Jacques was all alone in the apartment studio, barely large enough to accommodate a twin-size bed, a rather noisy refrigerator, and a few other essentials. Conspicuously placed on top of the entrance door was a massively decorated crucifix. Cold sweat was pouring down the back of his neck. His mouth felt awfully dry. For Jacques, there was no escape. Not even the talisman around Jacques' neck has been able to ward off the demons that have been pursuing him. He has just awakened from another one of

those scary dreams that have haunted his sleep over the past few weeks. Lord, it is back. That skull. That horrific-looking skull. Will that skull just go away? A black skull had suddenly come alive in Jacques' dreams. Oh, what a sight! A grin frozen in time. An inscrutable facial expression. It was hard to tell whether it was an expression of sudden grief or one of sheer terror. As if that was not enough, maggots were crawling all over the lower mandible. Those were the images flashing behind Jacques' eyes, like the frames of a short movie. And then, there was that voice. Lugubrious, cavernous, piercing the wall that separates the dead from the living, uttering an unforgettable and enigmatic curse.

".Maudit! Maudit!"

Something was wrong! Something was wrong! Jacques in exasperation, has torn up the shirt of his blue and white striped pajamas.

His bed looks as if a twister has gone through it. Jacques' fear has converted into an uncontrollable rage.

"Who are you?

What the hell do you want from me?

Why me?

Why don't you leave me alone?

Jacques yelled into the night. Not that he expected a response to his inquiry. Not that his yelling and screaming would be enough to vent his frustration. What good would that do anyway? Some invisible force had completely taken over. His words reverberated against the walls of the room and came back to him, foreign, distorted like a 33-rpm vinyl record playing out of tune. Jacques could not even recognize his own words. That timbre into the night was suddenly not his. It frightened him to even hear his laments. If he could only run away from this room? No, there was no escape. It seemed that this small room would be his coffin, his tomb all at once. Whatever was happening on that frightful night was not natural. How could it be? Jacques knew it but felt powerless to do anything about it.

Complete silence!

There would be no answer to his question that night. He could not understand why he was being persecuted. The macabre condemnation from the living dead had stopped for now. Maybe it was better that way. Jacques was not sure that he could deal with the answer to his question for now. The only audible sounds left were Jacques' heartbeats and his labored breathing. The room suddenly felt like a tank from which every bit of oxygen was slowly being sucked out. Jacques was suffocating. He needed some air very badly. Any time now, he would faint. Jacques felt as if his stomach was being turned inside out. He felt the bitter taste of gall coming up his throat. He held back to keep himself from vomiting. Thank God! He has not had a good meal for almost two days now. How much could a man take? He felt confused. He was a very tormented and troubled man. Something has gone awry. Jacques did not know what it was, but he just knew that he was completely under the control of a powerful and maleficent force. Jacques was afraid that inevitably, that night, the night after, and every night at the same time, this hideous black skull would reappear and take over the night. For interminable moments, Jacques would be slowly and methodically tortured by visions of an unknown and mysterious world. Jacques would be a haunted man. The past few days have not been any different. Somehow, Jacques had the feeling that he was forced into a battle for which he was very ill-prepared. Jacques was teetering on the verge of a psychotic break. He could hear madness knocking on his door.

Jacques mechanically reached for the top drawer of his nightstand. He could hardly read the fading label on some of the vials. Dilantin. Carbamazepine. He knew that there were medications that he should have been taking, but he has given up a long time ago.

"*Where are those stupid Tylenol?* ", Jacques was going into a frenzy. He finally found the container. It was empty.

What am I going to do about this throbbing headache now?" he said desperately. Lately, his migraines have been unbearable. He has tried every over-the-counter pill that he could find. Yet he seemed to have made up his mind that he would not return to his neurologist.

He needed some fresh air. He opened the window. A gentle breeze raced into the room bringing into the cubicle the decayed smell of the city. Anything was better than the mustiness of this room where the smell of sweat-soaked linen and Lysol contributed to creating a peculiar and unbearable stench. But that was not all. A large black butterfly almost the size of a bat, rushed into the poorly lit room, rhythmically flapping its wings. Jacques shuddered. Fear rippled through him. It was as if Jacques had suddenly gulped a large glass of ice-cold water that went straight to his stomach and just stayed there. Jacques' face was ashen. A cadaver well made up by a mortician for the final journey would have looked one hundred percent better. The line had been crossed. Somehow, he knew that he was no longer dealing with a simple dream, a mere phantasm of an insecure, stressed, and neurotic man. Was the black butterfly a final messenger from the other world? Or was it an omen that Jacques would not be in this fight all alone and that his guardian angels were ready to give him a hand? Either way, the forces of evil had landed, and wanted Jacques to know that they could not be ignored. In the small yard behind the apartment complex, the leaves from the dark olive trees have started to turn brown. Fall would soon be here, and the Miamians would finally get a break from the baking tropical heat of the last days of August. Outside, there were shadows. They took on different shapes and competed fiercely with the vanishing glows from the streetlamp posts. Soon though, all of that will not be necessary. The sunshine would take over. The outlines of the city would spring out of the dark. It will bring warmth and brightness into our hearts and maybe insurmountable challenges. And all the demons and goblins will have to retreat into their obscure shelters, awaiting more opportune moments to strike. Jacques will get a brief reprieve. He will be tempted to fall back into a false sense of security and start hoping... Hoping what? Jacques knew all too well that his troubles were far from over. His eyes glued to the red numbers of his digital clock; Jacques was lost in his thoughts. He was a man besieged. Night after night, he would have to face the same enemies. What would the future hold? Jacques wondered. He implored the Heavens to read David's Psalm:

"I am worn out from sobbing.
Every night tears drench my bed;
my pillow is wet from weeping."

Chapter 9

Jacques' fear went far beyond the frightful events of the night. To add to his misery, as if he did not have enough trouble, Jacques became aware of intermittent pain in his lower abdomen. Paralyzed by fear, he had ignored the signals from his bladder. Now, it could no longer avoid it. His bladder felt as if it was just about to bust. Jacques rushed to the bathroom. As he was urinating, he caught a glance of himself in the mirror. He stared at his image in the mirror for a very long while. He shuddered. What he saw frightened him. He did not like it at all. There were bags under his eyes. His face was pale like ashes. He was panting like a persecuted animal. He had the look of a terrorized man. "Who was this man?" he seemed to wonder. Jacques was even more afraid to look back and see what his life had become…

He had no choice but to return to Dr. Dickenson, the psychiatrist. He needed help. He went on to give more details about his recurring dream:

"I see myself in that big old house, he started. It looks like the place where I used to live in Les Cayes, a city in the Southern part of Haiti. I am lying in bed holding hands with other people who look like my brothers and sisters. The walls start to shake. The clay chips off the wall and starts falling off. Everyone is in sheer panic. It is storming outside. A skull as black as coal, pops out of a crack from the wall. What an expression on his face! An expression of intolerable anguish. Oh, these horrifying words out of his mouth echoing in the night: Maudit!... Maudit!... Maudit! They cannot seem to stop. The skull seems to have a crack in the occipital area. The name O'Connor keeps on flashing in my head. I am confused. I do not know what to do. I am looking for help. I have a dagger in my hands. I stab it. Fire comes out. It crumbles to the ground. Everyone is screaming. ... The horrifying words are still resonating in my head: *Maudit... Maudit... Maudit...*"

"I cannot tell you how many times I have had this dream until now. What is going on, Doc? Am I losing my mind? Can you help me? I am very scared. Please help me, Doc!" Jacques implored.

The expression on Dr. Dickenson's face was one of bewilderment. For a long while, the good doctor was speechless. He was nervously running his index finger through his greying mustache. He looked like he wanted to say something. No words were coming out of his mouth. That was a remarkable turn of events. A psychiatrist who had lost his usual loquacious ways. A psychiatrist that could not jabber away to get out of sticky situations. That was news. Dr. Dickenson seemed as agitated as Jacques was. If he were to continue to be helpful to his patient, he needed to quickly regain control of the situation. "What then shall I do? What then shall I do?" The bewildered psychiatrist seemed to wonder. The closest he has ever been to such an intense dream was from his reading of "Interpretation of Dreams" by Sigmund Freud. Somewhere in this dream, there was supposed to be some symbolism, a key that would give meaning to these disjointed somewhat nonsensical images. Where was that key? Dr. Dickenson did not have a clue. His vast knowledge and experience were being challenged. How was he going to get out of that one? He could not brush it aside as yet another manifestation of psychosis. That just won't do. He could not just say, "I will get back to you." No, this man in front of him was in too much distress.

Dr. Dickenson decided to be honest, and said, "I am sure that there is some very important meaning attached to this dream. The fact that you have been having it so many times is also significant. However, I must admit the meaning of it all escapes me at this time. Why a black skull? I do not know. I do not know what chemical phenomenon could cause a skull to turn black."

Once again Dr. Dickenson could not help it. He was hooked on the purely scientific explanation of the question. Any other approach would have been a great surprise. Dr. Dickenson could see an attempt at mastering an otherwise insurmountable challenge... He could also see Jacques' unconscious attempting to deliver a very important, life-threatening message to him. For now, Dr. Dickenson was particularly interested in giving immediate relief to his patient. Dr. Dickenson felt that he was in over his head with this case.

In recent years, psychiatrists to regain their footing with the other specialists of medicine, have moved away from what was perceived as the abstract field of the mind. No longer do psychiatrists passively sit in their comfortable chairs, while patients pour their hearts out. Solemn “uhm"..., and "I see..." followed by long pauses will no longer do. They have sought to discover the linkage between biology and behavior. Some of the newly trained psychiatrists - in the name of biological psychiatry and due to the tremendous success of drugs like Prozac, Paxil, Risperdal, and more recently Zyprexa - have given up on psychotherapy, a field traditionally covered by psychiatrists.

They have been reduced by managed care companies to the role of drug prescribers. No longer does the patient seem to get the benefit of extensive contact with a physician. As a result, the physician is unable to develop the breadth of knowledge and familiarity with the issues necessary to treat patients with complicated problems like Jacques'. First, Dr. Dickenson seemed to lack either the training in psychotherapy or the cultural competency necessary to deal with Jacques' situation. Jacques, therefore, was doomed from the start. No number of medications and no surgical interventions would be able to fix him.

It would be interesting to find out how a managed care claim reviewer would deal with Jacques’ case.
Dr. Dickenson was a good physician, and as such, he decided to

consult with Dr. Friedman, one of the few trained psychoanalysts in the area. It is doubtful that Dr. Friedman's psychoanalytical training included anything about alternative belief systems, even less so about Voodoo beliefs. These beliefs have long been discarded as barbaric and devilish. The Western world, especially the American society has developed vis-a-vis the Voodoo religion what Laennec Hurbon calls an "a priori attitude of scorn and rejection rooted in U. S. interpretations of Haitian independence, interpretations based on anti-Black racism."

Dr. Dickenson felt more powerless as Jacques's symptoms persisted. " I want you to learn the techniques of relaxation. You really can take control of your body and your mind with these exercises." He went on to demonstrate. "Just imagine yourself laying on the sand in a garden by the sea. The beach is deserted. You are all alone. The only sound you could hear is that of the waves breaking on the sand. You are feeling an irresistible feeling of peace coming all over you. You let yourself go. This feeling is taking all your troubles away. As you are laying on the sand, you feel in total control. The whole scene is under your control. You could change it as you wish. Do you want a little bit more sunshine? There! The place is all yours. Every single bird in this place is at your command. What tune would you like them to play? Yellow birds? Go ahead and ask them!"

Jacques was being very cooperative. He did not know he could respond to something like that. You learn something about yourself every day. This session turned out to be very helpful. At least, Jacques left much less agitated. He was still worried. What would he do when the dreams come back? Dr. Dickenson increased Jacques' dose of Xanax and added Ambien, a new sleeping pill. Jacques left with the feeling that his story was going to be all over the medical campus. Jacques remained very suspicious. His worst fear was that people would laugh at him when he passes by. Don't doctors discuss their cases over lunch all the time? Jacques was promised that everything would be confidential, but he did not quite believe it. All Jacques needed on top of everything was for some clerk to read Dr. Dickenson's notes and start talking about his problems.

What would have happened if Jacques had gone to a Haitian psychiatrist? Jacques believed that the problem would have been the same. Jacques did not believe that psychiatrists, despite their vow of confidentiality, can keep people from gossiping, especially when it comes to mysterious stories like his. People seem to be fascinated with the weird and the unusual. Jacques thought about discontinuing his visits to the psychiatrist altogether. What would become of him if he would? As it is now, he was not doing well at all. At least, Dr. Dickenson was someone to talk to.

Jacques was afraid that his story would perpetuate the stereotypes about his fellow Haitians. He was distressed about that possibility. Meanwhile, it has been many weeks now since he started to see Dr. Dickenson, and nothing seemed to be happening. He had turned on to the Bible in a ritualistic way." His mother did not give up on trying to find out what was going on with her son. At the dinner table, she told Jacques without hesitation:

"I will be coming with you on your next visit. I want to know what is going on. "

She was very concerned about Jacques' condition and wanted to hear directly from the doctor. Jacques did not have a say in the matter. Good luck trying to convince a concerned Haitian mother that psychiatric sessions, unless otherwise indicated, are somewhat restricted to the patient and the doctor Once Madam Maurice had made up her mind about something, it became useless to argue.

The situation was very awkward. Madam Maurice had difficulty understanding most of what Dr. Dickinson was trying to explain. To understand abstract psychological concepts would be difficult for everyone but was especially so for a sixty-four-year-old woman who spoke little English and had only a limited secondary education. A lot of the conversation was missed. Maybe it was better that way because Jacques would feel very uncomfortable if she could understand what Dr. Dickenson would later have to say at some point he was expecting Dr. Dickenson and Dr. Friedman to offer him their understanding of his persistent symptoms. "As I promised, Dr. Dickenson started,

I consulted with Dr. Friedman. He feels, and I agree, that the problem is sexual."

"What do you mean, sexual?" Jacques inquired, somewhat embarrassed by the insinuation.

"Well! You are over forty-four, not married and you live alone..."

"And you think this is why I am having these dreams." Jacques interrupted.

"You see Mr. Gaetan, dreams are sometimes like a safety valve, an outlet where we can vent our frustration without fear of ridicule or consequences."

"I still don't see the connection with that awful-looking skull. Go on!"

"You have remained sexually fixated and have not grown into a fully developed adult."

Jacques could not stand this psychiatric mumbo-jumbo anymore. In his mind, none of this made any sense.

"Sorry Doc, you are completely off. You are not even close. You missed it by a mile." Jacques was thinking, He suddenly lost all his usual combativeness. He would not share his thoughts with the good doctor. No, not this time. Instead, he decided to put an abrupt end to the session. He walked out, vowing not to come back.

"This was a charade, a real charade."

However, Jacques was still impressed by the ability of the

psychiatrist to capture a side of him that he has not been willing to face. How could Dr. Dickenson have possibly known about it? Jacques attended Catholic school as a child. Sexual issues were just not discussed. They were taboo. Everything that he knows, he learned from his uninformed peers. When puberty hit, he was completely unprepared. He could not understand his sudden urges and desire for intimacy. He felt confused about the wet dreams and the early morning penile erections. When he caught himself engaging in repetitive self-stimulation, he felt sinful and guilty. He would pray to God for forgiveness and would run to confession. He would recite hundreds of "Ave Maria."

"Ave Maria! Gratia plena. Dominus tecum. "Santa Maria mater Dei, ora pro nobis."

As the hormonal changes were intensifying, so were the sexual fantasies. Jacques caught himself lusting at anatomical parts in magazine pictures. Jacques started to take long walks to the riverside. There he would loaf around for hours, laying on the grass and watching some of the women taking a swim with their breasts exposed, while others were busy doing their laundry. Jacques would become quite aroused. He had no idea that he was subject to a natural phenomenon. Jacques became even more confused when he started to feel some tenderness in his breast. His mind would wander. Jacques was ripe for initiation.

Jacques was hesitant to ask his friends about their own

experiences, until one day, he was invited to a place named *Chez Michelle*. The place was packed with women wearing very tight clothes, outlandish hairdos, and heavy makeup. The group was greeted at the door with endearing names.

"*Mon petit cheri*, what is your pleasure tonight?"

Jacques was shocked. Never in his life, could he imagine women being so forward. He could not contain his nervousness when a lady who introduced herself as Maria came right at him and whispered in his ears.

"Are you ready for some action, mi amor? I can make you feel really good."

Jacques was taken aback. He did not know what he was supposed to say. Maria was extremely attractive. She stood about five foot-ten inches and had the facial features of a doll. Her nose was almost too perfect. Her full mane of jet-black hair came down gracefully and was gently caressing her shoulder. She looked like an Egyptian goddess. Before Jacques could say anything, Maria was sitting on his lap, nibbling on his ear and neck. Jacques felt a rush of blood going through his whole body. It was a feeling unlike any other that Jacques had experienced before. His friends seem very amused. Like spectators in a bullfight arena, they were rooting him on.

"Jacques, you are in luck! You have got yourself una *chica*. Maria likes you. She means business. Go for it!"

Was Jacques up to the challenge? It is unbelievable what

people can do when they are faced with peer pressure. Jacques found himself alone with the siren of the night. She had meant every word she said about making Jacques feel like a *conquistador.*

What happened after that, Jacques would never say. Jacques came back less than fifteen minutes later. Jacques could not perform that night. It was not for lack of stimulation. Maria had the most gorgeous pair of breasts that any man would ever wish to see, and that any woman would ever wish to have. They look like they were carved out by the creative hands of Salvador Dali. Jacques had succumbed to the momentous events of the night. A goddess had descended from heaven to quench the libidinous fire that has been burning inside of him for quite some time. The pressure was just too much for him to bear. He never told his friends what had happened. Rumor had it, that Jacques was afflicted with a not-so-uncommon ailment "premature ejaculation."

Jacques revisited that place quite a few times. Over the next year, he would try Theresa, Martine, and Soledad as if he wanted to have another chance, but always he would end up in some mishap. He was growing more ashamed and frustrated about his failure. How did he end up a regular customer at a brothel was hard to imagine. Jacques would hang out in the cafe on Saturday night and to mass on Sunday morning. Jacques was growing more disenchanted about his church affiliation. It had become such a routine and he did not feel that his heart was in it.

Jacques stopped attending religious services. A few years later, he would have another opportunity to broaden his sexual horizon. He met a girl named Suzanne. It was one of those stories that one does not hear often.

Jacques fell in love right away, at least he thought he did. For some time, Jacques felt like a different person. He found himself thinking about Suzanne. He would write long poems to her, professing his love. Suzanne responded to his love notes and acknowledged Jacques' poems. She was playing hard to get. Suzanne would tease Jacques enough to keep him interested but would fall short of accepting Jacques' advances. Jacques persisted. One afternoon, to Jacques' surprise, she accepted to accompany him to the beach. It was an afternoon that Jacques would never forget. Everything was going right that day. Jacques and Suzanne spent the whole afternoon together, they frolicked in the white sand and swam in the blue Caribbean Sea and then... and then it happened! Jacques was on fire. His body was alive. His shyness and many unsuccessful attempts at sexual intercourse seemed so far behind him. Suzanne surrendered. She responded to Jacques' relentless energy with vivacity. They kissed for a long time and explored each other's inhibitions that he had carried on his shoulders for so long. Like a dam under assault from an out-of-control avalanche, their young bodies gave in.

They came in unison, letting out a scream

A primal scream.

Dream fulfilled.

Thirst quenched.

Task mastered.

It was hard for Jacques not to fall to the charm of this woman whose body contours were almost perfect. He felt the tautness of Suzanne's inner thigh muscles and pressed hard. His heart was pounding out of his chest. She whimpered, making long and repetitive dove sounds. They kissed. They play with each other's tongues. No words could describe how it felt. It seemed that even the seagulls were fooled. They came by as if they were latecomers to a party to which very few were invited.

They joined in the celebration and started a concert of their own. It was time. The moment had arrived to join their body together in an ultimate demonstration of passion. He awkwardly tried to find his way inside of her. She offered some assistance.

They went on and on. Holding back, letting go in an unprecedented display of strength and control. It was all so natural. They were in seventh heaven. There would be no more self-restraint, no more self-denial. Jacques felt suddenly relieved of the weight of the body.

That experience was never to be repeated. Suzanne suddenly left town leaving Jacques wondering why. His heart was broken. Since then, he has gone back to unfulfilled fantasies, searching still for the lost moments. The sunset had forever taken Jacques' energy and soul into the depth of the Caribbean Sea. This experience had left him profoundly traumatized. He could not get close to anyone. So, when Dr. Dickenson suggested that Jacques' recurring dream was sexual, it was as if an old wound was suddenly ripped open without any warning. Jacques was not ready to deal with this unfinished business.

He left Dr. Dickenson's office more confused and distressed than ever. He was desperate. Jacques was afraid that if something was not done soon, he would indeed lose his mind.

Chapter 10

His sleep had not improved. Jacques would kneel by his bed every night and recite Psalm 91. He knew the verses by heart: *"Celui qui demeure a l'abri du Tres-Haut..."*

"Those who live in the shelter of the Most High, will find rest in the shadow of the Almighty... He alone is my refuge, my place of safety; he is my God, and I am trusting him. For he will rescue me from every trap...His faithful promises are your armor and protection..."

Jacques was raised as a Catholic, but it has been a long time since he went to mass. The last time he went to Sunday mass, things seemed so different. The songs were unfamiliar. He did not feel that he had much in common with the members of the church as if they were not from the same community. It was not that the pastor did not go out of his way to make everyone comfortable. He invited the congregation to shake hands and meet each other, but it all seemed so artificial. The sermon sounded more like a political action committee rally. For so long, Jacques had derided his Christian friends who went to Bible school every weekend that he felt ashamed to go to them for help. For the first time in his life, Jacques felt all alone. Maybe moving away from his brother Georges and the vibrant New York community was not such a good idea after all.

Something had to be done fast. In the past two months, Jacques had lost over twenty pounds. He felt extremely tired. In the mornings, he felt like he had just come back from fighting a raging bull. He felt exhausted. Jacques would not answer his phone. One afternoon, Pierre dropped by his apartment. He became worried that he had not seen Jacques at the soccer game the past few Sundays and that Jacques had not returned his calls. For a few weeks now, he had not reported to the taxicab hub. The owner had been asking about him.

Jacques tried very hard to hide the truth from Pierre.

"Tell me what is going on, Jacques. I have not seen you in a couple of weeks," Pierre asked.

"Nothing is wrong! I have been staying home with the flu," Jacques answered.

Of course, Pierre did not believe one word he said. Jacques and Pierre go a long way. Their friendship dated back to elementary school in Les Cayes, until Pierre's parents moved away. They met again almost twelve years later, and they have been inseparable since then. For Jacques not to stay in touch with Pierre was very significant. Pierre could not figure out what, but he just knew that something was wrong.

Jacques's mother stayed away from the conversation. Jacques did not want Pierre to know about his mental condition. She did not want Jacques to start feeling ashamed. Pierre just wanted to help his old friend and felt that his hands were tied.

He would not forgive himself should something happen to Jacques.

Jacques has always been jealous of Pierre's ability to confront situations head-on logically. Besides, Jacques could not get mad at Pierre, the one longtime friend who has always stood by him. Pierre did not want to push Jacques too hard, afraid he might get angry. He greeted Jacques good night and left, uncertain about what might happen next.

Jacques felt stuck. The cup of bitterness is filled to the rim, and he is forced to drink it. He has no escape. He has been cooperative.

He has attended a few therapy sessions with Dr. Dickenson even when he felt that this man of science was disconnected from the essence of his problems. He has taken powerful mind-altering medications to no avail. He has learned the technique of relaxation and imagery. Nothing has worked. He continues to have seizures. And the dreams! The dreams have persisted, relentless, more vivid than ever. Now, he has become familiar with the facial features of that threatening white man pointing a finger at him and screaming. Now he is even calling him by name:

Jacques! Jacques! Maudit sois-tu! Maudit! Maudit! You cannot escape me…

Jacques started to have a lot of self-doubt. Could it be true that his problem is sexual? Why is it that psychiatrists always find a sexual twist to any problems?

Never have the threats been so specific. Jacques has been a wreck.

Could it be true that he has not fully developed into a fully blossomed sexual being? Does that explain his feeling of frustration, his seemingly persistent dissatisfaction? What connection could that possibly have with the dreams about a black skull? Sorry, Dr. Dickenson! I feel you are navigating in unknown waters. If only you would admit it. Jacques' days and nights have been blending into a nasty-tasting potion that was slowly taking away his sanity. How does one escape from this feeling of nothingness? It was taking Jacques by the throat and taking the air out of him. He was gasping for air, and nobody would come to his rescue. He is a passenger on a ship that has gone adrift. No guiding light on the horizon.

Jacques is a soul tormented and shattered. He is battered by a black skull who wants to finish him up and claim victory. Game over!

He has prayed. He has lamented. His prayers have remained unanswered. He is a man forsaken.

I search my soul and I wonder:

Where shall I find an answer to my quest?

Who will offer me the cup of elixir that will quench my thirst?

Entrapped in my mortal fetters, I feel gnawing inside a genuine fear of the unknown

I search my soul and I wonder…

Lost in his thoughts, Jacques's quest for his soul went on unchecked:

Barely finding my way through the labyrinth,
In response to my wish or simply a mirage
I found myself ensnared in a giant plant.
Genesis? The factory of souls?
The working place of a whimsical god?

A clutter like no human eyes has ever seen:
Rejects. Misfits. Remnants. Recalled souls. Degenerated souls.

Jacques was delirious. He needed to do something drastic. It was with this frame of mind that Jacques decided to leave everything behind…

Chapter 11

Jacques decided he had enough. He wanted to be free or at least enjoy the illusion of freedom. He was going to take matters into his own hands.

No medications!

No, Dr. Coleman or Dr. Dickenson!

No watchful eyes of an overly concerned mother!

Early that morning, he walked out of his apartment empty-handed with a few twenty-dollar bills in his pocket. His plan was simple. He would get on the Tri-Rail train and head north until the last stop and return on the same train back. The destination is unknown.

Not that in his current state of mind, he could enjoy any of the beautiful scenery offered by the landscape and the extraordinary architectural design of the expensive mansions.

Off he goes on his trip to nowhere!

He engaged in a repetitive chant, *un cri de guerre* of sort, with words the meaning of which was only clear to him:

Ou Met Rele-m Shango

Pa di mwen gen madichon

Ou met rele-m Azaka

Pa di mwen gen madichon

Mwen pa konnen ki kote-m soti

Mwen pa konnen ki kote-m prale

Ou met Rele-m Legba

Pa di mwen gen madichon

Ou Met rele-m Damballah

Pa di mwen Gen madichon

Se we mwen we-m la

Mwen pa konnen ki-yes mwen ye

Mwen pa konnen ki kote-m soti

Mwen pa konnen ki kote -m prale

Bat chyin tan met li

Pa gen chyin ki pa gen met, tande

Make sa-m di-w la

Pa gen chyin ki pa gen met.

Ale-w vouzan monche

Translation

You can call me Shango

Don't say I am cursed

You can call me Azaka

Don't say I am cursed

I don't know where I came from

I don't know where I am going

You can call me Legba

Don't say I am cursed

You can call me Damballah

Don'tsay I am cursed
I just found myself here
I don't know who I am

I don't know where I am going

Beat the dog, wait for its master
There are no dogs without a master
Mark my words
There are no dogs without a master
Go away! Out of my face.

Was it bravado talks or simply boastful words of a deranged and foolish man? Only time will tell.

Jacques had just fired a shot across the bow of the ship. It was a warning to the old man in the dream. Jacques was ready to launch a fierce counteroffensive.

Jacques was lost in his thoughts. Some of the passengers were disturbed by the presence of this strange man with a disheveled appearance, mumbling and seemingly talking to himself in a language they could not understand. Jacques was becoming a nuisance, they soon started to move away from him. Not too many people in this country have tolerance for individuals they perceive as "other" or different. There have been reports of passers-by attacking and savagely beating homeless or mentally ill people just because such people did not fit how they imagine the world to be. It was enough. A passenger signaled Jacques to the train attendant and at the next stop in Boynton Beach, Jacques was evicted. Just like that! No explanation was given.

Jacques was now in an unfamiliar environment with no identification and only a few dollars in his pocket. He had to find a park or a homeless encampment where he could mix up with the crowd and go unnoticed. His adventure on the train was short-lived. Now he had to survive. Jacques figured that it should not be difficult to find a group of homeless people he could hang out with. They usually descend on the city near most of the major business buildings to claim their spot and will mark it with a discarded or stolen grocery cart, a piece of cardboard. Jacques was ill-prepared for what was coming to him. He must have walked at least two hours until he spotted a group of individuals with the usual characteristics of the homeless. He was exhausted. He bought a couple of bottles of water from a street vendor. If he was thirsty so were the people in the small group. He greeted them and offered each one a bottle of water.

Who are you? The leader of the pack asked with an air of suspicion.

"Find another spot. You cannot stay here."

The grouchy tone was only superficial. Before long, they were all cracking jokes and planning their next move.

Meanwhile in Miami…

Total pandemonium. Madam Maurice is worried sick. Almost eight hours after leaving the house, Jacques has not come back home or called. His whereabouts remain unknown. There was even more alarming news. Madam Maurice went to Jacques's room and noticed that all his medications, his driver's license, and other documents were still in Jacques's little pouch. What was he up to? Without IDs or medications, Jacques was in a danger zone. Madam Maurice needed to act right away. She still had the number of the officer from the last encounter when they came to the home. She was afraid; however, the police would stick to the 24-hour rule. Technically, the person is not missing if it had not been 24 hours. Did it matter at all that the individual had life-threatening conditions? Without his medications, Jacques could start having seizures and could die. Madam Maurice was thinking.

She dialed Officer Jones's number.

"Officer, she started, my son Jacques is missing. You came to the house a couple of weeks ago. He left the home in the early morning and has not taken his medication. I am afraid he might have a seizure out there."

"I remember him, Officer Jones responded. That's the fellow who did not want to take his medications. Did you get a chance to go to Court as we recommended?"

"No Officer! He has gone to his psychiatrist, and we have

been trying to manage it. He did not even take his IDs with him. "

"He cannot be very far, Officer Jones offered. Was he driving?"

Officer Jones was underestimating the ability of people to move around with the modern means of transportation available today.

He has not driven the taxicab for over two months now."

"It's still early. Let us give it another few hours. If he does not show up, I recommend that you come to the station with a recent picture and file a formal missing person report. In the meantime, I'll tell the guys to keep an eye out for him."

It was better than nothing, but Madam Maurice was not satisfied.

Maybe, I should call Dr. Dickenson's Office. They might be able to stress the danger that Jacques is facing and speed up the process with the police.

They sounded concerned but offered no additional help beyond what Officer Jones had already said.

How about Pierre? He should know where Jacques usually hangs out. She would have to break Jacques's secret and tell Pierre about the struggle his friend had been facing with a seizure disorder and mental illness. She did not hesitate, as she feels that the situation was dire and she needed to mobilize all the help she could get.

She briefs Pierre about the situation avoiding unnecessary

details about Jacques's condition. Pierre offered to help. He suggested that they should put a public announcement on the Haitian radio shows that have popped up everywhere in Miami.

Alas! All the private information would be out in the open, but it was worth a try.

Nothing happened in the next day or so. The police report has been filed.

Jacques's picture would be distributed throughout the county, in all the hospital Emergency Departments and Community Centers in Miami Dade and Broward for now. The search would be extended further North if there are no results.

It has been three days now and still no results. Madam Maurice has not been sleeping and eating and looked exhausted. Pierre has been around a few times and has brought some soups a few times. He was worried that Madam Maurice would get sick.

In Boynton Beach

In the homeless encampment, Jacques's encounter with the other homeless men did not last long. The same night, Jacques went into a full seizure episode associated with some of his psychotic symptoms. He was going into his chant:

Ou met Rele-m Shango
Pa di-m gen madichon…

When the seizure started. The group went into a panic and

called the ambulance. Jacques was taken to Bethesda Hospital in Boynton Beach. Jacques still would not reveal his identity.

Ou met rele-m Azaka

Pa di-m gen madichon

Mwen pa konnen ki kote-m soti…

Jacques was registered as an Unknown Black Male in his mid-forties. Discovering Jacques' true identity was in the purview of the police and social services. Now that a police report was officially on file, one would think that a search through the database would quickly reveal who this strange individual was. Not that easy.

At Bethesda Hospital, the ED physicians initiated treatment with Dilantin and Valium. They repeated some of the studies. They rehydrated him to bring the CPK down. It had gone to the roof due to the excessive walking.

Psychiatry was called into consultation. To everyone, this individual with no name was grossly psychotic.

When he got to the psychiatric unit, a fortuitous encounter helped resolve the mystery of his identity. Another patient said to the nurse in an innocuous conversation.

"Why did you bring this taxi driver here? The patient asked. Did anyone call a taxi?

What do you mean Mr. Robert, asked the nurse with her ears perked up.

This man drives a taxi in the Miami-Dade area.

The clue was enough for the police to go to work.

They called back in an hour. This man is Jacques Gaetan. They provided his date of birth, and his address, and even sent a copy of the picture that the mother had provided in the missing person report.

It was a match.

It was Officer Jones who gave Madam Maurice the good news.

"Mrs. Gaetan, we have found your son. He is okay. He is being treated at Bethesda Hospital in Boynton Beach."

Madam Maurice could not contain her joy,

Alleluia! Praise the Lord Almighty.!

"Here is the number of the unit that he is on. The nurse will be able to give you more details about his condition."

Madam Maurice wanted to call Dr. Dickenson right away so Jacques could be transferred to Miami under Dr. Dickenson's care.

"I am glad he was found, and that he is ok. Don't worry! We'll make the necessary arrangements for his transfer. I am familiar with Bethesda Hospital."

Madam Maurice was relieved. Time to call Pierre and share the news about his good friend.

At Bethesda Hospital Jacques chant continued, unabated:

Ou Met rele-m Damballah

Pa di mwen Gen madichon
Se we mwen we-m la
Mwen pa konnen ki-yes mwen ye
Mwen pa konnen ki kote-m soti
Mwen pa konnen ki kote -m prale
Bat chyin tan met li
Pa gen chyin ki pa gen met, tande

The transfer to University Hospital in Miami went on without any problems. Upon his arrival, Jacques was admitted to a specialized unit for Psychotic Disorder. He was maintained on close observation because of his agitation and unpredictable behavior. He was still upset that his great escape from Miami on the Tri-Rail had ended so abruptly. To Jacques however, every experience has a positive side. He has had a taste albeit short of life as a homeless person. Every homeless person has a story. It is not always what it appears. Rehabilitation would have to include an inventory of the talents wasted and the contributions of people that were prematurely discarded from the fabric of society. In the unit, Jacques was offered participation in different groups. He was able to realize that some of the patients had it much worse than he did. Young adults were disconnected from their families and have lost all hope of ever re-establishing the emotional links that they so desperately need. Professionals in a moment of poor judgment had destroyed careers that they have so carefully built over years of sacrifices. Like a masterful illusionist, the trained therapist holds the mirror in front of you, moving it when needed, and allowing you to see yourself in the best possible light. You also get to hear from your peers that not all is lost as they share with you their life experiences. You learn how to navigate the system and get help when needed. If successful, the treatment allows you to develop self-confidence in your ability to get well. Albeit at times short, this experience allows you to mend your life and put you on the rail to recovery. That is what Jacques was supposed to get out of the inpatient experience if he would let himself go and cooperate with the treatment team. In addition, the trained staff ensures that the patient is taking the medication properly while the side effects are closely monitored. To be helpful, the medication needs to target symptoms that will be responsive. The medications need to be taken at the right dosage and for the appropriate length of time. The treating physician has the unique opportunity to make the necessary adjustments. The question then is "Is Jacques benefiting from the treatment? After 5 days, Jacques is less agitated. His nutrition has improved. No longer has he felt the need to resort to continuous chanting to drown out the condemnation from the man dressed in black in his dream. They might not have gone away totally, but they are more manageable. Madam Maurice has also been involved and hopefully has acquired new skills on how to deal with an adult family member with mental illness.

Dr. Dickenson made daily rounds and seemed satisfied with Jacques' progress. By the seventh day of hospitalization, Jacques was ready for discharge. He had developed a new sense of purpose.

Chapter 12

Madam Maurice started to have some doubts about the approach they have taken so far to handle Jacques' condition. Jacques has been under the care of excellent physicians and prescribed different medications. He has been hospitalized and the results have not been that impressive. As the first-born son of the family, Madam Maurice always knew that Jacques would be the most vulnerable. The family had some debts to pay to the ancestors and maybe it was time to do so. They had been neglecting to pay their annual dues to their ancestors. When Madam Maurice heard about the dreams, she knew that there were some connections with this issue. She became afraid to contemplate the possible implications. With the children dispersed around the world, it has been difficult to keep up with this family tradition. Jacques unfortunately seemed to have been the chosen one. All the burden was being placed on his shoulders. Sooner or later the issue would have to be addressed. Despite Jacques's seemingly open attitude towards religion and spiritual issues, he has never accepted the fact that his family had connections to the ancestors that date back several generations. She never forgave Jacques for his ungrateful attitude and for not wanting to acknowledge how much he owed to the spirits. Now, he was paying the price. When the children were much younger, Madam Maurice would make regular trips to Carpentier, a small town near their birthplace to consult with the voodoo priest and would come back with all kinds of potions. Jacques remembered being awakened in the middle of the night along with the other children and being put through some rituals. Jacques remembered receiving massages on the extremities with a stringent smelling lotion, while his mother was mumbling unintelligible series of words. This was supposed to ward off evil spirits and keep the family alive and well, especially after the suspected voodoo-related death of Grandpa Giraud. Jacques was the first one to rebel against the practice. If the spirits were so powerful, how come they did not protect the Gaetan family from the sudden death of Grandpa Giraud and Jacques' father, Maurice?

It was rumored that Maurice, like Giraud Gaetan, had died of supernatural causes. Jacques must have been six-year-old. He still could remember vividly the rituals he was put through. There seemed to have been two ceremonies. There was the usual wake where all the friends, family members, and neighbors came and viewed the body. Jacques' father was all dressed up in his brown gabardine suit with a rosary around his wrist. But the night before, all the children were suddenly awakened in the middle of the night. A man, "Ge-klere" must have been the name, had created a circle in the middle of the living room using a long-threaded sailor's rope of sisal. The room had been emptied of all the furniture. There was a strong smell of asafetida and incense in the air. One by one, only in their underwear, the children were carefully introduced to the circle where a transfigured Madam Maurice was awaiting. Complete silence! No words were spoken! At least, none that Jacques could remember.

For seven nights, all the children had to wear an undershirt made from bright red material. Around all the children's necks hanging from a shoelace, a little red pouch containing different items. Jacques was dying to open it up and find out what was inside, but he would not dare. Jacques found out much later that this pouch usually contained items such as pieces of parchment with a pentacle, special prayers written in symbols, and sometimes garlic among other things. Why red? The triumph of brightness over darkness, of life over death. In such difficult times, anything to give the bereaved a sense of power and mastery over death was welcome. Spending his days in Catholic Church and school by day, and involved in Voodoo rituals by night, Jacques was set for the ambivalent feelings he would carry well into his adult life. Staffed for the most part by missionaries from Europe, the church during Jacques's childhood showed little understanding or respect for local beliefs, These European clerics would display overt prejudice and contempt towards the African attributes of Jacques' cultural heritage. Jacques was made to believe that everything about the Catholic Church was good and everything about Voodoo practices was bad. Jacques also learned that in the early forties, the Church in alliance with the State, went into an all-out- war with the Voodoo believers, destroying their temples or *Hunfor,* and making it a crime to practice Voodoo. Jacques would have memories of a Belgian priest in his all-white soutane, walking down the mountain in the small town of Roche-a-Bateau, the heart full of missionary zeal and singing:

"Woy Woy Pe mission prale
Sa ki nan mission laprye pou-yo
Sa ki pan nan mission madichon pou yo
Sa ki nan vodou madichon pou-yo."

("Father Missionary is leaving
Blessed be the ones who joined the mission
Cursed be the one who did not
And cursed be also the ones who practice Voodoo!)

One is reminded of the directives given by King Leopold II of Belgium to departing colonial missionaries on their way to Congo in 1883:

"Your action will be directed essentially to the younger ones, for they won't revolt when the recommendation of the priest is contradictory to their parent's teachings. The children have to learn to obey what the missionary recommends, who is the father of their soul. You must singularly insist on their total submission and obedience, avoid developing the spirit in the schools, and teach students to read and not to reason…"

"Teach the n… to forget their heroes and to adore only ours. Never present a chair to a black that comes to visit you. Don't give him more than one cigarette. Never invite him for dinner even if he gives you a chicken every time you arrive at his house."?

What a hateful and arrogant speech! Where is the love taught by Christ in all these words?

It backfired. Since then, Voodoo has benefitted from an ideological and political movement that promotes a return by the Haitian people to their African roots. Haitian music and arts depicting Haitian beliefs have flourished.

In his adult life, Jacques had to deal with many deaths among friends, family members, and acquaintances. Always, he would find an excuse not to go to the wake or the funeral.

Jacques had also developed a strong aversion for anything that would remind him, even in the most remote ways, of Voodoo practices.

After meeting Jacques' psychiatrist, Madam Maurice became more convinced than ever that a trip to Haiti was necessary. As she learned more details about Jacques' dreams, she became perturbed in a way that only a mother could. She knew right away that her son was in a lot of trouble. She was not too sure about the meaning of the dream herself but was determined to find out. There would be no delay. Jacques in her mind had wasted too much time already, going to that white man. What could such a man possibly know about the roots of people like us? Was it possible for them to learn? Of course, they could. But would they? Probably not. It seems like an unspoken law of Nature that learning about, or acceptance of a foreign culture is almost always guided by self-interest and some hope of ulterior gain. Therefore, there was almost no chance that Dr. Dickenson would become so interested in Jacques' problem to delve into its real root. It was all up to Jacques' mother now. She would have to guide Jacques out of this quagmire, comes hell or high water.

For Jacques, it was a real dilemma. His first option was to remain in Florida with very minimal family support and face inevitably a downhill spiral. Like many others, he would drift away and end up on the street, alone, homeless. He would be lost amongst the growing numbers of individuals that seem caught in limbo, rejected by everyone. He would run the risk of losing whatever little bit of dignity and self-respect that was left in him. The writings were on the wall. Jacques could either heed them or face more calamities. He had lost so much weight now, that his cheekbones were becoming more pronounced. His eyes had sunken a bit in their sockets and were reddened from many sleepless nights. Not only had Jacques was losing his physical strength, but he was also extremely close to losing his mind. He was still being tormented by the horrific dreams. At times, he found his mind wandering. Often, Jacques questioned whether or not he would survive this ordeal. He started to see shadows and to feel suspicious about everything and everyone around him. Jacques felt powerless. He could just picture himself in a long-term psychiatric ward lost among so many faceless patients. He felt horrified by that prospect. The second option seemed a bit more promising. It would be quite challenging for Jacques to finally confront what was, according to his mother, the source of all of his torment. It would take some acknowledgment that there is a world out there that expands well beyond the limits of the rational. A world where power is shared by many gods. A world where the fainthearted were not welcome.

"Why?

"Why me?" Jacques wondered.

He felt that he had always been good to everyone. He has never harbored any ill feelings against anyone. Why did he deserve such a fate? Jacques wanted an answer fast. He was willing to pay a hefty price if he could only find out.

He had avoided being close to anyone, afraid that people might see through him. Jacques felt that he had always come up one penny short. Jacques was running out of time. The game was almost over. The final seconds were ticking away at a vertiginous speed. He could no longer run away from himself. He needed to find answers to his queries. The time was now.

He has made up his mind. Now, he was eager to get started.

Jacques could not help but compare himself to his siblings. Georges is happily married to a beauty queen from Trinidad. For some reason, he has never been one to show some social conscience. Nothing seems to bother him. He does not seem to care much about what goes on around him. He always chides Jacques for being so politically driven. He migrated to the US a few years later than Jacques and bought right into the entrepreneurial American spirit and has been involved in different businesses and has settled into electronics. He is now the proud owner of a thriving electronic retail store. He owns a duplex in Brooklyn and is quite happy. Why couldn't Jacques have the same carefree attitude? What a difference in personality between two brothers born only a couple of years apart! Jacques felt like a child who is being assailed from all angles on the school playground. He has to put up a fight or else his self-worth will forever be lost. Jacques knew that when the fight was all over, he might have to nurse his bruises and disguise his black eye, but the alternative was much more difficult to tolerate.

At this time, there was only one person Jacques could depend on to help him with this very important decision: Jacques himself. He knew that he was about to draw the curtain and immerse himself into a whole different new world where all the rules were different. He was about to test the limits of his senses.

Where he could not see or hear, his imagination and beliefs would have to take over and make up for it. He was entering a world of animism where everything could suddenly come alive and take symbolic meaning completely beyond the understanding of the Western way of thinking. Jacques was left with very little choice. He was seating on a divan in the small living room. He turned to his mother, his voice shuddering.

"Mother, I have called the travel agent. I am trying to book a flight on American Airlines. Is that okay?"

"Try for a Wednesday," Madam Maurice replied, "It is easier to get transportation to the countryside on market day. We could catch the bus on the next day."

Madam Maurice felt relieved that Jacques had finally made up his mind. She could be a forceful person, but she knew that she needed to be careful. Jacques had been known to blow his top and make hasty and sometimes, irreversible decisions. Madam Maurice just could not run that risk. This time, there was no getting away. It was as if Jacques was driving through the mountain with pits on both sides and suddenly found the road blocked by a giant boulder. He just knew that travel through life would not be possible until he figured out a way to remove this colossal roadblock. His destiny was ahead of him. The moment had arrived to get some answers. He did not have a tea leaf. He could not read oracles from the sky. He did not have an assortment of colorful votive stones. Even if he did, they would be no use to him. For the first time, Jacques wished that he could read into the future. How would his life be any different? He did not have the gift. A sense of powerlessness came upon Jacques.

No amount of love could fill that void. No amount of comfort could make him wholesome.

It is time.

It is time for Jacques to partake in the fountain of knowledge.

It is time.

It is time for Jacques to drink out of the cup of bitterness.

It is time.

It is time for Jacques to face the ultimate challenge.

If the dreams that had been tormenting Jacques' life were any indications, a very unsettled world was about to unravel. Evil was looming on the horizon. Jacques could feel it in his bones. They felt like icicles ready to melt. For a while, they did not feel like they serve any purpose at all. Jacques pulled his legs against his chest assuming a fetal position. Somehow, he felt that he needed to garner all the energy that he could. Once again, he found himself in the unusual position of knocking on a door, afraid of what he might find behind it. But then again, Jacques' whole life has been anything but normal. If it were true that it was man's destiny to toil and suffer because of Adam's original sin, one man seems to have to endure more than their fair share.

Jacques was one of those men.

"From childhood hour, I have not been
As others were; I have not seen
As others saw; I could not bring
My passions from a common spring."
Alone, Edgar Allan Poe

...

"And on my birthday, a black butterfly lay on my crib..."
Coriolan Ardouin

Seek and you shall find!

Madam Maurice had decided. After Sunday mass. She sat with Jacques at the kitchen table and made a long speech. Jacques did not have to say much. As he was searching for words, his mother stated:

"Jacko, it is true that you have not followed the recommendations of Dr. Coleman and Dr. Dickenson. I have spoken to both several times. They are good doctors, won't you agree? They have tried their best to help you but there is an aspect of your condition, I do not expect them to understand. They know nothing about the matter if you know what I mean. The time has come "poun-n met pie-n nan dlo" (meaning to set feet into the water) to seek alternative treatment for your condition.

Such treatment, we can only find back home in Haiti.

I can no longer watch you suffering like this. This condition is destroying your life right in front of my eyes. I cannot allow that to happen. We have no choice. We must make that trip.

Jacques was caught off guard. He always knew that his family had some connection to cultural traditions in Haiti, but he did not expect his mother to express it in such a way. There did not seem to be a simple explanation for the persistent and recurring dreams that he was experiencing. How about the seizures that were so hard to control with the usual medications? His mother had a point. They needed to explore other explanations. To go back to Haiti, under those circumstances, he needed to prepare himself mentally and physically. It was not going to be easy.

PART II

OUT OF THE DEVIL'S FANGS

What is the meaning of our lives, the meaning of the life of all living in general? To have an answer to this question is to be religious.

Albert Einstein

Chapter 13

Heureux qui comme Ulysses, a fait un long voyage
Ou comme cestuy la qui conquit la toison
Et puis est revenu, plein d'usage et raison
Vivre entre ses parents, le reste de son age!. . .
Joachim Du Bellay

Happy he who like Ulysses essays
A glorious voyage or wins the Golden Fleece
And then returns home to dwell in peace
Both righteous and wise the rest of his days.

Jacques had a hard time deciding how he should feel as he was negotiating his way through the long registration lines at the airport. The words that came to his mind were nostalgia, confusion, doubt, and overall fear. His fate was going to depend on the purported power of one man. What if that man was a scam? The preceding weeks have been a real rollercoaster. The seemingly unrelenting dreams. The return of the seizures. The precipitated trip of his mother from New York. And now this trip on this overbooked plane. The scene on the plane seemed surreal. The flight attendant was having a hard time getting some of the passengers to limit their carry-on luggage. Toward the front, a toddler was expressing rather loudly his displeasure about separating from grandma. No toys or promises of a quick reunion would console the poor lad. He was crying at the top of his lungs. His eyes heavy from sleepless nights, Jacques was watching the passengers through a dirty window on a rainy day. While all these events were unfolding, Jacques could not get his mind off the mysteries that were ahead of him. How would he receive a suggestion from a voodoo priest? How would he manage his doubt about the practices of this religion without offending his mother? The moment of truth was upon him. Jacques knew that trying to escape from what seemed inevitable would only add to his anguish. The quest just had to go on.

"You have often

Begun to tell me what I'm; but stopped

And left me to a bootless inquisition,

Concluding "Stay, not yet."

The Tempest, William Shakespeare

It was only eight in the morning, and the day seemed so old already. Clearing the airline counter at Miami Airport was not an easy task. It seemed as if the travelers were trying to outdo each other.

"Madam, the American Airways agent started, your baggage is way over the limit."

The middle-aged traveler would not have any of it.

"Cherie toutou, I have to get these items to my daughter that is getting married. What am I supposed to do?"

"You have to check this box in for an extra $ 60.00."

After much pouting and teeth-hissing, the woman came up with $50.00. A compromise was reached. The long line was finally able to move.

For Jacques, it was the first trip back home. He wished he were taking this journey under completely different circumstances. He had a really busy schedule ahead of him. Everything was planned, if one can ever plan well enough for Haiti. He had kept abreast of the daily events back home. Which Haitian does not? Jacques, as any other Haitian American living in South Florida, was fed with his daily fare of news broadcast directly from the remote corners of Haiti. Not that you believe everything you hear. That could be very deceiving. Since many individuals have embarked on the information business with little or no preparation, they often play on the emotions of the masses and tell them whatever they want to hear. Most people listen not for information but for entertainment. One feels connected to Haitian culture through Haitian radio stations. When he left over a decade ago, Jacques had hoped that he would one day return as a different person. He expected at the very least that he would have completed his education and would be on a better financial footing. Alas, to the many friends and cousins that would find their way to him, Jacques did not have much good news to deliver. There would be no feast. There would be no hero's welcome. The circumstances were much too somber for this kind of celebration. However, despite all of that, Jacques could not help from giving in to a feeling of exhilaration. It was still a bittersweet event. No, he was not sporting the latest hip-hop fashion. Nor did he speak with a Brooklyn accent. He did not walk with a cadence. He would not be easily picked as a member of the diaspora. At least he did not think so.

When he finally made it to his assigned seat on the airplane, Jacques was exhausted. His heart was pounding. He felt restless. He was moving about his seat as if some fire ants had found their way into his trousers. He extended his neck towards the plane window. He did not want to miss it for the world. After a little over an hour of flight, the plane was ready to make its final descent towards the macadam of Port-au-Prince airport. Jacques was treated to a breathtaking view. Magnifique! Absolument magnifique!

Underneath the cobalt-blue Caribbean Sea, like a giant quilt, lay Port-au-Prince in all its splendor. In that potpourri of colors with all the shades represented, the milky white color of the *Palais National* stood out. How could one miss that architectural wonder? Surrounded by a well-manicured lawn, the construction sprawled over several hectares of land like two giant breasts inviting anyone with the guts for a final melee. The winner takes all. Right at the center of the compound, as if it wanted to remind the Haitian people of their destiny as a nation, the blue and red flag was gracefully waving to the whims of the Caribbean breeze. In contrast, the rusty color of the tin roof in the Bel Air section, the ashy smoke of the soap factory, the forest green color of the trees witnesses to the last rainy season of the tropics, the denuded spots of the hills fallen victim of unwary construction suppliers were telling a much different story. A story of inequality. A story that was not at all clear to unwary visitors. Finally, in the middle of all this chaos, a consoling note of piety. Pointing to the heavens in permanent prayer, stood the twin towers of the national cathedral. What would Port-au-Prince be without this majestic display of its devotion? Haiti is a very pious country. Like a slide show, this kaleidoscope of colors was presented to the traveler in a vertiginous series of snapshots. In a matter of minutes, it was all over. The bird's eye view was gone. No longer would the visitor have a chance to look at this unbelievable fresco. Before Jacques could get over his marvel at the aerial display, the comforting voice of the captain came on the loudspeaker.

"Mesdames et Messieurs, l'equipage tout entier voudrait vous souhaiter la bienvenue a Port-au-Prince. The temperature is 86 degree F."

The tracks left by the rubber from the jet's landing gear were visible on the runways. As he was getting off the plane, Jacques was overcome by a flood of memories. Finding a trigger for these memories shouldn't be difficult. By the main door, four musicians clad in their colorful Hawaiian shirts were singing *Choucoune,* a Haitian favorite folk song accompanied by a marimba, a pair of maracas, a hand-made guitar, and a goat skin-covered drum. That is all it took to create a rhythm that made you want to tap your feet and dance.

"Choucoune ce te you marabou , ge li klere kou 'ou chandel..."

The words were not new, but it did not matter. They had the same exhilarating effect each time. The flight from Miami lasted a little over an hour. Jacques and his fellow travelers found themselves quickly ensconced in a very different world. The realities of Haiti would grasp the visitor at the throat like the acrid smoke of a burning dumpsite. In a matter of seconds, all of Jacques' senses would come alive. There was the reverberation of the early morning sun on the ground that mirages of water everywhere. There were pockets of smoke that seemed to come from every corner. And then, there was that characteristic smell. It was hard to dissect it and find every single element that contributed to it. But everyone knew it was the smell of Port-au-Prince, a centuries-old city that had developed a personality of its own. Emanating from the nearby ocean the odor of seaweed mixed with decaying and burnt rubbish.

What an experience it had been!

Jacques had made this trip and visited those pictures so many times in his mind. He was there now. Jacques could not help but wonder how much his homeland had changed over the years. Many leaders had emerged and fed the masses with grandiose plans for the country.

They have promised to build a long bridge to connect downtown Port-au-Prince to Carrefour. Revitalization plans were drawn to be quickly forgotten. They have all promised to bring Haiti back to its glory and opulence of yesteryear. Yeah! Yeah! Yeah! Those "Spartacus who would save the masses has fallen into oblivion after a couple of years. Port-au-Prince had not changed. Same narrow streets! Same overcrowded slums! The same will to survive by industrious and resourceful merchants determined to make a sale. A whole family's survival was dependent on every sale. No sale! No dinner! And then there were the children. They seemed to be everywhere. Shirtless, wearing only pants, or naked. What insouciance! The epitome of innocence. But alas, the symptoms of everything that was wrong with that society.

Against all odds they still carried hope. For now, they were just one mouth too many in need of basic foods and immunization.

They too, are very much a part of the commerce. They had lost their childhood before they could even enjoy it. No time to play! Life is a serious business. They too have something to sell. The children of industrialized countries had their survival training skills to trade.

Madam Maurice and Jacques caught a taxi to the bus station on the south side of the town. With a little bit of luck, they still could make it on time to catch a bus going to Les Cayes, the third most populated city in this country of over twelve million inhabitants. The city was abuzz with activities. It seemed that the whole town had taken to the streets in response to an invitation to a huge block party. However, everyone seemed to be going in a different direction. The noise level was extreme. Merchants were peddling all kinds of fruits like mangoes, pineapples, *cachiman*, and other produce. Some were quite pleasant and would approach with the most attractive smile you will ever see. Others were darn right hostile.

Especially when the prospective buyer did not fall for the vendor's charms. Not too far away a set of powerful speakers were blaring out the sounds of *compas* music.

"Ti gason, ou pa we ou tro jeune

Pou ou passione de lamou?"

(Young man, don't you think you are a little too young to be passionate about love?)

It had always amazed everyone, how Haitians could be going through the worst time of their lives and yet find the spirit to sing and dance as if nothing ever happened. Any mishap from a politician or infidelity from an indulging spouse is quickly captured and transformed into the theme of a popular song. Wait until the next carnival season!

Jacques felt quite estranged from his old environment. On the one hand, he was feeling very much at home, as he went down the crowded roads of Port-au-Prince. On the other hand, something indescribable was missing. Jacques was heavy-hearted over the opportunities that he had lost. Somehow, Jacques had the feeling that the years that he had spent chasing his dreams would never come back. What if he had never left the country? What if he had never suffered from this chronic ailment? A feeling of profound anguish came over him, and he found himself holding back tears. In the States, he never had an extravagant life, but it seemed to him that some of his needs and wants were created by just being there. For some reason, these people on the streets living off their daily commerce did not seem concerned about the apparent lack of sanitation, the scarcity of running water, or the rationing of electricity. They did not seem to be under any pressure to keep up with their neighbors. Everyone seemed full of vitality. Nothing, but nothing could bring down their enthusiasm, not even the baking heat of the mid-afternoon tropics. Under what guise would a social scientist try to convince the lady in the sugar sack frock sitting behind an assortment of candies, cigarettes, and other foodstuffs, that five children just about a year apart were a little too much? Under the guise of civilization or some borrowed ideas from the Western world? Did anyone bother to ask that lady what she wanted? One only needs to look around to see that only a two-hour plane flight away from America, a far different philosophy of life was at play. No need to rush, tomorrow will wait. It did not matter that the life of every passenger on that overcrowded bus was endangered. *"Bon die bon"*. The Lord is great and will protect everyone. The colorful signs, a spontaneous display of popular art, tell the whole story.

L'Enfant prodigue (The prodigal son)

Dieu seul qui donne! (Only the Lord provides!)

Bon Die Bon! (Lord is great!)

Everyone seems to carry with him a sense of uniqueness and invincibility emanating from his armpits. Jacques could use a long and relaxing hot shower. The trip from the airport to the bus station took as long as the plane trip from Miami to Port-au-Prince. No problems. It was only 3:00 PM, but for most public employees, the workday was over two hours ago. The roads were impassable. The taxi finally made it to the bus station.

Jacques and his mother retained a pair of seats on a large, modified school bus, en route to Les Cayes. Jacques was much too exhausted to enjoy the lush vegetation and the green pasture that seemed to be running away from him as he was zipping through National Road No. 2. This part of the country did not suffer from the erosion that has been so much talked about.

Chapter 14

Jacques' trip went very well. There was something very soothing about the breathtaking landscape passing by. It felt like only yesterday when on August 15, Jacques went to Petit-Goave which was celebrating its official patronal Saint. *Notre-Dame de L'Assomption.* The band Bossa Combo had just come out with one of its hit songs and everyone seemed in a very festive mood until the dance had to be stopped due to a brawl between two men over a girl. A constant stream of memories passed through Jacques's mind. They were so vivid. On that August night, Jacques remembered being a bit drunk. No one could stop him from talking and making up stories where he always had the best role. Jacques was suddenly pulled out of his reveries by a feeling of nausea. The smell of the diesel gas added to the 85-degree temperature did not sit well. Jacques was sorry now that he ever ate that prepacked breakfast on the airplane. He could just feel the taste of sour omelet in the back of his throat.

"*I wish this bus would stop soon,*" Jacques thought.

He was also starting to feel cramps in his left leg. He needed to stretch out.

Madam Maurice did not seem bothered by the old man sitting next to her. The man had an unlit pipe in the corner of his mouth and was dozing off with jerking motions of the head.

His head would tilt forward repeatedly. At the last minute, as he was about to hit the front seat, he would catch himself. He would wake up, look around and go right back to sleep. The cycle would start over. He looked like he could sleep standing up. The bus was remarkably quiet considering the number of children among the passengers. It did not last long. The driver announced, "We will be stopping in the next five minutes. There is a small restaurant around the corner. If you are getting off, please return promptly."

Only a couple of blocks away, a fading sign of Cola Couronne was now visible.

Jacques walked around and felt invigorated after he washed his face from the river. He started to feel the effects of the Prestige beer he had at the last stopover two hours ago. Jacques could not tell exactly, but he got the feeling that he had been in that place before. The scene was so characteristic. A heavy-set man in his early fifties was slouched in a high chair behind the counter. He greeted the customers with an overly warm smile. His eccentricity and exaggerated gregariousness stroke everyone as disingenuous. He was wearing a blue kerchief around his head, barely covering some ashy hair. His face was covered with sweat despite a large ceiling fan which was turning rapidly with an annoying squeaky sound. This man, it was said, had quite a reputation among travelers in the area. He was known to be very up-front about his attraction to younger boys. He would tell anyone who asked that he was born gay. He has never hurt anyone. He would sometimes be seen hauling large boxes from the supply truck. He lived like a hermit. His mother, after attempting for many years to have him exorcized, had given up and has now accepted his sexual orientation. Jacques decided on a soft drink and picked up one for his mother who did not get off the bus. Jacques also bought some hashed coconut sweets. They were still warm. Delicious! There was a line at the cashier. Jacques needed to get back to the bus. The old man next to Jacques' mother was fully awake now. They seemed to be engaged in a lively chat.

"Jacques! You are back! Meet Joseph. "

" Joseph? The name when matched with the face sounded very familiar."

Jacques was trying to remember.

"He reminded me that he used to live only a few blocks away from us in Les Cayes, Madam Maurice said.

Jacques could vaguely remember the features now.

"Tonton Joe! Of course! You used to wear a *Fu Manchu* mustache, right?"

Jacques did not expect the old man to acquiesce and acknowledge an earlier life of flamboyance and eccentricity. He is sporting a more conservative look now with his hair trimmed short and his closely shaven face. Tonton Joe used to walk his dog every afternoon at the same time. The children in the neighborhood did not like him very much. He had earned quite a reputation as he used to report all their mischiefs to their parents. Tonton Joe was the official neighborhood "snitch." He was the cause of many spankings. Imagine a middle-aged man, dressed in all white with a long mustache and a suspicious look ready to tell on every kid on the block. There were quite a few not-so-nice names assigned to Tonton Joe. Often, the children would dare each other to run under Tonton Joe's window and sing the following song:

Beware of your neighbors
Beware of your neighbors
because they are snitches
Tonton Joe, Tonton Joe
Go and… your mother!

One day, Tonton Joe decided *"Enough is enough"* He was ready for these brats. Like a feline stalking for his prey, and standing on its paws, Tonton Joe waited. He stood *en garde* by his front door. As soon as Jean-Claude started the famous song, Tonton Joe sprung out. Aha! Gotcha! Oh boy! What a spanking Jean-Claude got that afternoon! As always, a *martinet* nicknamed Josephine was kept on the wall in full view of everyone. It was meant to remind every child that no misbehaving would be tolerated. The *martinet,* Josephine, went into action that evening. And worse of all, as part of his punishment Jean-Claude had to apologize. We still could remember the voice of an infuriated woman, Jean-Claude's mother.

"You will apologize to Tonton Joe, or you will stay on your knees in the corner until you do." So much for Jean-Claude's *amour propre.* What choice did Jean-Claude have? He went to Tonton Joe presented his excuses to a man that seemed so happy to have finally stuck it to these miscreants."

Jean-Claude was not done. He was not going to concede victory to the enemy that easily. He met with his friends *en seance extraordinaire* and took the solemn vow that they, *chevaliers sans peur et sans reproche,* would have the last laugh...

By the time the bus reached Les Cayes, it was half empty. Most of the passengers had gotten off to awaiting family members. The final stop on the bus was *Arniquet,* a small town that seemed to come alive on market day when all the farmers from the vicinity brought in their produce for distribution. The bus entered the village at about 6:30 PM. The sun was still high. Jacques and Madam Maurice's journey was not over. They had arranged to rent a pair of healthy-looking horses. Jacques had an opportunity to test his horse-riding skills. He was quite nervous at first as he approached the black stallion. Would he be able to handle it? Madam Maurice did not seem to have any difficulty at all. Riding a horse is like riding a bicycle. One never quite forgets. Jacques was going to do just fine. He was full of fear. He did not know what this trip would uncover. He was feeling the weight of a day that started what seem to be thousands of miles away. The roads were extremely dark and deserted. Occasionally, they would hear the gallop of an approaching horse and before one could distinguish who the late-night traveler was, a well-covered shadow would zip by. Far away, one could see a scintillating camping light. Absolute silence was in order, for the moment was too solemn to be spoiled with trite comments or unnecessary chit-chat. The silence of the night was only disturbed by the musical sound of *cha cha,* as the breeze gently caressed hundreds of pods from the gigantic Royal Poinciana, causing them to flutter harmoniously. The *flamboyant* trees stood majestic with their large scarlet flowers popping out as if the gods wanted to keep a watchful eye on this troublesome land. It was an Eden-like but eerie atmosphere. Jacques felt a knot in his stomach. It was a scary night, but the prospect of the challenges Jacques was about to face was even scarier. Jacques' head was pounding. His heart seemed to be jumping out of his chest. He felt as if two armies of butterflies were about to engage in hand-to-hand combat with his stomach as the battlefield. Jacques knew they were close to the end of their trip, as they started to come across more and more people. A faint and continuous series of drumbeats seemed to welcome friendly visitors and ward off unwanted thrill seekers.

Chapter 15

Carpentier was a very serious town. It was the hometown of Ge-klere, the Voodoo priest of all Voodoo priests. The chosen one. The recipient of the *Gift*. The one, whose advice has been sought by presidential candidates, presidents losing popularity, civil servants seeking promotions, and disenchanted employees seeking to silence demanding supervisors.

Oh yes! Many visitors from the Haitian Diaspora have made the now-famous journey. And now Jacques was about to meet his destiny. He was still very skeptical. After all, he was still under the influence of a one-God religion. So, he has been told all his life. How could it be any different? In his mind, there could not be any room for participation and belief in a cult that recognizes the power of many gods, where every ancestor who dies could potentially be added to the pantheon of gods and goddesses whose only role is to protect the living. Or was it that Jacques had been so blind that he failed to recognize all the mysteries that surround him? It was too late for Jacques to pull back. He was in Ge-klere's territory. His presence could be felt miles away. As if someone wanted to remind the traveler of that fact, drumbeats echoed over the mountains and came cascading down to them. Make no mistake about it, they were already under Ge-klere's spell. For now, Jacques' anxiety was all gone.

That was a good omen. After all, there was a chance that everything would be okay.

No one knows exactly how Ge-klere came to gain prominence. Rumor has it that his mother was chosen by a dying Voodoo priest among his *Hounsi* to bear his child. The villagers did not believe it could ever happen. The chosen *Hounsi* was in her late forties. She stood a mere five feet 8 inches, but she was an ebony woman, a siren of a woman with eyes that would make any man go gaga. A pregnancy at this late age was definitely a risky proposition. Everyone was worried except for Ge-klere's father because he could read the future. Ge-klere would come to this world to carry the gods' mission and nothing was going to stop him. "There was no way she was going to successfully carry a pregnancy to completion", some thought. Well, she almost did not make it. Almost, that is all it takes sometimes. The *chosen one* was never seen in public for the nine months the pregnancy lasted. It is said that she was put through very rigorous training, and it was during one of the final exercises that Ge-klere came into this world. A name had been chosen for him: Saint-Home (Holy man), like his father. Unbeknownst to his mother, on the day Ge-Klere was to come to this life, his father suddenly made the final trip. Just like that. As if someone had simply blown his candle out. They say that Ge-Klere had the most beautiful smile on that day. Maybe because he knew that he could not go very far. He would be somewhere among the stars watching over his newborn son. He would be there at his son's beck and call. Ge-klere's mother received specific instructions from her man. Ge-klere's mother was to spend the night by a special pond with tall *Mapou* trees all around it. It is believed that the *pie mapous* served as a residence to dozens of gods. Some *shanpwel* society[7] held regular meetings inside the giant trees. If your travel takes you in their vicinity, you are to keep on going. And if you happen to hear your name, you are not to pay any attention. Never tell a stranger your real name. Never find yourself in the shadow of the sacred tree. The expectant mother was to sing special incantations seven times and wait for some special signs. The only signs the lady received were labor pains. For hours and hours, the area which looked like an open-air temple, was filled with screams from a forty-nine-year-old woman going through labor for the first time in her life. No other souls were in sight. No one was there to help her cut the umbilical cord. She managed to tear it away with the edge of a sharp rock. Would Ge-klere make it? He did not cry at first. His mother slapped him. He started to breathe. His troubles were not over. They were found many hours later. Having fulfilled her sacred duty to bear the one through whom the gods would communicate with their brethren, the mother bled to death. Since she was

---

[7] Folk beliefs in Haiti have it that the shanpwel are a society of Loup-garous who go out at night and engage in human sacrifices and cannibalism. Children can be protected from the loup-garous by a special talisman or madiok prepared by the Voodoo priest or Hougan.

honored by the voodoo priest to bear her precious child, it was only appropriate that she would join him in death. As to the newborn, no doubt that he was going to beat the odds and survive. He was found covered with meconium. Like a crown, the remnants of the amniotic sac were still covering his head. How could it be any different? He was as close to royalty as one could ever be. With his supernatural power, he would rule the world. A great destiny awaited Ge-Klere. An heir to the throne was born! Would he live up to the reputation of his father? After surviving several bouts of infections including Tetanus, Ge-klere beat the odds. Raised by relatives, h soon showed signs of developmental delay. Many names were tried like *Potovi,* a Creole word for retarded. And then one day while playing with another child well known for his abrasive ways, Ge-klere astonished him with the depth of his answers. The other children were amazed and started to call him Ge-klere, literally "bright eyes" to mean clever and astute, a guiding light. An eye, a light that would guide Voodoo adepts through the mysteries of the centuries-old religion from Africa.

Physically, Ge-klere was very unimposing. He was quite awkward. He could not jump or kick balls like the other children. He grew very isolated and would spend hours and hours with his father's mementos, bottles, talismans, and potions. Soon he was starting to mix remedies for common ailments. His reputation was built in a matter of months. When it was time to christen him, his adoptive parents just whispered to the catholic priest. His name will be Ge-klere. For better or worse, he was stuck with the name. This is the story of Ge-klere and how it has been told and probably embellished hundreds of times. Ge-klere, the guiding light, had become a legendary figure, an icon better and grander than life. Ge-klere is well-known among all Voodoo adherents, but very few know the real story…

When Madam Maurice and Jacques entered the little hamlet of Carpentier, they were greeted by a group of people who seemed to be expecting them. The road to Ge-Klere's dwelling place was decorated with palm branches on both sides. The mood of the town was solemn. No one would utter a word. It was like a mournful procession. The children stopped their play as they passed by to give them a very inquisitive look. Something very serious was about to happen in this town. As they entered the compound, a servant took away their bags and showed them to a reception area. They offered them water and food. Jacques' stomach could not take much of anything. What he wanted was a place to lie down. They were then shown to their sleeping quarters. Two army green cots were prepared for the guests. Jacques was very grateful. Everything was very clean, and the linen smelled fresh. Jacques unashamedly threw himself on the bed and went right to sleep. He was beaten. He drew quite a snore. Jacques could not tell how many hours he had been sleeping. Jacques saw himself sitting by a pond in the yard of a very beautiful castle. Seven nubile girls were swooning over him, feeding him with grapes and washing his feet. From the bottom of the pond rose a woman that looked more like a goddess. As she was about to speak, Jacques felt like someone was shaking him.

"Wake up! Wake up! You have to get ready now, sir."

When he opened his eyes, a woman in her twenties was talking to him. "The ceremony will start before long, and you need to change into this." The woman handed Jacques an all-white outfit that included a bottom with lace at the waist and a top that looked more like a kimono worn by a karate fighter. Jacques took the clothes automatically. It took him a while before he was fully awake. For a moment he did not remember where he was.

The roosters were announcing the day with their concert of cock-a-doodle-dos, even though there was at least another couple of hours of darkness. The place was abuzz with activities. People were moving about just like bees. However, a mature-looking woman, dressed in long multicolored garb and a red kerchief holding together what appeared to be a wig, was clearly in charge of the situation. Everyone was moving to her commands.

"The master is ready to see you and your mother now," the lady said.

"What time is it?" Jacques asked. The large basin of cold

water he used to wash up did not quite wake him up, but he felt refreshed. He was now fully dressed in his new outfit.

The moment of truth was finally here. Jacques shuddered and felt his heart hammering inside his chest. Sweat was running down the back of his neck despite the early morning breeze. Jacques' sense of smell was suddenly awakened by the aroma of fresh coffee mixed with that of the burning resin from pine woods. He took some comfort in the fact that he was among friends. No matter how frightening the situation was, that smell reminded him that he was indeed home.

Chapter 16

They were asked to wait in a small indoor yard with a pole right in the center, the *poto mitan.* The pole was heavily scorched by the heat from burning candles. One could easily notice residues of variously colored candles, black, yellow, and white. On the clay floor, elaborated designs traced with a mixture of flour and cornmeal were inviting the different loas, all the loas. A poor soul was in distress, and they were being summoned to this sacred place for its rescue. For that, the help of Ge-Klere was necessary. The supplicants would make offerings. They would sing and lament. They would pray and dance. Should the gods be agreeable, they would soon manifest their presence by using some of the participants as a medium. The more gods would show up, the better. Each design represented a different loa or god. Jacques seemed quite puzzled by the meaning of all of this. Soon all the activities started to take shape as they slowly wove into a giant animated fresco of colors, sounds, and human tragedy. It was an edifying display of unity. This congregation had come together for a common cause and if Jacques was lucky, he would be the beneficiary.

Jacques's destiny was unfolding in front of his very eyes and beside the bewildered look on his face there was very little he could add to this dramatic event. Some of the women were rolling handmade candles. Some were preparing food. A lot of different foods. Chickens. Pigeons. Goats. They were getting ready to feed the whole village. Or maybe, they were expecting all the gods to join the feast. The men were tuning their drums, a whole set of them in different sizes, and the hush-hush conversations. All of this was going on simultaneously. They were preparing for a special ritual. What would he do if he was asked to drink some bloody-looking potion? Jacques was becoming nauseated at the simple thought of that possibility. What could he do at this point? Not much. He imagined himself being put into a trance and losing all his faculties. What was going to happen? Jacques wished someone would tell him something. No such luck!

Suddenly! The shaking of a bell. The master was here. The one who could communicate with the gods was here. His presence filled the room. He walked with an extremely slow and cadenced gait, barely touching the ground. A rolling of the drums saluted his arrival. All the women, dressed in long white frocks and their hair kept together with a white scarf, went to the ground one by one as he passed by. They were ready. They were awaiting his orders. How could a man inspire so much awe? If you ever meet Ge-klere you would know why. How old was this man? It was hard to tell by his demeanor. He was still quite athletic and lean. As soon as he opens his mouth, an indescribable feeling seizes you by the stomach and ties it into a knot. However, there was nothing evil about this man. How could it be? He has built a reputation for kindness and caring. Should any of the villagers find themselves in trouble, they only needed to ask. Ge-Klere will be there to help. All the children refer to him as their godfather. In his presence, you find yourself spellbound, ready to follow him wherever he might decide to take you. This time the audience was ready to be transported into the supernatural world. The rules of engagement were known only to one man and to one man only, Ge Klere. His stare at times seems empty, as the world around him was a mirror through which he had the power to see way beyond what any one of us could see. He spoke in a very soft voice. So soft, that you were almost forced to lean toward him to catch a few words. That is if your courage will allow you to get close to him.

"What troubles bring mother and son in our temple? Do you have brightness in your heart?"

Jacques did not know how to respond or whether he was even supposed to respond.

Jacques' mother did not seem as disturbed. Her eyes were riveted to the old man's face, interpreting every motion and every expression.

"We do not know, and we humbly seek your help because...", Madam Maurice started imploringly. Before she could finish her sentence Ge-klere stopped her, raising his hand gently.

"Say no more! I see clouded skies. I hear the rumbling of thunder. I smell the scent of burned flesh. The water is muddy and awaits divine intervention. A tree cannot grow when it does not have any roots. Your little boy has lost his roots…"

Jacques did not understand that Ge-klere was referring to him. He did not want to understand. A clear interpretation of his troubles from a clearsighted individual or a direct message from the gods? Ge-Klere had no hesitation in his voice. Jacques quivered at the idea that maybe more troubles were ahead of him. Ge-klere was right at least in one aspect. At this time, Jacques felt very much like a man that had been uprooted. To someone of Ge-klere's charisma, every man probably looks like a little boy. His face was very smooth and looked almost carved out of a baccarat crystal, were it not for the perfectly shaped brown eyes that suddenly became alive. Gone was the empty stare. His eyelids were fluttering as if he was disturbed by the specters of events of the past or of happenings yet to unfold. Jacques thought for a moment about running out of the room, but he had nowhere to go. The women seem now more organized. They were standing in a perfect half-circle around Ge-klere. Outside now, one could distinctly hear the rhythmic beats of the drum. Ge-klere was in séance. Once more, he was about to make his divination. Jacques would not admit this to anyone, but he was about to have a physiologic reaction of the digestive type. He anticipated that his long fugue away from his cultural heritage was probably ending. Ge-klere would probably remind him of things, that for some unexplainable reasons, he had always felt but would not admit. There was no going back.

The women were in a frenzy. They were moving very gracefully. Their hips and shoulders were involved in an amazing contortion. They twirled and twirled. Their blouses were open revealing their well-shaped breasts. At any other time, this lascivious scene would have triggered a hormonal surge, followed by libidinal urges. One of the dancers caught Jacques' attention. The features were exaggerated, she was wearing eyeliners which accentuated her eyebrows. Her hair seems unusually straight. She was overly graceful in her steps. There was something weird about this character. Suddenly, it donned on Jacques. Drag queens! One, two, three…

Jacques counted at least five of them for sure. We're not for the black bushy mustache above their lips and their hairy chests, Jacques would never know. The cross-dressers moved as graciously as the women and could easily fool the most astute observers. They seemed as light as the fine garment they were wearing. They probably could teach Dennis Rodman or Elton John a lesson or two. How did they come to find their niche in this very select and powerful group? Jacques would later learn that it was a very common practice in the Voodoo community for gays and lesbians to become members of the high priest's immediate entourage.

Some of them were not even homosexuals. It is not a bit unusual for power seekers, politicians, and the like to participate in homosexual orgies to achieve ultimate power. Men would have sex with men, and women with women, according to certain rites. Nothing could be allowed to stand in the way of special requests from the gods. The Voodoo community is probably the most tolerant sector of the Haitian community. Everyone is welcome.

The drumbeats had reached a frenetic rhythm. They sounded as if they were talking in a language that only the initiates could decipher. The dancers were no longer themselves. There was one with the music, one with the singing, one with the environment. The whole scene was a giant display of harmony. It was like a long bridge on which the gods would travel. And suddenly, as if they could no longer bear the intensity of the repeated strokes on their senses, the dancers yielded. They surrendered to the loas. Triumphantly, they entered the temple one by one. Came *Papa Legba* the guardian of the gates, controlled and subdued. Next came *Baron Samedi* of the *Guede* family, lewd, sexually provocative, petulant, and bratty, his mouth full of filth. You wouldn't want your children to hang around with him. Then came *Damballah*, weaving his way into the crowd, on the floor like a snake, a drunk snake. And then more came, *Papa Zakka, Erzili, Grann Brijit*. They were all there because Jacques was in a jam, and he needed their help.

The dancers were now falling at Ge-klere's feet one by one, completely possessed and transfigured by the different spirits. Some were crawling like snakes. Some were making weird guttural sounds. Ge-klere would touch them on the forehead with one hand while holding the ceremonial *asson* in the other hand. They were still in a trance but controlled. There were more than a dozen different spirits in the room. What could be going on for all these gods to show up in this place? What earthly mortal could have such power as to summon the gods? Madam Maurice let out a long, piercing sound. She started to go around in a galloping motion. Madam Maurice sang many songs that night. Some of them were unintelligible. Some of them were not songs at all. They were laments. They were more like endless utterances of pent-up anguish and unfulfilled dreams, of denied desires and self-immolation. This time, Madam Maurice wanted to leave every fiber of her heart completely exposed. She wanted the gods to probe the depths and crevices of her heart. Her son's torments had become hers for now and she was feeling all the sorrow. As a mother, she did not know what else to do than to beg and throw herself at the mercy of the gods. Madam Maurice knew that without their divine intervention, her son Jacques was doomed and would certainly sink into the entrails of madness. Would the gods listen, or would they turn a deaf ear to the plea of a mother in pain?

Madam Maurice laments went on and on:

"What did I do, O god for you to claim my first-born son.

I will be your servant for the rest of my life.

I'll give you incense and myrrh.

I'll give you all kinds of sweet liquors, but O god, I cannot give you my son. "

Other songs seemed more poignant.

"Damballah--Wedo Ce bon, Ce bon
Damballah-Wedo Ce bon, Ce bon
Le ma monte chwal mwen
Gen moun ka Kriye

Le ma monte chwal mwen
Gin moun ka Kriye
Damballah-Wedo, Beware! Beware!
When I ride my horse (medium)
Some people will cry."

The songs sounded very sad. Madam Maurice's facial expressions were telling the whole story.

Fright.

Despair.

Dread.

She no longer sounded like herself. She had the voice of an old hoarse man. She was completely transfigured as if the god had descended on her shoulders. She was moving nimbly on her feet as if this woman in her sixties had just turned thirty.

The words kept on coming out rhythmically, in perfect synchrony with the buffered stomping sound of her steps on the clay ground. I will be damned! Madam Maurice was possessed too.

Then complete silence. Ge-klere was talking.

"The Gaetan family is in trouble. For many years, this family has ignored the advice of the *loas*. They were cursed by a white man. A man from afar! A very powerful man! A very rich man! After so many years, the Frenchman's soul is still looking for its final and eternal resting place. Only *Baron Samedi, Baron Simitye,* and *Baron Lacroix* can help you and your family. You must ask for forgiveness. If you do not, your son's neck will be broken! I see more trouble ahead! Papa Guede is extremely angry! "Pwen fe pa, mo red. (No Mercy! Sudden death!) I see that your first-born son is in a lot of torment. You need to find the skull of the French man. The gods have spoken! This man's soul has been haunting your first-born son."

The words came out, grave, solemn as if they were being etched in stone by a knowing and skillful hand. Once they were spoken, they could not be taken back. They would live forever. They did not sound human at all. They seemed to echo in the area as if they had been amplified through a sophisticated stereo sound system. The drumbeats started again. They were now reaching a deafening level, almost drowning the remaining words spoken out of this holy man's mouth. They did not even sound the same. All the joy was gone. Now they sounded as if they were part of a *Requiem.*

Jacques could not take it anymore. He felt as if a death sentence was just placed over his head. How could this man possibly have known about the skull? He never asked Jacques any questions. Jacques had been careful not to share such information with anyone. Since he came to that little town. he had hardly spoken a word to anyone. Jacques' worst fear was right before his eyes. He never believed that one could read his past or his future. For some reason, he felt that the armor of steel that he had so carefully built around himself was falling into thousands of small pieces. Gone was his façade of invincibility! Gone was the philosophical attitude about alternative beliefs. He felt as if a dagger had been plunged right in the middle of his heart. Jacques could no longer discount this revelation as pure mumbo jumbo from a drunk or oversexed old man. What happened after that was quite confusing.

Suddenly! Pandemonium! Jacques was completely out of control. He became as strong as a raging bull. He could not be contained. He picked up a stool and flung it across the room. He fell to the ground. He was foaming at the mouth. His whole body was shaking like a tree finding itself in a sudden tropical storm. This was by far the worst seizure episode that Jacques had ever experienced. Some blood was streaking from Jacques's lower lip. A few men came with a sisal rope. They wrestle

Jacques to the ground. After putting up much resistance, Jacques surrendered, sore, vanquished.

Jacques' head was inches away from hitting the charcoal-burnt rock used for offerings. The seizure episode lasted more than ten long minutes. To the priest, it was yet another manifestation of unsettling forces gone unchecked. Like a chief surgeon in his operating room summoning his residents, Ge-klere ordered: "Go and fetch. . . . "

He did not need to complete his sentence. His servants moved in unison. Less than two minutes later, they were back carrying long green branches from the Congo peas tree, a white bowl with oil and water, and some other unidentified items. Jacques was thrust to the ground as one of Ge-klere's delegates started to whip him with the branches. The rest of the women did not budge. They continued their singing and their incantations were understood only by the initiates.

It is doubtful that Jacques had any awareness of what was going on. The words from Dante in The Inferno would have been appropriate:

"I saw new torments and new souls in pain
about me everywhere. Wherever I turn
away from grief I turn to grief again."

He seemed limp as the flagellation went on for over ten interminable minutes. The whole audience was in a trance. No evil spirits were supposed to survive such a shock treatment.

They were supposed to flee in terror beaten at their own game. Let them inhabit the black pig in the pen or this three-horned goat next door, but" By the power of *Ogou Fer*ay and *Ogou Balenjo* and in the name of justice stay away from this poor soul" The drumbeats changed to a war march. The smell of *clairin* mixed with incense created an acrid odor that imbibed the air. The moment was not appropriate for laughter. *Guede* the trickster did not go quietly. He attempted to lighten the atmosphere with a few jokes of his own. Nothing worked. The tension persisted. Jacques was still being beaten. As far as Ge-klere and his entourage were concerned, Jacques was under the influence of a very evil spirit, and he needed to be exorcised. Who was best placed to perform this delicate task than the powerful Ge-klere himself, the one who could talk to the gods and knew just the right incantation to appease them or get in their good grace? Did it matter that Jacques was in severe pain? Did it matter that Jacques was no longer responding? To great ills, great remedies! Jacques was under attack and extreme measures were needed to save him. Came Ge-Klere to the rescue! Jacques was in shock. Once the flagellation was over, his forehead was anointed with oil and a white turban. An assortment of leaves was wrapped around his head. The treatment lasted close to an hour. Jacques was no longer seizing. The ushers seemed as exhausted as Jacques was. Jacques went into a profound state of narcolepsy. The instructions were clear.

Jacques was to go on a three-day-and-three-night fasting. No one would talk to him, lest someone wanted to become the medium for the evil spirit which was being removed from Jacques.

Very dangerous proposition. No one would dare. He would only be given water and honey. Ge-klere was done with Jacques for now. The spirits have been warded off. The next step would be a more complicated one. It was all up to the Gaetan family. There was no other reason for Jacques to stick around at Ge-klere's place for now. He was free to leave the premises whenever Madam Maurice was ready.

Jacques was in no condition to travel on horseback as he came. A cot made up of dried-up fibers from banana trees and some large pieces of wood was assembled. Jacques was placed on it and transported to Roche-a-Bateau. Ge-klere made sure that Madam Maurice obtained all the help she needed. She was given a bag full of potions and condiments with specific instructions. Jacques and Madam Maurice were in good hands. Transporting a wounded man down the hills on this rather primitive couch was very tricky. Any misstep and the whole caravan could find itself in the ravine on both sides of the tortuous dirt road. Not to worry. The carriers knew every inch of the heavily vegetated area. Roche-a-Bateau was situated only a few kilometers from Carpentier. The trip on foot lasted about an hour and a half. Almost thirty years after he last visited his birthplace, Jacques was back, carried over four men's shoulders like an African king making his triumphant entry into his city. However, there was nothing regal about Jacques' look. His long journey and ordeal had left him, bruised, and exhausted. He was barely conscious, aching in every fiber of his body. There was no marching band. There is no loudspeaker blasting the Ninth Symphony of Beethoven. The only welcoming party: the birds singing their morning prayer in salute of the rising sun. Jacques was home, a much different man. A man who had gone and seen but had not yet vanquished.

Chapter 17

Jacques did not know for how long he had been in this semi-conscious state. He could vaguely remember the events at Ge-klere's place. Was it just another dream? The soreness he was still experiencing all over his body was there to remind him that every minute of his ordeal had been real. He was torn between two feelings. On the one hand, he felt that he had been violated. On the other hand, he was surprised that he did not feel any anger towards the group for the rough treatment that he had been subjected to. There was something very comforting about Ge-klere and his followers who seemed to have come out in full force to help him. Jacques could feel his naked body underneath the white sheet. His body had been imbibed with an oily substance and to his surprise the sheet was not sticking to his skin. His sweat had cooled off his body and had broken his fever. Who would have thought that Jacques, the skeptic *par excellence*, would join the list of the few who have benefitted from this rare form of treatment? His body was sore all over as if some Tabasco sauce had been poured all over his bruised body. He could feel a persistent tingling on his back. He attempted to touch it but realized he had better not, as he felt some sharp pain over his left shoulder. He did not know how long he has been there, days maybe weeks. He did not exactly know where he was. Usually, his sense of hearing would have helped him decipher all the sounds around him. Not this time. All he could hear was a persistent humming sound and a tingling in both ears. There was a very characteristic and pungent scent filling up the air. For a while, Jacques was trying to figure out what it was. Then it came to him. *"Ilang Ilang."* How could he ever forget? As a child, he ravished this perfume that became part of his everyday life.

Jacques and the other children would sit under the tree, unaware of the time until the old church bell would remind him, it was way past his curfew. What excuse was Jacques going to have this time? There was only one place that could bring so many memories. How did he get there? Jacques was not quite sure. The memories started to come back gradually. He could see himself running around half-naked, trying to sneak out to play in the rain. *"Come back here Jacques! You are going to catch pneumonia!"* His mother would scream. His futile attempts at outsmarting his mother would always end up the same way. She seemed to always know how to catch him. Nobody got away from Madam Maurice. She would roll up her eyes in exasperation and scream at the top of her lungs. *"When I am done with you Jack"* That is all it took. That firm but caring voice. Until next time. After a while, Madam Maurice gave up on trying to chase the children around.

Jacques started to wonder.

"If my family was involved in some kind of unresolved conflict,

why should I be the one to carry the curse? Why?"

It did not seem fair. Jacques felt that a great injustice had been done to him. Why should he have to carry the burden of past generations? Jacques' mind was getting clearer every day. Jacques could not give up to despair. He felt that he no longer had a choice. He needed to regain all his physical strength. More challenges lay ahead of him. As the days went by, the pain in his back became more and more bearable. He just knew that Ge-klere had not heard the last of him. Once he was fully recovered, he would take a trip to the Petit Seminaire research library in Port-au-Prince. If the person Ge-klere was referring to did exist, there should be some trace of him at that library. Jacques did some volunteer work in that library one summer. There were books on just about every single event in the history of the country. There were documents dating back to the colonial period. If there is any validity to O'Connor's story, the answer should be there. The history teacher at the school, Father Adrien, if he is still around, should be able to help. First, he would have to convince his mother that he needed to make that trip. Now, Jacques could barely feel any pain. Jacques was having some flashbacks about the events at Ge-klere's place. He remembered vaguely being held while a few people were dancing around and singing while hitting him with some branches.

"I must have passed out," Jacques thought.

He tried to take a few steps. Oops! He must have been drugged. He had to hold on to the head of the bed. This bed must be over fifty years old. It was made of massive mahogany wood, and one could almost see the different layers of varnish that have been applied over the years. Jacques took some steps closer to the door. Somebody was coming. Jacques rushed back to his bed and lay down, feigning that he was sleeping. He did not know what to expect. He closed his eyes halfway. He could distinctly recognize the features of a face ravaged by years of usage. This face expressed joy, amazement, and pain. She was carrying a tray and the aroma of crab soup filled the air. This face had seen the Gaetan's family moments of pride and moments of sorrow. "It was the face of..." Jacques could not help it.

"Amelia!" He yelled in amazement.

Jacques had thought about this old comforting and motherly face many times. She had aged quite a bit, her hair was all grey, but she was still wearing her characteristic smile. Oh! That smile. A smile that revealed the big gap between Amelia's front teeth. Her face had not changed much, except for a few added wrinkles. Whoever said that aging was not beautiful has never seen faces like Amelia's. Grace. Elegance. Dignity. Those were the words that came to mind to describe Amelia. Claude Dambreville, the renowned Haitian artist would have a great time putting this face on canvas for posterity to see.

"You are awake!" she said, "You must have been very tired, you have been in a deep slumber for four days now," as she placed a large bowl of steaming soup on a small table by the bed.

Jacques rose and gave Amelia a big bear hug. He did not need to say much. It was most appropriate that Amelia would pop up on the scene at this time in Jacques' life. She had wiped many tears from his face. When he was a youngster about to leave school for the first time, Amelia was there. She had also shed many tears on her own. Jacques remembered a particular event. Amelia was extremely sad after she learned that her husband had died in Havana, Cuba. "What day is today?" Jacques asked.

"Today is Thursday," Amelia responded with a lisp.

"How did I get here?" Jacques continued to wonder.

"Hush! Enough talking! You have been very sick," continued Amelia.

"Sit up and eat! I brought you some soup. "

Jacques was feeling less estranged now. Amelia's face could only spell good news. Amelia has always taken good care of him. When his mother went on trips, Jacques and his siblings were left under the watch of Amelia. She would always threaten to get the *martinet* to get the children back in line, but Jacques could not remember Amelia ever getting angry at anyone.

Jacques pulled himself closer to the table. The aroma of the soup took away the last traces of sleep from his bruised body. Jacques attacked the soup with a loud slurping sound. He felt pain in every single muscle of his face. The soup was a mixture of legumes including carrots, turnips, red tomatoes, sweet potatoes, dumplings, and crabs. The whole thing with the right balance of garlic and pepper-based seasonings.

"Yummy! Delicious!" said Jacques, as he continued to make a slurping noise with his lips. The soup was steamy hot. One could always count on Amelia for a delicious meal. Soup was her specialty. Crab soup, squash soup, or cow foot soup. On some Saturdays when she prepared her *Chaka* soup, people would invite themselves from all over the neighborhood to have a bowl. Amelia never turned away anyone. This place was familiar to Jacques. After his family moved to the larger city of Les Cayes, Jacques would return every summer to Roche-a-Bateau for vacation. He would play in the woods by the river *'Les-islets,'* hunting ortolans and nightingales, setting traps for crab while his mother was doing the laundry. From afar, one could hear the beetles on the linen, only interrupted by some mothers yelling at their lads not to go too far. All of this was coming back to Jacques suddenly. It seemed as if the memories were competing. Jacques was starving. He was starting his third serving.

“Easy!” said Amelia, “there is plenty more where this came from.”

Jacques could not retain his joy. He leaned towards Amelia and kissed her, thanking her for the meal. Tears were pouring down Jacques’ cheeks. Jacques was reminded about his wounds, as he felt the tingling on his back. Amelia sat at the foot of the bed. They had a very long chat.

"It has been such a long time," Jacques said.

"I know, I know," Amelia replied.

"Where is everybody?"

Amelia avoided the question. "Jacko, child! You are going to be fine Jacques was reminded that Amelia was one of a few people that called him by the nickname of Jacko. It was unusual for Amelia to avoid a direct question. Jacques asked even in a more direct way:

"Where is my mother?"

"Oh, your mother? She has gone back to the States. She wants you to stay here until you are fully recovered. She feels that you are in good hands here. What do you think? Uhm, Jacko?"

It was an astute way for Amelia to put it, to signal that she did not wish to discuss it any further. At least, not now. Jacques felt put on the spot.

"You're right. I am in very good hands, Amelia. "

Jacques knew that he was not being told everything, but he did not insist. He would find out the rest of the story in due time. If anyone had a secret to hide, Amelia was the person to confide in. She knew everything about the family. She did not read or write. She did not keep a diary, but she could tell you all the important dates about the family, birthdays, and anniversaries with precision. She had been around in good times and in bad times. She had witnessed the birth of most of the members of the Gaetan family, as she had the weddings and the funerals. She was a modern-day version of the African matriarch.

Jacques was enjoying his stay in this small town. No telephone. No traffic jams. He knew that many arduous steps lay ahead of him. Every day, he would wake up in the early morning hours when the dew was still covering the grass. He would take a long walk through the woods until he felt completely energized. As it got warmer, he would go by the stream and take a swim. He would throw himself on the grass in meditation. He wondered what his life would have been like if he never left the country. So much had already happened. He had seen how much violence has been done to the environment in the name of civilization. Jacques was becoming quite philosophical. Was it worth trading this pristine environment for life in the cities? Jacques had seen barges of garbage produced in a couple of weeks by large cities go around the world from port to port like a moving museum of urbanization gone mad. Would you trade this beautiful landscape for the smog and pollution of cities like Los Angeles? Jacques also knew that human intelligence had taken man to places that no one could ever imagine possible. It was now possible for a man to create a virtual world where his every need can be satisfied.

Jacques sat there in ecstasy, his questions unanswered. What would life have been like if he never left this land? Maybe he was asking the wrong question. A better question would be: What choice did the farmers of this small town have to be condemned to a life of abject poverty, with no hope of seeing their fiftieth birthday or for their children to ever complete basic education? The question was too deep. Was this question even necessary? Besides who the hell was Jacques to even raise the question?

The farmers, it seemed, had developed a completely different attitude, one of avoidance. They despised agronomists who come to the small town with their heads full of social theories but ran to their condos in the cities when famine and drought struck. Jacques could think about his fellow men's problems besides his own. That was indeed a good sign. He was getting better. If one ever asks Jacques what he had rather be in his other life, he knew what his answer would be. He would probably be a politician. Don't ask why. Politicians are sacrificial lambs who dare to confront their ideal, knowing from the start that if elected they will fall far short of the mark. Why would anyone want to kill his/her dreams? On the other hand, special talents or not, what could be more exhilarating than putting oneself at the service of your fellow men? Jacques had always been fascinated with the writings of Plato, Machiavelli, Gandhi, and Martin Luther King. Different eras, different methods maybe, but one common thread, an obsession to explain the political behavior of human beings. Man is a political animal. Jacques was an avid reader of Nietzsche's moral theories and Jean-Paul Sartre's brand of existentialism. He was also somewhat of a visionary who dreamed of a more perfect world. Jacques was feeling good. He had not felt that good in years. The wounds on his back, thanks to some home remedies from Amelia, had healed rather quickly. The scars were barely visible. Jacques could run, jump and throw balls with both hands without difficulty. He had fully recovered.

He rushed back to the house, as he wanted to pack a few items. He wanted to go to Port-au-Prince and get back here as soon as he could. Tomorrow, he would make the trip back to the next town and catch the bus to Port-au-Prince. Amelia prepared him a nice dinner consisting of red snapper fried crispy dry with onions, rice and kidney beans, and fried green plantains. Jacques had a very large appetite that evening. Amelia told him stories and trivia about every member of the family. Some of them he had heard hundreds of times over the years, but no one could ever tell a story like Amelia could. They chatted late into the night, sipping cinnamon and ginger tea with condensed milk. It was almost 1:00 am when Jacques decided to call it a day.

Chapter 18

Instead of Nature's living sphere

In which God made mankind, you have alone,

In smoke and Maud around you here

Beasts' skeletons and dead men's bone.

Faust by Goethe

Jacques woke up very early that morning. He could hear the crowing of the rooster. Cocorico! As he was saddling up his horse, the strong stench of manure got into his nostril, he sneezed repeatedly. That was a good omen. Maybe after all, the gods have come around. Maybe now, they were in Jacques' corner. These were very comforting thoughts. Most of the people in the town were already awake. Jean-Pierre used to live in that house at the end of the dirt road. Whatever became of him? Jacques wondered. Some of the people were loading up their donkeys. They were getting ready to make their weekly run to the market. They greeted Jacques enthusiastically as he passed by. "Bonjour Msie!"[8] He would respond in the same cordial manner. Jacques was happy to see that the people from this town had not been touched by the distant and cold attitude that people tend to have these days. He made it to the next town in good time. He was able to catch the bus *Dieu si bon*. It was very crowded, but the passengers on the second row made room for him. All around were merchants trying to make a last-minute sale of homemade sweets (*douce makross, coconut gran feuille and tablet pistache*) before the bus pulled out in fanfare with three long sounds off the horn. The smell of diesel oil filled the air. The moment was magic. If everything went well, they should be pulling in the dock in Port-au-Prince in about five hours. Along the way, the bus made quite a few stops.

Jacques did not pay much attention to the landscape he had seen only a few days ago. It is quite surprising what a few days of rest can do to one's mind. Jacques was not as anxious as before. He was more curious. If that Frenchman, Mr. O'Connor was such a socialite, there should be some trace of him in the library. Jacques was eager to find out. The trip was uneventful. It was about four o'clock in the afternoon when the bus reached Port-au-Prince. Jacques caught a taxi to The Palace, a small hotel near the Champ de Mars, the main park of the city.

---

[8]Good morning, sir!

It was within walking distance from the *Petit Seminaire* library.

Jacques used to have a lot of acquaintances in Port-au-Prince. Now he is like a stranger in the town. Jacques attended secondary school at *Petit Seminaire,* where he developed a taste for liturgical and classical music. Jacques' only regret was that he never learned how to play a musical instrument. Jacques' hotel room was small, but well furnished. It even had a thirteen-inch color television set. Jacques just realized that for the past few days, he did not keep up with current events and to his surprise he did not miss it a bit. He turned the set on. An old Bruce Lee movie was on. Jacques fell asleep while watching. Maybe it was better. He had seen that movie at least five times before.

Jacques presented at the school gate at about nine thirty in the morning. The old clock was still ticking. The buildings were still painted in a characteristic light green color that seemed to be on everything pertaining to the school. In the front panel of the main building, one could read the words 'Dei Virtus,' the motto of the school. Jacques was greeted at the front office by a priest dressed in regular clothes except for the white clergyman band around his neck.

"Father, I want to look for some information in the library. Can anyone help me?" Jacques asked awkwardly.

"Certainly, the library is in the building across the yard," the priest said. He had a strong smell of tobacco. His front teeth were stained with nicotine residue.

"Thank you, Father..." Jacques hesitated.

"Father Paul," the priest quickly added, "and what is your name, son?"

"Jacques Gaetan...I attended this school many years ago. The place looks the same..."

The priest was not listening, he was already moving along to wherever his pastoral duties would take him. The librarian showed a lot of patience. He methodically searched through the newspaper publications of the era. Any references to the name would be welcome. Jacques and the librarian were about to give up until... Bingo! A picture of Claude O'Connor with a group of businessmen. The plan to exploit some gold mine in the mountains in Les Cayes region was announced in grand fanfare. There he was, with a broad smile on Mr. O'Connor's face. Mr. Entrepreneur himself.

"Always at the right place, at the right time, smiling for the camera. This kind seems to always come across opportunities that the local people never seem to be able to find."

It was later discovered that O'Connor was in possession of some old maps indicating where treasures were hidden from colonial time. Jacques was able to find a few documents, including some more clippings from an old issue of Le Nouvelliste referring to a businessman named Claude O'Connor. What Jacques discovered was the profile of a drifter, a con man maybe, but one with a vice, very strange habit, a compulsion to run after teenage girls. After further tracking, this is the story that Jacques was able to reconstitute. Claude O'Connor reportedly came to Haiti via Martinique. Rumor had it that it was an assumed name. O'Connor might have had a criminal record back in his native country of France. He was wanted by the police for embezzling large sums of money from businessmen with the promise of large return by exploiting gold mines. Others believed that O'Connor was his real name and that he was born in Toulouse in the South of France to an Irish family heavily involved in practice of witchcraft. He accumulated an immense fortune. Some say that he might have sold his soul to the devil.

Nobody really knows which version of the stories to believe. One thing was certain, Claude O'Connor was very rich. He lived a very lavish lifestyle. He visited with the rich and powerful. He wore expensive clothes directly imported from Europe. He was often seen sitting in the outdoor cafe sipping on Martini with his trademark designer sunglass on the tip of his nose. One night, he had one drink too many and let out another important piece of information to complete his profile. He had been arrested before for some sexual crimes and got off after bribing someone. A trip out of his native country was quickly arranged. He spent some time in Martinique, got on a ship as a stow-away enroute to Port-au-Prince. To Jacques, it seemed that it was like filibuster and buccaneer time all over again. It was like a trip through a time machine. Right in the middle of the century, another pirate had targeted the Caribbean Island as his destination. Soon Claude O'Connor developed a reputation as a womanizer, especially the much younger ones. He was never known to hold a steady job, nor did he seem to need one. Claude O'Connor was a very handsome man. He had a very imposing posture. He stood six feet and three inches tall, he had the muscles of a gladiator, like a young Richard Burton out of a Roman Empire movie. He often carried a tennis racket in his sport bag. Claude O'Connor had violated many taboos, like getting into bed with both mother and daughter. He had also broken the hearts of many girls in the prime of their lives. It had been rumored that over two dozen girls might have been violated by this man, including the sixteen-year-old daughter of the police chief. O'Connor was also believed to have magical powers. He could be in two places at the same time and always managed to get away from jealous and angry fathers.

One hot summer afternoon, however, Mr. O'Connor would meet a very violent death. Genevieve Gaetan, a beautiful and promising graduate from a Catholic school, fell victim to O'Connor's insatiable sexual appetite. She was lured into the park one evening and savagely raped. Unlike the other girls, Genevieve decided to speak up. She went straight to her father, Mr. Giraud Gaetan, and told him what had happened to her. Mr. Gaetan went into a violent rage, picked up his gun and went about the town. After asking a few questions, Mr. Giraud Gaetan had some idea where he might find O'Connor. He followed him for about three hours, and as he was taking his evening stroll in the park, Mr. Gaetan went to his face and shot him right through the nose. Mr. O'Connor went backwards and hit the pavement. Nobody knew what happened afterwards. There was no police report, no investigation. So many people wanted him dead. No one shed a tear at his sudden disappearance. It is said that Mr. Gaetan was never the same again. He lost interest into everything. He no longer enjoyed cock fighting which has been his hobby for years. Mr. Gaetan was never seen in public again. He might have lost his mind. Revenge did not bring him any happiness. He was full of guilt. It felt as if a dark cloud was always looming over his head. He was cursed. Mr. Giraud Gaetan died a couple of years later.

That is all the confirmation that Jacques needed. He decided that he would go back to Ge-klere and do whatever he had to do. What a burden, Jacques had to carry. To Jacques, it started to all make sense. There have been very few males born to the family since his great-grand-father, Giraud Gaetan, died. His own father, Maurice, died young under strange circumstances. Jacques was the first male born in his generation. This was very serious. Jacques owed it to himself and to the Gaetan family to have this curse removed once and for all. Jacques felt obligated to notify all the members of his family of his intent. Should he fail to control the curse, it could have very deleterious consequences. There might be more deaths. Jacques remembered the words of Ge-Klere to his mother *"Your son's neck will be broken. Pwen fe pa. Mo red!"* (No mercy. Sudden death).Was Jacques up to the task? At this point, Jacques felt he no longer had a choice. This would be his duty, his mission. Jacques stopped at the school chapel dedicated to Notre-Dame de la Victoire. The glorious chapel has fallen into disrepair. In the back, symmetrically situated, two mahogany staircases led up to a mezzanine with circularly arranged rows of pews. Filling the whole area with its imposing presence, an old pipe organ. It was quite a piece of workmanship. The long brass-colored pipes handsomely crafted, bore the signature of Wurlitzer. One could hardly imagine that an instrument that has animated so may celebrations, was so still and so awfully silent. It just stood there *en garde* ready to roar and marvel at the musical virtuosity of Bach, Mozart and Beethoven at the next holiday celebration. The choir area also was deserted. There were no long rows of alto and soprano boys dressed in their ceremonial costumes, innocently singing how "the beauty and the immensity of the firmament proclaims the glory of God". The sunlight was filtering through the multicolored stained-glass windows creating very strange designs on the ground. The etchings on the windows were depicting important events in the history of Christianity. The dumfounded faces of the higher priests when Christ presented to their temple at age twelve and baffled them with the depth of His knowledge, or the scene where a beam of light descended upon Saul on his way to Damascus causing him to be blind and Saul's statement of faith, "He is indeed the Son of God. . . " One is reminded the words of Cuban poet Jose-Maria de Heredia in his masterpiece "Vitrail" (Church Window):

Cette verrière a vu dames et hauts barons
Étincelants d'azur, d'or, de flamme et de nacre,
Incliner, sous la dextre auguste qui consacre,
L'orgueil de leurs cimiers et de leurs chaperons ;
Ils gisent là sans voix, sans geste et sans ouïe,
Et de leurs yeux de pierre ils regardent sans voir
La rose du vitrail toujours épanouie.

Translation

(Translation was obtained from: www.PoemHunter.com.
The World Poetry Archive)

This window has seen dames and lords of might,
Sparkling with gold, with azure, flame, and nacre,
Bow down, before the altar of their Maker,

The pride of crest and hood to august right;
All still are they, voiceless and deaf, while e'er
They gaze, with stony eyes that ne'er see more,
On window's rose blooming forever there.

At the other end of the church hall, a display of white marble with the altar in the middle immaculately dressed like a virgin ready for sacrifice. Silence and emptiness filled the small chapel. Jacques sat there, pensive, alone in cold sweats. Nothing that Jacques remembered could compete with the solemnity of the moment. What would be the outcome of his quest? Jacques wished he could, like in ancient times, read the oracles in the sky. And since he could not, he did the next best thing he knew. He prayed. Just like a Roman warrior ready to go on a campaign, Jacques lit up a candle and implored help from Heaven using the following words:

"Oh Lord, you created me in your image, and I am who I am!
The son of a country born out of two continents
My ancestors from Africa had so many needs that you let them have one God for each one of those needs.
My mentors from Sorbonne and St. Germain des Pres, have taught me your Holy Word
"Oh Lord! You created me in your image, and I am Who I am!
When I hear drumbeats, they resonate through my stomach!
When I hear the "Messiah" by Handel, my heart palpitates!

Oh Lord! You created me in your image, and I am who I am!
When I watch women being possessed, I feel trepidations!
When I listen to a Gregorian mass, I am in seventh heaven!
Oh Lord! You created me in your image, and I am who I am!
Oh Lord! Now I am confused, scared, and possibly cursed.
Please help me, so I do not lose my soul.
Because you created me in your image, and I am who I am!"

The statue of the Virgin Mary in her blue gown ornate with gold trimming seemed to be smiling. Was the Virgin Mary smiling at the audacity of Jacques' prayer, or was she giving a sign from above that the inhabitants of Heaven understood Jacques' dilemma and it was okay for him to proceed?

> *"And the Master said to me: "Soon you will be*
> *where your own eyes will see the source and cause*
> *and give you their own answer to the mystery."*
> *(The Inferno, Dante.)*

Jacques left the church, relieved. All he needed to do now was to notify everyone in his family of his decision. It was only fair. The waters will no longer be still. Possibly, the crows would take a pause in their pilgrimage around the cornfields. Maybe, only maybe, the vultures in the sky would give a reprieve to their preys. Beware! Jacques was about to ruffle some feathers. Stillness of the water, no longer! Giant Sea monsters who live among the corals at the bottom of the sea, wake up from your long slumber, you are invited to this galactical encounter. He would need some resources. Jacques called his family asking for financial support. After all, the mission he was about to undertake was on behalf of the whole family. He will leave it up to his mother to further explain the situation. The family responded immediately. Funds were wired. He collected the cash at a nearby bank. Jacques had no idea how much it would cost for Ge-klere to help him. By the time Jacques finished running his errands, it was already six o'clock. It was no time to be on the street with so much cash.

He rushed back to his hotel room and called the international telephone operator. He wanted to make sure everyone was onboard with his plan because if unsuccessful, it carried the risk of unleashing more calamities, more curses on other members of the family. Evil has no friends and never forgives. To his surprise, he was connected rather quickly. Jacques got Georges first. "Hello, Georges, this is Jacques. I guessed you know what happened, don't you?"

"Yes, mom told me. What is the next step?"

"Well, I wish all of you could come down. We need to have Ge-klere resolve this problem once and for all. "

"I don't know, I will discuss it with everyone. I doubt that Jean-Paul will be able to take time off now."

"Try your best, Georges! I really need your help on that

one."

They were cut off. Jacques hoped that he was able to convey to Georges how grave the situation was. If anyone could convince Jacques' brothers and sisters, Georges would be the one. For some reason, Georges had always been taken seriously, unlike Jean-Paul who was seen as a debonaire, a *bon vivant.* It seemed that all Jean-Paul was interested in, was nice sports car and parties. If they did not show up, Jacques would have to do it alone. Jacques attempted to get connected to Montreal. No luck this time. All the circuits were busy. After waiting for over an hour, Jacques gave up. Jacques could not remember when last the whole family was reunited. Jacques was not very hopeful it would happen this time. Jacques felt very tired. He stopped at the hotel bar and ordered a Prestige beer. The award-winning version of Roberta Flack's song by 'The Fugees' was playing:

"Singing my life with his words
Killing me softly with his song. . .
Telling my whole life with his words"

It was a hot steamy night. Soon, the whole town would be paralyzed with daily torrential rain. Jacques would have Amelia contact Ge-klere as soon as he gets to Roche-a-Bateau.

Chapter 19

Jacques left Port-au-Prince the next morning at about ten o'clock. This trip was even more pleasant than the first one. The bus was brand new, and Jacques was allowed more leg room. It was quite a different atmosphere, as Jacques was more decisive about the steps ahead of him. He made it back to Roche-a-Bateau right after the sunset. On the porch of the tin roof house, some families were gathered for an evening snack on charcoal roasted ears of sweet corn. The rest of the town was already asleep. It was the time when grandparents sit with their grandchildren and tell stories about time long, long time ago... The stories would be embellished, but it really did not matter. These moments were invaluable. Later, these memories would be valued and remembered. They would be cherished like old treasures. They would inevitably take on more values with the passing of time. But never, would they be forgotten.

Amelia greeted Jacques at the door. "Jack, you are back? How was your trip? You must be exhausted. I will fix you something to eat."

"Thank you, Amelia! I am not really hungry, some tea and a piece of bread will do just fine."

Amelia disappeared toward the back of the house where the small kitchen was located. The sweet aroma of cinnamon filled up the room. Amelia was back in no time, carrying a tray with a large pot of hot tea and some sweet homemade biscuits. Jacques sipped on the tea very slowly, as he discussed with Amelia, how they would contact Ge-klere. Amelia had been careful not to push Jacques into making a hasty decision. She knew all along that Jacques would eventually come around. If the first trip to Carpentier, Ge-Klere's hometown was traumatic, this one would even be more so. Amelia did not want to alarm Jacques too much. They talked about old times. Unlike the first time, there was no tension. Jacques no longer seemed paralyzed with fear. Now he was more determined than ever to face the mysteries that awaited him. Amelia decided that she would send someone to talk to Ge-klere as early as tomorrow morning. Jacques would stay put and wait for instructions. It was already Tuesday, Jacques anticipated that nothing would happen until the following weekend. Ge-Klere's emissary came back the next day with his master's instructions. The preparation for the days ahead would be very arduous. Jacques got to work right away. It included long hours of confinement, special incantations, and consumption of special foods, at specific time. The rituals were very detailed and specific. This time, however, Jacques was ready to take on the challenge.

Chapter 20

But when the mind is overwhelmed by mighty fears,
we see the spirit is upset and shares in the terror:
for sweat and pallor now appear throughout the body
the speech is indistinct; the voice begins to fail,
the eyes to swim, the ears to ring, the limbs to falter;
This terror of the mind, these shadows must be dispelled.
not by the sun's bright shafts nor by the brilliant daylight,
but by an understanding of the laws of Nature.
On the nature of the Universe, Lucretius

Dong! Dong! Dong! Dong! . . Twelve o'clock! The strokes of the bell of St. Michel church broke the monotony of the small town. Jacques was standing by the door, ready to walk out of the old stucco house. He was instructed to start his walk precisely at noon on that day. When he set foot outside, the sun was supposed to hit him directly on the head, causing no shadow on the ground. Jacques looked like a monk out of a sixteen-century monastery. His head and his face had been cleanly shaved the night before. He was wearing a loosely fit two-piece suit made of white satin material. Around his waist, a hanging cotton cord with seven knots. On his left shoulder, he was carrying a large white sack containing among other items, a bottle of rum, a vial of Florida perfume, and three small bags containing each seven hundred seventy-seven dollars and thirty-three red pennies. For the three days preceding this trip, Jacques was instructed to sleep on sugar sacks on the floor. He was not to get into his bed under any circumstances. For days he was visited by a huge black butterfly. Jacques did not know how it got there. It did not move and did not seem to be bothered by the changes in temperature or brightness in Jacques small bedroom.

Jacques felt comforted by its presence, because according to Amelia, it could only mean that Jacques' good angels were here to assist him in the challenges that lay ahead of him. He would remain indoor, not get exposed to either sun or dusk. He had abstained himself from meat, fish and any sexual contact. He took repeated baths, using rough laundry soap. The used bath water was to be poured in a hole in the center of the yard. On the final night before the trip, he bathed himself in milk drawn from a white cow and anointed his head with crosses in seven different points with antimony unguent. Jacques felt no shame at all, walking with decisive steps towards his destiny. He paid no attention to the strange looks he got from the old legion of Mary ladies on their way to their mid-day meeting, nor did he notice the frightened and puzzled expression on the face of some children. Other children were much bolder and yelled a few derogatory names at Jacques. They were quickly pulled by the ears and reprimanded by their wary parents. The steamy heat of the early summer day was unforgiving. Jacques realized that he was not in as good a shape as he used to be. Covering the ten-mile trip to Ge-klere's habitation, would be quite a feat. He measured his steps. Jacques was not allowed to speak to strangers or comment about the purpose of his pilgrimage. After almost forty minutes, Jacques paused a few moments to have a drink of coconut milk that was being sold by an old man with a donkey. Only a couple of words were exchanged.

Jacques did not accept any change, afraid that bad luck might come from the coins he collected from the old man. Jacques was slowing down again. He was out of breath. He sat on a large rock by the road. Was he tired or was he scared? A little bit of both... Jacques knew that he did not have a long way to go. The beats from the drums were becoming more distinct. The habitation could be seen taking shape, maybe about two miles away at the top of a rather steep hill. Jacques gathered all his energy and began his final climb. Jacques has no idea how long it took him, but he made it to the top. The whole habitation looked much different. The streets were swept clean of all trash and the dusty ground was watered down. The trees on the side of the road leading to Ge-klere's temple, were festooned with long bright yellow, red, green and blue banner. The children were dancing and singing at the rhythm of an old vaccine, while another man was blowing away at a long tube of bamboo. The town was in a very festive mood. As Jacques approached the group upon the leader's signal, he was saluted with a customized version of Hail to the chief (Aux champs). To what did he owe the honor of such welcome, Jacques did not know. Jacques knew too well that he was no chief. For the next few days however, all the gods would rush to this corner of the globe to rescue one person: Jacques Gaetan. Jacques had no idea how it would happen, but it felt very good. This blessed town would be the theater of events that would mark Jacques for the rest of his life. It seemed like the whole town had been invited to the celebration. It all started with an invocation to *Papa Legba*, the god of the gates and of the crossroads, the one through whom every request must pass.

"A Legba, vanyan, sanyan
Wa di yo na pe tan' nou
A Legba, vanyan, sanyan
Wa di yo na pe tan' yo
Wa di yo na pe tan' yo
Translation:
(O valiant Legba, Sir

Go and tell them, we are waiting.
O valiant Legba, Sir
Go and tell them, we are waiting for them).

Like a Bishop adorned with his most beautiful vestments for a holiday celebration, Ge-klere wore his white ceremonial garb with dignity. His head was capped with a large, well ornate tiara with fake stones of all colors. Flanked by two assistants, the *laplace* and the *hougenikon*, Ge-klere kept a tight grip on everything that was going on. Everything was well choreographed. The participants moved with the precision of the parts of a Swiss gold watch. *Papa Legba* was asked for permission again and again, for they could not afford to offend this most powerful god. The whole endeavor would be all for naught, should *Papa Legba* shun their request. The *laplace* implored insistingly.

"Papa Legba souple, ouve barrie ya pou mwen
Ma rantre, Ma fe ceremoni lwa mwen,"
And the audience responded in chorus,
"Legba ouve barrie ya pou mwen"9
Translation:
Papa Legba please, open the gate for me
I will enter. I will perform my ceremony

After all, they could not afford for *Legba* to get angry. He was much too important a personality to make him mad. He was married to the graceful and sensuous goddess *Erzili Freda*. *Erzili* liked nice perfume and could be very flirtatious at time. Once they were sure that their supplication was heard, the *laplace* under order from Ge-klere, started the presentation of water. Water was thrown east, west, north and south, three times before the peristyle, before the *poto-mitan* (center post). The three drums (manman tambou (Assoto), seconde tambou and Kata) were blessed three times with water under the watchful eyes of the *Hounsis*. The other sacred tools were then introduced one by one by the l*aplace* and two *hounsis*. Once Ge-klere kissed them in sign of approval, they were ceremoniously placed on a well decorated altar. Then there was what seemed like an interminable procession of voodoo flags. All the loas had their symbols proudly displayed and shown to the supplicants who bowed and showed their respect. *St Jacques Majeur, Danballah, Erzili Danto,* Baron *Lakwa,* all were invited with good measures of swaying, gyrations, and sensuous sounds according to their liking. The ceremonial Voodoo flags were held high and presented to the four cardinal points, to the *poto-mitan* and the sacred drums. Ge-klere then slowly and masterfully traced some special design on the ground, the *veve,* using white flour. The ceremony had officially started.

All the supplicants then became involved in a long litany

of prayers where every single inhabitant of Heaven was summoned down to this sacred place. Some of the prayers seemed right out of the catholic missal:

"Vierge sainte exaucez-nous
Notre espoir est tout en vous
Chere Dame, portez la garde
Tres digne mere de Dieu
Voyez, nous sommes de garde
Pour vous defendre en tout lieu."

They called St. Philomene and St. Francois. They asked for mercy. They called St. Antoine de Padoue and St. Andre known for their compassion for the innocent, the defenseless. They asked for protection. They departed family members must now be in heave. Now they were gods themselves. Their support was sorely needed in this momentous occasion. Come on down now! Do not delay, for tomorrow it might be too late. The spirits of renowned and powerful houngan and mambos now departed were asked to make one last trip on this wretched earth. People in limbo, people waiting to be canonized, come on down now. I mean now. Situation critical. Why would it matter? Do not take any chances, invoke them anyway. Ge-klere was very forceful in his imploration:

"Apo lisa gbadia tamerra dabo
Apo lisa gbadia tamerra dabo
Apo lisa gbadia tamerra dabo
Awan gansie,
Lissa dole zo,
Granma Silibo vavoun,
Agassou Mahoude."

Ge-klere's face was completely transfigured. What used to be the white portion of his eye was injected with blood. His eyelids were going into rapid, repetitive contractions. His mouth was spraying spittle. Ge-klere was in full command of his troops. His own assistants were staggered and stood still, like Queen Elizabeth's royal guards in attention in front of Buckingham Palace. This was a critical moment for the whole process that was to take place that evening. If the gods did not respond to Ge-klere's magical formula, nothing else could happen. Jacques would be doomed. They could not proceed with the ceremony. That would spell trouble. The supplicants would have to wait for more favorable time. Every single spirit from everywhere was summoned. The situation was very grave, the more saints, the better.

Suddenly, bedlam! The long-awaited sign came. The whole audience went into a frenzy. People were shaking. Heads were falling back. Hands were clapping. It was almost as if everyone was struck with a moment of collective folly. It was chaos. Everyone seemed to have lost control. In the small temple there was a cacophony of sounds, a mixture of screams, irresistible laughter, weeping, feet stomping, women screaming in pain as if they were in labor, babies crying as if suddenly born in a world full of terror. The whole place was out of control. It was as if someone had let open the gates of a gigantic dam and all the gods were running loose. The gods were here, there and everywhere. Damballah was dancing on the ground like a snake. His wife, *Ayida Wedo,* the rainbow spirit, had joined him. They were now enlaced in a lascivious embrace and falling to the ground and mimicking sexual intercourse. *Papa Zaka* looked very elegant in his denim outfit. The gracious and sensual *Erzili* was flirting again with the men, teasing them by throwing kisses and exposing her breast. She was a goddess in rut. *Papa Loko* arrived tired, as if from a very long journey, afraid to be late for dinner. At the other end of the room, *Papa Guede* was at his trick again, joking around and making indecent gestures. He never seemed to have enough, recounting his sexual prowess. He had men and women holding their side from laughing too much. The drums could not keep up with the official salutations. As soon as they started with one God, another one was there awaiting jealously and impatiently for his introduction. What a meeting it was! People were falling, gasping for breath, exhausted, begging for a sip of clairin or water. Anything would do.

Anything to quench their thirst. They were talking in tongues understood only by the initiates. Jacques was suddenly enthralled in a brand-new world, a world where he could risk only baby steps, lest he wants to find himself in the abyss of death. The only words that came to Jacques' mind were the following verses from the Scriptures:

"Suddenly, there was a sound from heaven like the roaring of a mighty windstorm in the skies above them, and it filled the house where they were meeting. Then, what looked like flames or tongues of fire appeared and settled on each of them. And everyone present was filled with the Holy Spirit and began speaking in other languages, as the Holy Spirit gave them this ability. "

In the middle of all of this, Jacques was there, sitting and hoping that once this was over, and so would be his troubles. As the ceremony continued, the confusion reached its paroxysm. More bedlam. The words were now unintelligible. The roll call of the spirits went on and on, interrupted only by Ge-klere's quick drink out of a bottle of tafia. He would bring the bottle to his mouth in a rapid motion and make a horrifying grimace, shaking his head as his oral mucosa would encounter the over proofed alcoholic beverage. The gods were being called according to a certain order understood only by the initiates:

Ago, Ago, Ago,

A nou Manyan vodou,
Hounto Allada
Toutou Hans, Dja Hounsi,
Nou la dogwessan. . .
Legba Atibon. . .
Damballah wedo
Maitresse Erzili Freda. . .
Bossou Komblanmin. . .
Ogoun Badagri. . .
Baron Lakwa, gardien de tous Les morts…

The list went on and on. There could be lot of trouble if some god was left out of the party. Ge-klere knew better not to offend the powerful spirits.

The gods would have to be deaf not to hear this noisy but pious invocation. They heard it loud and clear. They came in great numbers. Who could believe that such a small place could accommodate so many deities? At any one time, there were at least five people going into trance. Ge-klere did it again. He had summoned the gods into his temple, and they were here. There could not be any doubt. Unmistakably so. One could feel their presence. It was up to Ge-klere to keep them here under check. The moment had arrived for Ge-Klere to join in with his congregation and make a very convincing plea. The gods can be very whimsical and temperamental. They do not like to be disturbed from whatever divine activities they were engaged in. Now, it was essential that all the gods be fed and treated in a way commensurate with their importance and according to their particular taste. No one was to be neglected. It was particularly important that the gods who had been guarding Jacques be given special treatment, the *"ti bon zange and the gro bon zange."* Whether or not Jacques wanted to believe it, they had offered him protection against all evil spirits this far. So Jacques was told not too long ago by his mother. Could there be any more doubt in Jacques' mind? He might as well surrender now. Jacques' soul was right before his very eye, naked, vulnerable ready to be stripped from all insecurity, all fear. Surrendering at this very moment could only lead to a future of strength and unlimited conquest. What is it going to be Jacques? Are you ready to proceed, Jacques?

Jacques had to admit that despite his turmoil, he was still standing. Wounded, weakened but not yet vanquished. He was still surviving. Thus far, he had survived this horrifying curse. The moment had finally arrived for Jacques to take an active part in his own salvation. This step was Jacques' and Jacques' only.

For a long while, Jacques seemed to be lost in his thoughts. He was so very aware of the importance of the moment. And suddenly, Jacques was no longer afraid. Gone were the memories of the frightful night. Gone were the feelings of panic that had grabbed him at the bottom of his stomach. An aura of strength was now emanating from a transfigured Jacques. Like the burning bush on Mount Sinai, Jacques was gleaming. He was now ready.

He threw himself at the feet of Ge-klere and asked for blessing. He joined in the incantation.

"Papa nou ki nan siel-la nou a genou nan pie
Koute prie-nou
Pitit ou engaje, vi-n sove nou souple"
Translation:
O Lord, who is in Heaven, we are on our knees
Listen to our prayers.
Your children are in a jam, come to our rescue."

And then one by one he pulled different sacred items from his large sack. Among other things there were gourmet items bought especially for some of the spirits. They were bottles of five-star rhum Barbancourt, a bottle of Moet champagne, a dagger, a bottle of honey, a bottle of Amstel beer and some Toblerone chocolate bars. These items were to ornate the altar erected for the gods. They were to find their places among more common and modern foodstuffs like Pepsi cola bottle, Chivas whiskey, and a lot of different meals especially prepared by the best cook in the small town. Finger licking and delicious black rice, griot, banane peze, and macaroni *au gratin* to be washed down with jus de cachiman, were all part of the menu. The excitement reached its paroxysm when a black cow made its way in the room. It was bought on Jacques's behalf. It was brought in with grand fanfare. It was wearing a red scarf around his neck, and two long lit candles were attached to his head. The cow could hardly walk as his legs were tied up with long red pieces of cloth. The cow seemed drunk as it moved around in very unsteady gait. It was saluted with a special beat from the drums. Incense and asafetida were burned. Jacques was asked to make some characteristic salutes, throwing water and flower in the four cardinal points. When Ge-klere was satisfied that the Gods were ready to accept the offerings, he signaled to his *laplace* to proceed. The *laplace* without hesitation plunged his sharp dagger into the neck of the unsuspecting animal. It went straight to the carotid artery. Blood spurted out. Life was taken right out of the unfortunate animal. The gods were hungry and were invited to a feast. The animal fell to the ground like a huge sack of victuals, listless. Only half of a gasping sound was uttered. Surprisingly, very little blood reached the ground. The blood was collected in a large calabash container. Jacques was numbed, he no longer knew how to feel or what to say. Was it repugnance? Was it fright? Well! Every single hair on his skin was standing. He was ready for battle, like a wild animal whose territory had been violated. It was too late for him to flee. The reality of the moment was upon him. Fear was no longer going to be part of it. Jacques had just crossed a path from which he could never return. It was as if a giant gate had just been slammed shut behind him. There was only one way to proceed. He could only move forward. Gone was his innocence! Gone were his hesitating moments! So ended Jacques dreams of everlasting candor. The rite went on... Some of the blood was saved in a golden chalice for the altar, and the rest was offered to the participant starting with the host of the night, Jacques Gaetan. After a few seconds of hesitation, he took a few sips from the calabash and quickly passed it to the person next to him. How did it taste? Jacques could not even tell. Jacques taste buds were in shock. Jacques thought he was going to pass out. The world that Jacques had just entered was not for the fainthearted. He might as well get used to it. Jacques held on. This first hurdle was too crucial. He thought about spitting the whole thing out. Not a good idea!

Jacques has come too far now. He swallowed the cow blood along with his disgust and his fear. How could he ever hope to move on if a few sips of blood were going to stand in his way? Not a chance! He let out a scream that carried very far into every corner and into every cave of the fully awakened town. Every single bat, every single owl joined in and let out their own characteristic cries. To Jacques, it was like the sound that would start a war with enemies invisible, enemies whose strength Jacques could not measure. The cow was dissected in no time.

Some of the meat was placed in the middle of a *veve*. Some of the meat was prepared in a special way known only to the initiates. It was then placed in a large utensil mounted on three large rocks with a very lively fire underneath. The glow of the fire reflected on the supplicants' face. They were barely recognizable. They no longer look human. They were simply actors of a giant play. They were bearer of energy that was no longer under their control. The whole scene was choreographed by a punny-looking elderly man, Ge-Klere. Other delicacies were placed on the altar together with the various liquors. It was obvious that the gods were being spoiled. They were offered Havana cigars imported directly from Cuba, and some chocolate all the way from Belgium along with roasted peanuts, mango Francique and tablet *lakol.* The menu was a testimony to a marriage between two worlds, the ancient world of Europe that claimed to hold the key to civilization and the New World with implants from an even more ancient world, Africa. The altar started to look like a Christmas tree on Christmas night. Were not for the picture of *Erzili* in the center of the table and the burning candles, one could easily mistake the altar for an overcrowded supermarket shelf. One could find about everything on the altar, from expensive French cologne from Givenchy to cheap *Samedi Soi*r bathing powder from the grocery store. No matter how weird or eccentric their taste was, the gods would be pleased. This group certainly knew how to make the gods feel at home. The gods were entertained all night long. The young and the old alike sang, danced, and laughed at each other. Papa Guede joked all night and was not afraid to make a fool of himself. After all, he, like the dozens of gods present that night, was a guest of honor. The gods were coming and going through their medium as they pleased. *Baron Lakwa* was here with his lugubrious demeanor. The plat de resistance was yet to come. For now, everyone was exhausted and trying to catch a cat nap in between the different events. The drums told the story on their own. The rhythm changed from *Yanvaloo* to *Petro*, from *Mais* to *Congo* depending on the god being ushered into this crowded peristyle. This was the place where all the gods got along, and so did most of the followers. The neighbors' squabbles over the position of fences and damages caused by goats and pigs, were temporarily put aside if not forgotten. For the moment, it was life as described in the primitive commune: a large family where everyone took care of everyone. Foods and laughter were shared, so were sorrow and the gravity of the moment that would follow. The ceremony was far from over.

Jacques was advised to stay indoors, and not to communicate with anyone. He had gone earlier in the week through the process of purification, but he was put one more time through the ritual of *laver tete (head washing)*, just to make sure. Jacques wore a long white shirt, while Ge-klere with the help of his inseparable assistant repeatedly washed Jacques' head with water. He was made to lay on a *natte* (a mat made from large dried up banana leaves). Some cane syrup and white flour were used to attract the good grace of the spirit. Jacques did not move from that position until he was summoned to the next phase of the ceremony.

Chapter 21

"Tell me, Master, is it permitted to see
the souls within these tombs?
The lids are raised,
ne stands in guard."
Inferno, Dante

The next part of the ceremony started to look more and more like a funeral. The decor had changed into more somber colors. Black drapes were placed all over the place. The women head were now wrapped with lavender kerchiefs. The drummers were beating to a different rhythm. The frenetic motions of earlier had changed into slower pace. The crowd had been drained of its energy. A large coffin made of acacia and decorated in black with a white cross, was placed in the middle of a room lit up only by the flicking light of a candle. The *Hounsis,* usually very animated, were humming what sounded like wake songs, while going in a snake like motion from right to left and then from left to right. Ge-klere was dressed in a long robe that look more like an old missionary tunic. His face was covered with a piece of satin material. One could barely see his shining eyes with their piercing and disarming look. His long ankle-length white chasuble was embroidered with designs representing angels and wreaths in lavender colors. A black sash went from his left shoulder to his right side. The drummers seem to be simply scratching the goat skin covering the top of their drums producing a prolonged lamenting and ghoulish sound. Now one could understand why no children were allowed in this part of the ceremony. Suddenly, Ge-klere exclaimed:

"Jacques Gaetan, where are you? Come forward and meet your master!"

Jacques was caught by surprise. He hesitated before he uttered.

"Who is calling this name? Friend or foe? I do not know anyone by this name. If you are a friend, I will help you find him, if you are a foe, return where you came from. Alleluia, Satan Je renonce! Tell them there is no one here by that name."

Ge-klere called again, trying to trick Jacques.

"Jacques Gaetan, if you do not come now, you are as good as dead!"

It was not the right call.

Jacques repeated:

"There is no one here by that name. Return to where you came from, Alleluia, Satan, Je renounce! Return to where you came from."

This exchange was repeated seven times, three times Ge-klere's voice became impatient. He said angrily, stomping his foot on the clay ground.

"Gade foute! "(Watch it!)

"Jacques don't mess with me, you insolent young man! Gran moun pa joue! (Grown-ups don't play around!")

Despite his tone of voice, Jacques knew that he needed to keep his cool and not give in to Ge-klere's tricks or else it would be the end of Jacques. Death could come as quick as lightening. So Jacques was instructed, so he did.

Ge-klere needed to clearly state to the gods the purpose of the ceremony before Jacques respond positively to Ge-klere's call. And then, it came. The *laplace* came in and cracked his whip three times. The noise caught everyone's attention. Complete silence! Ge-klere raised his asson and his bell in the air and gave his commands:

"Ayibobo!"

The audience responded:

Ayibobo!"

Ge-Klere continued:

"In the name of Baron Lakwa guardian of all dead, the only one that can go through purgatory. I order you to come to the help of Jacques Gaetan your servant! He is tormented and only you can help him."

He came towards Jacques and gave him a special embrace,

touching Jacques' shoulder several times and ordered:

"Are you Jacques Gaetan, the gods are waiting, and they will help you." Pwen fe pa, Mo red! (No mercy! Sudden death!).

It was okay for Jacques to answer this time. Ge-klere had taken him under his protection. With a firm voice, Jacques responded:

"I am here master, and I am at your service!"

Jacques was ready to proceed. He could now receive the help he so sorely needed. The *laplace* checked the room one last time. He made sure that all children were out of the room. What was about to happen was not for the faint hearted. Anyone who could not handle it was asked to leave the room. The *laplace* cracked his whip seven times. Jacques was ordered to lie down in the coffin with his head facing the Orient, the position of the rising sun, while Ge-klere chanted and prayed in long verses intelligible only to highest ranking priest:

"In the name of Met Kalfou
twenty-nine pwin (charms)
Grinned Bwa
twenty-nine pwin
St Michel
twenty-nine pwin cemetery
who command the four parts of the world."

Jacques' heart was pounding away. He shuddered. His

palms were sweating like they never did before, and it was not from the heat. In fact, he was cold like ice. A shriver went down his spine. It was maybe the last opportunity for Jacques to show common human feelings like fear, dread, or anxiety, for the moment was far from being common. From now on, Jacques would have to be extremely brave. Any fiber of cowardice left in Jacques had better get out immediately. The moment of truth was here. Only the brave would survive. What Jacques was feeling could not be described. It was indeed a surreal experience. It was more a feeling of resignation that one could only feel when one is faced with a sense of inevitability. Somehow, Jacques found comfort in this emotion. Things could not get any worse. If he survived this, he could savor the exhilaration that comes with victory. Ahhh! What a moment it will be! The lamentations from the *Hounsis* had resumed. The sounds were very distinct. They were humming the Auld Lang Sane.

"Ce nest qu'un au revoir mes freres. . .
Should old acquaintance be forgot?
And never brought to mind,
Should old acquaintance be forgot
In days of Auld Lang Sane
For Auld Lang Sane my dear
For Auld Lang Sane
We'll take a cup of kindness yet.

For auld lang sane

Ce nest qu'un au revoir!"

The singing was getting louder and the expression on the *Hounsi's* face clearly depicted the gloominess of the moment. Their voices were trembling through the notes. Jacques felt that the end was near. What *jeux macabres* were being played at his expense? He had probed the depths of death. He was about to stare it in the face. Death would have to blink. Because Jacques was not about to surrender. And now, he was watching his own funeral. The cover was placed on the coffin.

If the process was successful. Jacques would be armed with a third eyes allowing him to scrutinize the other world and see what common human beings cannot see. He could penetrate a world forbidden to the livings. Under the cloak of the dead, he would be like among peers.

Jacques could no longer see what was going on around him, but he could still hear everything. He was instructed to carry with him some of his earthly possessions, especially his little bags of money to which some *madiok* beads and some cloves were added. Jacques felt the coffin moving. It was lowered in a shallow grave barely three feet deep. The sounds from the group sounded more distant and reverberated to the acacia wood of the coffin. Ge-klere was presented with some sand. He took a handful of dirt and spread it over the coffin while opening his finger in an exaggerated gesture as to signify the fragility and the temporary nature of life. He repeated the same slow movement seven times. A mixture of oil and alcohol was placed on a large metallic pan and a fire was started. Ge-klere was handed some frankincense and myrrh. He sprinkled the mixture over the fire, causing it to take a reddish shade. The pan was positioned over the coffin for a few moments. The temperature in the small room had reached an unbearable level. Jacques' name was mentioned many times as supplications after supplications were made on his behalf. The *Hounsis* chanted and danced. They wept and wailed continuously not just for Jacques but for all the loved ones who had taken the trip to the Great Beyond. Life and death were being celebrated at the same time. To this pious group there was really no difference between life and death.

They were but two necessary steps towards the true essence of everyone's existence in our perpetual quest for meaning. Claude today, Christina tomorrow, and Yours truly sooner or later. Behind that invisible wall we shall all meet one day. No matter when. No matter where. We will find the way. No doubt! No directions or GPS needed.

Yet wary and throbbing we remain. The heart full of trepidations, every single day we muse and wait in vain, wondering if today would be the day.

In vain we await a response to our query:

Shroud of Death

O Death, under whose commands do you so stealthily move?

Have you no shame?

You show up at our doors, uninvited.

You cut down old and young alike.

You make exception for no one.

What horrific grin, what insouciance

Do you conceal behind your black veil?

Did it matter to you at all

That Claude showed us every day the true face of friendship.

and that he nursed back to health thousands of children?

You waver your scythe and leave your gruesome marks all around us:

Orphans, widows, and childless mothers.

What thrill do you seek in bringing pain and sorrow?

What sadistic pleasure do you revel in, destroying our hope?

O Death will you ever give up your mysterious ways?

Will you for a fleeting moment let us penetrate your secret?

Will you let us cherish once more the memories that we have so carefully sown?

...

The gods descended on many of the supplicants as if they were competing for the best seats in the small temple. The Hounsis went into trance again and again. After what seemed to be an eternity, Jacques heard the characteristic voice of Ge-klere call his name.

"Jacques, Gason kanson (brave man), will you leave all your fear behind you?

"Jacques, valiant man, are you ready to crush the head of your enemy? If you are not ready, let *Baron Lakwa* find you a place amongst the dead!"

Jacques could hear the faint cracking of the ceremonial whip. This time it was Jacques being summoned from the dead. Once again, it was essential that Jacques does not respond to the wrong call. Jacques heard a coded knock on the coffin. Wrong code! Jacques's perspicacity was being put through some serious tests. Jacques was drenching in his own sweat. There was no time however, for him to pay attention to his own physical discomfort. It would have been very easy for Jacques to give up and accept defeat. No way! He needed to keep his spirits up and avoid sinking into confusion and disorientation. All throughout, Jacques was visualizing his own triumph. He imagined himself suspending in the air, levitating above the common mortals. Jacques felt the cover of the coffin move. Was he delirious? Was he losing his minds? Jacques held on to the thought of raising above his troubles. Yes, the cover was moving. The audience in the small temple stood in awe. The cover of the coffin went up about a foot in the air untouched by anyone and then after about half a minute it went down to its original position. Never had the audience witnessed such display of supernatural power. The drums went silent for a while. Maybe the drummers did not know how to salute the force that had suddenly been unleashed in their mist on the account of one man, Jacques Gaetan. Or didn't they? The drumbeats changed into muffled thumps separated by long pauses. It was like a knell toll. Why was the knell tolling? There could not be any doubt in any one's mind. The old Jacques had to die if a new one was to rise and walk away from a past of torments. How long would he be kept in that position, lying in the casket? The time did not seem to matter to Jacques anymore. Finally, seven knocks followed by a long scratching noise and seven more knocks. That was it! Jacques responded with three knocks followed by complete silence.

What if Jacques did not respond appropriately? For some long moments, Jacques thought he had made a mistake. What a costly mistake it would be? The cover of the coffin was finally pulled away. Jacques was never so happy to see human faces in his life. It did not matter that the faces looked more like monsters who had just escaped from hell. The flickering light of the candles was reflecting on the sweats rolling down the cheeks of the *Hounsis*. The flour had now mixed with the mascara creating that ghostly look that would scare away the bravest man. The rhythm of the drums changed. It became more rapid. All the people in the audience came around to shake Jacques' hand, starting with the master. It was more of an embrace. Ge-klere touched Jacques right shoulder, then the left and then his forehead. Ge-klere thumped three times on his chest.

"Ayibobo!" he yelled!

"Ayibobo!" the audience responded.

It was a very exhilarating moment. Everyone was rejoicing. The drums were telling a story that could be heard many towns away.

The *Hounsis* were holding quite well after so many hours of singing and shouting. A sensational event had occurred on Ge-klere's habitation that night. A native of the area has come back to his homeland to confront his enemy and has triumphed. The Hounsis and the drag queens were dancing the night away in their colorful garments. The moves were so gracious and well-choreographed, that one would think that they had been going through extensive classes and rehearsals. Nothing of that sort. It was just a spontaneous display of talents and creativity that could only come from the heart and soul of people who believed. They believed that their gods would not forsake them in time of need. They believed that their gods would rush to their rescue whenever they called. It was, therefore, appropriate that they expend all their given talents to please the eyes of their gods. On that day, they had good reason to celebrate. One more time, the gods have answered their supplications. On that day, they felt ever so close to their gods. Their gods were very real. Thanks to them, victory was here for them to savor. Hosanna! Victory of good over evil, of courage over fear!

Jacques' prayers were heard. He had survived death, albeit in a symbolic way. Jacques could only be stopped by his own self now. Jacques was reborn. He was a much stronger man now. It would be indomitable His face was beaming with confidence.

He could wash up now and wear clothing more in line with his new status. He could now be counted among the brave men. The celebration went on for the next three days. From now on, it would be all up to Jacques. He would carry his experience that night like a badge of honor. The statement made about people of Jacques' caliber would ring true.

"Li mouri, se santi Selman li Pako santi."

("He is dead, he is just waiting to decompose": to mean (" Things can never get worse for him")

There could not be possibly anything in Jacques' future worse than what he has already faced and vanquished. At least, that was what Jacques understood.

He was given instructions on how to proceed with the content of his dream. He now had the protection and the support of all the gods that have so graciously acquiesced to Jacques's imploration. Jacques placed the bags of money on the altar, and under the direction of Ge-klere, prepared his own lampe rogatoire. Jacques also received some special gifts from Ge-klere. He was now the proud owner of a staff, a dagger and some other items from which he would never separate. Jacques would take this lamp with him and would set it up at a place of his choice. Whenever he wanted to make a special request, Jacques would light it up and all the gods who were present that night would come to his rescue, provided he kept his own promises. The whole ceremony lasted a total of seven days, and long after all the sacred objects were put away and the ceremonial drums have gone silent, the town was still talking about the bravery of Jacques who looked at death in its face and did not blink.

Little did they know that Jacques yet had another important step ahead of him? This time he will take his challenge alone. Or will he?

Chapter 22

The truth was that Jacques would never be all alone again. He had a whole pantheon of gods at his beck and call. He felt confident that he could call upon them, whenever he needed. For the first time in his life, Jacques felt whole. It was a feeling of serenity and internal bliss. Jacques was radiating with energy. Jacques felt like he could take on the world. Gone was his anxiety! Gone was his fear! Jacques was exuberant. This feeling lasted well into the next evening. However, Jacques' forty-four-year-old body would catch up with him. He was exhausted. He then realized that he had gone through this ordeal without any members of his immediate family being present. Jacques did not get back to them as promised. No one made the trip. No one contacted him. He did not hear from Jean-Paul or his sister. Maybe, it was better that way. The challenge he faced and the one still ahead of him were very personal now. No one was going to stand in his way. No one, not even his brothers and sisters he loved so much were there to offer him support. Jacques decided he was not going to let this sour note bust his balloon. He was surviving very well alone so far. He would march on. It was his life and his destiny on the line. He found himself thinking aloud about Job's verses so beautifully interpreted by Handel:

"I know that my Redeemer liveth, and
that He shall stand at the latter day
upon earth. And tho' worms destroy this body,
yet in my flesh shall I see God.
I know that my Redeemer liveth: For now is
Christ risen from the dead, the first fruits of them that sleep."

Those were the joyful and grateful words of a man who had descended into the entrails of death and by the power of his gods had come out victorious and rejuvenated. What could Jacques possibly be afraid of, now?

Nothing could ever stand in the way of Jacques and his most secret wishes. He felt empowered to go at the conquest of his every single desire. No longer would he put his head down and accept defeat before he fights with every fiber of his body. Jacques felt elated, almost invincible. Never had he felt so confident in his life. Then came the clamor of a man who had found his soul, a man who felt he could no longer pretend. Jacques imagined himself climbing on top of the highest mountain of the land and proclaiming:

Oh! Don't I know who I am!
Gauche and primitive
But proud and relentless
Oh! Don't I know who I am!
A man of many gods
But attuned with the beauty of the world.

Oh! Don't I know who I am!
I seem totally burdened at times,
but like a willow, I kiss the ground in veneration,
and never break.
Oh! Don't I know who I am!
Yes! I do feel the pain of my fellow men.
and long for a world with equality and justice.
Oh! Don't I know who I am!
I revere you O gods,
for You have shown me your grace
through the beauty of this land, Haiti my country.
You have endowed this land with infinite splendor,
but also, with an indomitable temper.
You have made this land capricious, seemingly foolish,
but often unforgiving.
Abundance and health have escaped us,
while creativity and hope haunt us forever.
O gods, I ask you
will you let this land be "Perle des Antilles" again?

Jacques felt that his integrity had been restored. He was ready to take the ultimate challenge. All the steps he had taken so far would be meaningless, should he fail the next one. He needed to cross that thin line where the real and the unreal, the visible and the invisible become parts of the same cosmic reality.

Jacques had long come to the realization that not everything that exists is visible through our naked senses. Few are those who are endowed with that "third eye" and the power to scrutinize and probe the other world invisible to most. He also believed that one's physical being extends well beyond the definable contour of one's body. Jacques' ultimate challenge would be just that, test the border between our narrow and limited physical existence and the rest of the world. Didn't Aristotle, 350 BC, recognized that connection when he stated that when the object of perception has departed, the impressions it has made persist, and are they objects of perception? He continued in his treatise "On Dreams" to say that we are easily deceived when we are excited by emotions. The coward when excited by fear sees his foes, the amorous person excited by amorous desire thinks he sees the object of his desire. Jacques, therefore, saw no reason why he could not confront the content of his own dream. Jacques had reason to believe that energy from O'Connor's departed soul was still being directed towards him, and that he needed to free himself once and for all from that nefarious energy. Now, that Ge-klere had put him back in touch with his own inner strength, he felt ready to face the next ordeal.

Chapter 23

The stars' course then you'll understand
And Nature, teaching, will expand
the power of your soul, as when
One spirit to another speaks.
Ye spirits, ye are hovering near;
Oh, answer me if ye can hear!

Faust, Goethe

Jacques was not feeling as elated as he did when he left his birthplace. He has allowed himself to feel sad about leaving the bucolic town one more time. He did not know when and if he would ever return. He had seen Amelia against all hope and had reopened a chapter of his life he did not dare believe still existed.

He could not hide his emotions when he hugged her good-bye, knowing it could well be the last. Amelia was over eighty years old. He was ready to bury his memories one more time. He tearfully hurried out of the town, en route to Les Cayes which would be the theater of the final test. The plains of Les Cayes, as it is often called, had very original geographical characteristics.

It is an area irrigated by many rivers. It has managed to maintain very rich volcanic soil. Jacques was greeted by the lush vegetation as he approached the city. The city had changed very little over the years. One could clearly distinguish some colonial style houses with spacious front gardens, with a mixture of white and red hibiscus masking elaborated steps coming from both sides of the house and meeting in the center under a beautifully designed porch. The houses were mostly whitewashed and could be smelled as you pass by. Other houses had been damaged repeatedly by flooding from La Ravine, and water marks could be noticed on the walls as high as four or five feet. The downtown area was surprisingly very busy. Some very muscular men were busy unloading a ship at the dock. The sea seemed unusually dark and was quite agitated. A small sailboat could be seen fighting the high waves as it was trying to make its way to the dock. Jacques was looking for 111 Rue Toussaint Louverture. Amelia had made arrangement for Jacques to rent the home for a couple of weeks. It was quite easy, as the real estate market was extremely slow in the city. As the tap-tap turned into the street, Jacques was becoming quite nervous. There stood the house that he has seen so many times in his dreams. Jacques was shocked. He remembered living in this house when he was a teenager. The house was a two-story building made of oak wood. It was situated right across the official residence of the bishop. At nights, one could often hear the nuns' voices as they prayed at the stroke of Angelus. Sometimes one could see the bishop taking a stroll in the long hallway, while reciting his breviary. To the left there was the main park of the city situated in front of the cathedral. The park was the site of military parades and concerts on Sunday nights. On New Year's Day, there would be special games and contests including the traditional *mat suife*. Young men would compete to get on top of the slippery pole where await enticing prizes including money and coupons for new motorcycles offered by the businesses of the city. The revelers would gather, encouraging their chosen competitors, clapping their hands, laughing, deriding, or using colorful whistles collected over the holidays. The whole scene creating a very festive atmosphere. The back of the house was facing the sea. Jacques remembered watching the fishermen coming home in the evenings, with tales about the big one that escaped. The house was still covered with traces of what used to be light green pastel paint. Electrical wires went directly from a large black cistern attached to the pole to the wood fascia in the front of the house. The front patio was quite high to protect the ground floor of the house from flood. This was the house that Jacques has visited over and over in his dreams. This is where a black skull has come back time after time to torment his soul. This is the house that he could not get out of his mind. If Jacques had a chance to ask around, he would learn quite a few interesting bits of information. This house, for the past twenty years, has had quite a turnover. No tenant had ever lasted in this house more than a couple of months. There have been many stories about loud laughter being heard coming from the house late into the night, after it had been unoccupied for months. There had also been reports of a rocking chair moving back and forth on the balcony without anyone sitting in it. The last tenant, after attempting to have the house exorcized, gave up and accepted the fact that the house was haunted. The young couple left the house one morning terrified vowing to never set foot in there again.

When Jacques opened the door, the dampness of the room hit him in the face. He opened all the doors and windows letting the Atlantic breeze circulate in the house. Jacques flipped the light switch on. Jacques was dumbfounded. He knew he had lived in this house before, but it was more than thirty years ago. The walls have gotten very old and have probably been patched and repainted many times over the years. The memories he had were much more recent. There was no way he could have imagined the walls being in their current state. He had recently been haunted by these walls. For the past few months, he had seen them so many times in his dreams that Jacques could describe them in minute details. Like an artist, he could analyze the texture of the walls, their different shades and values, the tracks left behind by ants and termites, the peeling paint and the long sinuous crack that went across the wall as if Andre Pierre, the famous Haitian artist, had tried to capture on it some etchings made by a bolt of lightning.

How could Jacques' mind have imagined the walls with such precision? As Jacques was examining the walls of his new residence, his attention was drawn towards a familiar dark shape on a beam in the ceiling. A black butterfly awfully similar to the one that he first saw in his small studio in Miami was there watching over him. Jacques shuddered and felt goosebumps cover all his extremities. How could that be possible? Jacques was not going to even try to find out. He quivered at the thought that he was sinking ever so deep into more mysterious coincidences. Jacques was lost in his reveries, when he realized that he needed to get to the store for some necessities. The heat was unbearable. He grabbed a piece of paper and started to make up a list:

Fan,

Sheets,

Towels,

Bread,

Coffee,

Milk,

Sugar,

Incense,

Candles,

Garlic

Lavender

Salt

Vervaine

Bergamot

Kerosene.

As he was going through his list, he realized that spider webs had taken over strategic corners of the house. The electricity was still on. It must not have been that long since the last tenant was here, he thought. He turned on the faucet. Good! He thought. He had electricity and running water. Well, Jacques said to himself, if I could only get this place clean, I would be all set. It was getting late. Jacques needed to get to the market. He needed to claim the premises and ward off all evil spirits. He went around the four corners of the house, threw some water to the gods.

On a piece of parchment, he wrote the following words:

Four nooks in this house for holy angels,
a post in the midst, that's Christ Jesus
Lucas, Marcus, Matthew, Johannes,
God be in this house, and all that belongs us.

He placed his thurible right in the center of the room and started to burn some incense. Seconds after the aromatic smoke started to fill the air, something very bizarre happened. A bronze framed mirror that was hanging on the wall, fell to the ground in a loud crashing noise. The mirror broke in a thousand and one pieces. The message was clear. Evil had already claimed this place. There was going to be a fight. May the best man... Sorry... May the best god prevail! Not now, Jacques thought, as he rushed out of the house. He would clean up the mess later.

Jacques went down to the perimeter of the park, down Grand' Rue (Main Street) and was in the market in no time. He managed to keep away most of the merchants who wanted to sell him all kinds of knicks-knacks and picked up the items on his list. Jacques was a much-disciplined shopper. He completed his errands in a very short time. He picked up some "zo-devan" just in case. The sun was on its last leg on its way to set. When Jacques got back to the house, a very puzzling phenomenon was waiting for him. The house looked as if a sudden storm had gone through it. Everything was turned upside down. Some of the glass utensils were splashed on the floor, the incense container was tossed into a corner, and the contents of his suitcase were thrown all over the place. Interestingly, nothing of value was missing. There was no sign of intrusion. No break in! The locks on the door were intact. Wait a minute! Jacques could not believe his eyes. He was shivering. He had goose bumps all over his body. The bronze mirror he had left, less than two hours ago on the floor in pieces, was back on the wall, at its exact original place, intact. Was it some kind of joke? Jacques resisted the idea of examining it more closely. He needed to choose his own battles. No! Not yet, he thought. The forces of evil had made their statement. Loud and clear! It was the turn of the forces of good to make theirs. We shall see! Jacques would take no chances. He considered himself warned. The hatchets of war were unburied! Jacques was reborn. His newly found strength was being put to the test. It was like a full declaration of war. Winner takes all. Let the band start the military march! Oh, how appropriate would the dramatic words of Jehoiada to the Levites in Jean Racine's "Athaliah:"

> And you to arm yourselves, come, follow me
> To where lies hidden, far from the profane.
> This terrible array of swords and spears
> Which once were drenched with blood of Philistines,
>
> And which victorious David, crowned with years,
> Has consecrated to his Savior, God.
> Can they be wielded for a nobler aim?

How appropriate would be the musical interpretation:

> "War March of the Priests" by Felix Mendelsohn:
> "See that at once the martial trumpets sound
> Spread sudden fear throughout the enemy.

O sacred Levites, priests of God,

Surround this place, but do not show yourselves.

The stage is set, let the battle begin!"

Chapter 24

Jacques had one more task for the night, and then he would wait for the appropriate time to begin the confrontation, or so he planned. One of the many instructions he was given by Ge-klere was to go to the cemetery and retrieve seven pinches of dust. This would be another trying test since this was an essential ingredient of the rest of his travail. It was up to Jacques to use his perspicacity to get into the cemetery that evening, get his samples and be off the street before the stroke of midnight. He was to make the trip alone, lest he wanted to be distracted in this very delicate task. Jacques changed into more somber colors and put on a black cap and a pair of shades. It did not matter that it was half past ten and that it was pitch dark outside.

He met several late strollers but uttered no words to anyone. He was not supposed to. He felt some sweat going down his back as he approached the graveyard. The smell was unique. The mixture of the smell of old decomposing bodies with more recent ones, together with the degrading flowers created a stench equal to none. No amount of sunshine, no amount of tropical breeze, could clean up the air of this pungency. Jacques would have to ignore it for now. He had more serious matters at hand. He passed an old woman who looked homeless and had set up her bed for the night. She seemed as frightened as he was about the unusual encounter. No words were exchanged. Jacques took a more leisurely pace as if he was on a normal evening walk. When he became sure that no one was around, he jumped over the fence and landed on a freshly moved heap of dirt. Jacques recited some magic formulas:

In the name of *Osiris* and *Baron Samedi*
I enter this place.
Ye who dead, stay dead.
From this place, nothing I want except what I want.

He then moved according to a certain pattern grossly creating the shape of a star, and at each tip of the star, he bent over and collected a handful of dust while still reciting verses only intelligible to the initiate. He retrieved his seventh sample at the center of the star. He carefully placed his precious collection in a small bag especially prepared for the occasion.

As he was completing his task, Jacques thought he heard a voice that sounded like a young woman calling his name. He startled for a moment and caught himself just in time as he was about to turn in the direction of the voice. It would have been the end of Jacques. The instructions from Ge-klere were very strict:

'Your name will be called very distinctly. You will be offered eternal life. You will be made very attractive promises. Do not even flinch! Do not turn your head! Do not answer! If you do, Adieu! Pwen fe pa! Mo red!' (Goodbye! No second chance, sudden death).

Jacques could still hear the warning from Ge-klere, as he was about to leave Ge-klere's habitation.

In the ghostly full moon Caribbean night, temptations loomed. They took different shapes. They seemed to go at the very core of the Haitian soul. As the Haitian proverb goes, three things are important to a Haitian man's success - money, power, and sex. The Creole words were a bit more graphic -

"Twa bagay, Ce twa bagay ki fe you fan-m rinmin nonm li
Lajan gnoun, pouvwa de, domi kole twa."

The dead were all aware of that. Something was out there that night. It seemed to come from under the ground. One of the tombs, maybe? Jacques did not know. He knew what he heard. A female voice, very clear. Seductive and voluptuous it started: "Come to me, Jacques. You will be the most handsome man on this land. You will have all the women you want, marabous, brunettes, grimeles with hair falling to their butts. No one will be able to resist your charm."

Hum! Jacques commented to himself. Very interesting prospect! Imagine what it would be like!

Jacques could see himself surrounded by T-bikini-clad women, with all kinds of looks, marabous, brunettes, and grimeles with hair falling to their butts. They would be leaping in his Olympic-size swimming pools with crystal clear blue water. The pool would be in an Eden-like environment with latanier plants, water lilies, and coconut trees. All around the deck, there would be white Italian marble and Roman pillars. An atmosphere fit for a king.

The girls would be all over Jacques tending to his most secret sexual desires.

Nah! Impossible! Jacques? Jacques! Come on! You are neither Denzel Washington nor Morgan Freeman.

Jacques offered no response to the sensuous voice from beyond.

"Come here I say," continued the cavernous but sexy voice! "You will be the most popular man on this land. More popular than Titid! More popular than Michael Jordan. You will be president for life! Better yet, you could become Emperor like Jean-Jacques Dessalines or Faustin Soulouque. The people of this land will be at your feet."

Hum! Emperor Jacques? Or King Jacques! What a thought!

It had a nice ring to it. Jacques' narcissism was being put to the test. He was almost delirious.

He remembered the words of Paracelsus in Paragranum:

"I shall be monarch,
and mine the monarchy shall be,
and as monarch shall I rule."

Jacques was already imagining himself dressed in royal

clothing and being crowned king in the national cathedral with chiefs of state and dignitaries from all over the world present. The Te Deum would be played with all the pomp and circumstance. What a celebration it would be!

The voice of reason came to Jacques' rescue because he was losing his mind:

Jacques? Hello! Get a grip! You don't seem to get it, do you Jacques?

Monarchy is out!

Popular elections are in!

Kings, no more!

Emperors, no more!

Presidents for life, no more!

One man, one vote!

Oh no, Jacques! Get a grip! We have gone that route before. You know that if you should run for any office, members of your own family might not cast a vote for you. Wake up, Jacques!

Never again, Jacques!

Never, again!

This is the post-Duvalier era!

Vive la democratie!

Jacques came to his senses and gave no response to the voice. The woman's voice became ever more convincing. There was a sense of desperation:

"Come to me, now! You will be rich. All the hidden treasures of this land will be yours. You will have gold, diamonds, and everything. No one on this land will equal you in wealth!"

How tempting! Jacques envisioned himself, dressed in tight black pants and guayabera, walking around staff in hand, inspecting his estate, and making changes to the exterior of his mansion. This white color would do just fine. Oh no! I changed my mind. I think I will go peach this time. He could just imagine the mile-long driveway. The heliport would be to the left. The garage should be three cars wide with the Lamborghini and the Maserati as alternate cars. They should be plenty of Australian pine trees and a real green lawn with a waterfall moving up and down at the tune of classical music.

Okay! Okay! Jacques, you need to get off. You have gone out of your mind. Jacques, you are not a drug kingpin. You are not an Arab emirate. You are neither Donald Trump nor Bill Gates. Too bad! Jacques thought. He offered no response to the dying voice.

There were drumbeats, yes drumbeats! How sweet was the *compas* rhythm? It sounded like Tropicana. It changed into classical music. A philharmonic orchestra? Come on! A lot of laughter! How far will they go? They were certainly having a good time. The dead seemed to be having an orgiastic celebration. How inviting!

A man took over from the woman, this time attacking Jacques' machismo:

"Come here, you little sissi! Aren't you man enough to take it? Come here before I break your neck!"

Jacques was getting a weird angry feeling. Yet, he did not succumb. No response from Jacques.

"Come here!" he continued, raising his voice. This mortal earthly creature was not budging!

"Come here, the women are waiting! Can't you get it on?"

Now, wait a minute! Wasn't that going a little too far? Jacques was tempted to just turn and clobber the imaginary creature, but he resisted. As he always does when facing imminent danger, he took some deep breaths to relax and went on to recite his famous and powerful Psalm 91:

"Do not be afraid of the terrors of the night,
nor fear the danger of the day. . .
If you make the Lord your refuge,
if you make the Most High your shelter,
no evil will conquer you."

This was a terrifying experience. It was Eros and Thanatos (love and death) competing to bring Jacques' demise. His lust for women, money, and power, along with the aggressive feelings brought out by the provocative male voice from beyond, were being used with only one goal: To cause him to trip and fall into the abyss of death. The plan was even more Machiavellian than Jacques thought. The voices were also there to distract Jacques and make him forget the time. One way or another, they figured they would get him. *"Off the streets before the stroke of midnight..."* Jacques suddenly remembered. What time was it? Jacques exposed his wristwatch to the glow of the full moon. Eleven minutes to midnight! Jacques repeated his verses hurriedly and jumped off the fence into the night, using the same route he took going in. His heart was racing. His chest was thumping. His mouth was dry. Would he make it? He started to run. He never looked back.

Run for your life, Jacques! Run Jacques! Run! One could hear Jacques's heart racing. Would his legs give out? What if he was mistaken for a burglar running away from the police? Jacques could see the house half a block away. A few more houses. Jacques was not an athlete. His legs started to hurt. Run, Jacques! Run! You can make it. Jacques imagines himself in the Summer Olympics. Hundreds of people on both sides of the track rooting for him. Go, Jacques! Go! You can make it! There would be a bouquet of roses at the finish line. There would be congratulatory words from the officials. Yes! Jacques had to make it. And he did.

Jacques made it to the house with less than ten seconds to spare. As soon as he passed the front door of his house, the bell from the chapel at the bishop's residence broke the silence of the night. Twelve strokes, Jacques counted. He was inside, safe. Or so, he thought! Just like the gods, the devil often does not like to wait.

Chapter 25

Jacques imagined that maybe it was too late that night for him to get ready for the final confrontation. However, his decision to wait could be a regrettable one. What would happen to him if he were caught unprepared? Jacques did not like the idea at all, given the signs that he was given earlier in this house. Jacques needed to buy some time. Ideally, he would like to prepare himself for at least two nights and make his interpellation on the third one. Among the items he had brought to the botanica was an iridescent crucifix that came directly from Italy and was blessed by the Pope himself. Jacques pulled it out of his bag and placed it on the main entrance door.

"Oye! Oye! Let it be known that this house is protected by God."

Jacques washed off a large white enameled washbasin and filled it with water. He added some boiling water bringing it to a warm temperature. He threw in a few drops of oil of lavender, oil of rosemary, oil of peppermint, oil of thyme, and a few pinches of a powdered poppy seed. He added more incense to the water together with some camphor, some jasmine, and some pulverized cucumber seeds. It was very relaxing. The only thing missing was some relaxation music, but Jacques could easily make up for that with his reveries. He saw his third eye going inside his body and visiting every organ, just like a pilot going over a checklist before take-off. Heart rate? Check! Blood Pressure? Check! Breathing? Check! Oxygen saturation? Check! There Jacques was in his favorite spot under the Red Poinciana tree again. The birds were quiet and listening for a change. Internal harmony was near. The gods were with Jacques. It was a good omen.

All is well! All is well! At least for now.

The mixture that Jacques prepared for his bath was supposed to help him induce prophetic dreams. Jacques had a few unanswered questions. He wrote his questions on a piece of white paper:

Claude O'Connor, are you here?

If you are here, are you alone?

Who else is here with you?

He placed the paper under his pillow and went to sleep, not before he, one more time, recited some verses from his favorite Psalm. Jacques passed into a very deep slumber. Retro Satana! (Stay back Satan!)

Jacques' sleep was not as restful as he had anticipated that night. He had numerous dreams. Much too many to remember them all. He dreamed about coffins and being visited by people dead many years ago. He thought he saw the face of a man that vaguely reminded him of the face of his father. Was he here to lend support since Jacques was about to knock on the other side? Or was he here to warn Jacques that he was getting in over his head and to stay away? Jacques like the former possibility better. Having departed very early in Jacques' life and left all the responsibility of Jacques' care to Madam Maurice, the least that his father could do was to be supportive in this trying time.

Jacques also had a dream about O'Connor again. It was ever so vivid, ever so real. It seemed more like a revelation than a dream, as he felt he could reach and touch the area of the walls he was seeing in his dream. His questions on his paper could have easily been changed to: Where in this house, are you hiding? Well, Jacques had better leave those questions for a little later.

There were also weird noises throughout the night, like a repeated encoded knock on the door, the creaking of the bathroom door followed by the flushing noise of the toilet bowl. Jacques was no longer afraid because he had accepted the fact that he was sharing the place with ghosts. The question was, were they friends or foes? Jacques was hoping that at least some of them would be friendly. But he was not counting on it. When he was ready to call them, they had better show up. Ditto! Jacques, the brave one, the one who descended in the entrails of death, the one who survived temptations from cunning and menacing ghosts. Jacques woke up that morning with the feeling that he never went to sleep at all. He felt that he had been in a palace war room the whole night, meeting with his generals and strategizing about his next move, for he had a war to fight, a war to win. Many battles were fought and won, now he needed to win the big one, the one which would decide the outcome of the war. He wanted total surrender from the enemy. He also had the feeling that on this wall, he was facing at this very moment, a message was hidden for him to discover. He tried to concentrate and revisit every frame of that dream that he has had at least a dozen and a half times. He approached the wall and looked more closely. He thought he saw the shape of a circle. He was not sure. He reached for his pocketknife. He used the handle to test the wall. He knocked in different spots. A hollow sound. Jacques turned his knife around and proceeded to scratch the wall. There it was. An old dark bottle, covered with mortar. One could easily see in some areas the inside of it. A message was included in the fashion of the sailor lost at sea, but this time it was in the wall of an old, dilapidated house, a house full of ghosts. Jacques was visibly excited about his finding. His relaxation exercises were not working. Jacques felt as if he was just struck by a bolt of lightning. He could feel his pulse going wild.

"Calm down, Jacques! This message was always meant for you. Your destiny is right here in front of you."

Jacques was talking to himself as loud as he could, given his state of shock. He looked for a hammer. None to be found. He went to the next best thing way before the tool age, a rock. On second thoughts, No! This bottle is a historical artifact. It has been here for well over fifty years. Jacques patiently and painstakingly went through the process of removing the cement around the neck of the bottle one little bit at a time. He revisited the idea of just crushing the bottle with the rock but did not. Patience Jacques! Patience is the mother of all virtues. After over an hour of hard labor, his efforts paid off. He freed the neck of the bottle and could easily see a piece of paper inside with some pale characters handwritten on it. Now the next task was to remove the paper without destroying it. Jacques looked for a large paper clip. He opened it up, making it longer. He turned the bottle upside down. The paper moved. Jacques pulled it out using the paper clip, like a burglar trying to pick a lock. Yes! The paper was out. Large drops of sweat were falling off his face. Careful! Not on the paper. Jacques paused for a moment and went for a towel. He dried up his face. The moment of truth was here. Jacques's eyes were filled with emotions. He had to fight the tears.

On the piece of paper, he could see some fading characters. The writer must have used one of those fountain pens. The handwriting was beautiful. Jacques could decipher the following message:

"Ici repose Claude O'Connor qui a porte la honte sur notre famille. Peut-etre que j'aurais du laisser la justice dans les mains du Seigneur et que je serai maudit pour mon acte. Que le Dieu de bonte me pard. . . "

The rest of the message was not legible.

Signed G. G. (Giraud Gaetan).

Translation

"RIP Claude O'Connor who humiliated our family. Maybe, I should have left justice in the hand of God and that I will be cursed for this act. May the Good Lord have mer…"

The answer to Jacques' question could not be any clearer than that. He was granted permission to proceed. The exciting and revealing moment both at once. Jacques was holding in his hand a memento of things past, of people long gone. What a privilege! In his hand, a trophy! Jacques would need to safeguard this precious relic very carefully, lest he wants to unleash the forces of the past. There is no telling what might happen should Jacques successfully complete the next phase of his long and trying quest. Tonight would be the night...

What irony! Claude O'Connor the sexual perpetrator par excellence ended here. The man whose misdeeds and reputation went from continent to continent, the great wizard of witchcraft ended up encased in the wall of this old wooden house. Yet he could not find peace. Even Satan, his master to whom he had sold his soul could not save him.

Chapter 26

Jacques spent the rest of the day going over his plans for the night. He needed to keep his ingredients and his formula in order. He wished he had some assistance to keep everything organized. First, he had to make sure that his triangle was pointing in the right direction. He needed to construct his triangle in such a way as to allow O'Connor's spirit to enter it. Should O'Connor not come alone, there might be a lot of trouble. He had decided that he would use the wooden floor as an altar. He polished the floor carefully and used a long sisal cord to make a triangle. He put all his ingredients and paraphernalia on a small table nearby for easy access. All the items given to him by Ge-klere, including his special dagger, would be put to use at some point during the long night that awaited Jacques. In a workbook on the table, he had all his magic recipes and formulas. Jacques also placed plenty of incense, garlic, Sulphur, vinegar, and some rotten apples. When everything was ready, Jacques took another bath, adding some garlic to the earlier mixture. He dressed himself in a white tunic and lit up his lamp rogatoire. It would remain lit for the next few days. It was like raising the flag to notify the gods that their supplicant Jacques was on active duty. Jacques sat down in meditation and awaited his moment.

At the first stroke of midnight when the moon was still full and all the spirits were ready to wander the streets on their proverbial outing, Jacques started his invocation. The room looked like a small temple, where Jacques was playing the role of the officiating priest. He looked very fervent as his shadow floated on the walls of the smoke-filled room. The incense burner was continuously alimented with church incense moistened with Palma Christi oil, and even at the beginning with a drop of Jacques blood. Jacques' goal was to get the ghost of O'Connor out of his hiding place. At the corners of the triangle, Jacques placed three small white saucers with lit white candles. Jacques' voice rose into the night, tremblingly but decisively:

Vassago! Vassago! Vassago!
I conjure thee to descend and help us.
You the master of all wandering ghosts
Be here to mediate our meeting with Claude O'Connor
He has been wandering amongst the living,
Causing mischief after mischiefs
Only you can help us put him in his proper place.
Amongst the dead where he belongs.
Vassago! Vassago! Vassago!

Jacques was concentrating the best he could while his eyes were locked focusing on the center of the triangle. Then he summoned Claude O'Connor to appear:

"Spirit of Claude O'Connor deceased, I come in peace and demand that you approach this gate. Berald, Beroald, Balbin! Gab, Gabor, Agaba! Arise, arise I order you!"

Jacques repeated the above command at each corner of the triangle, raising his voice and catching his breath as the strong smell of the burning incense and asafetida got into his throat. He cleared his throat with a few coughs, and suddenly without much warning, everything in the room started to shake. The walls cracked open, and only a foot or two away from the triangle, a black skull appeared. In great pandemonium, it rolled out onto the ground, penetrate the triangle through the east, and stopped right in the middle of the triangle. The skull looked precisely like Jacques had seen it so many times in the past. It had a very dark grey color, almost charcoal as if someone had tried to burn it. The deep orbital space still carried an expression that cannot be described. It was as if someone had stunned the deceased in the middle of a hideous act. For over half a century, this wall has guarded its secret very jealously. By some inexplicable power, the spirit of this man had conjured a whole army of ghosts to help him guard his secret. Their mission was to scare away everyone from this place until the chosen person came along and helped Claude O'Connor complete his journey. What a twist of fate! Jacques' mouth was still open in amazement at the sudden apparition. He felt he had just found an old friend. Maybe he had. For years he had carried a curse, and for months now, he had been tormented by this horrifying dream. He had lost hours of sleep and had lived almost like a shadow, losing taste in life. Now, his old acquaintance was here, and Jacques needed to deal with it accordingly.

Jacques added some vervain and some garlic to the incense burner. In a matter of seconds, Jacques was transfigured. His eyes were full of rage and were like those of a dragon ready to shoot jets of fire at its prey. Right here at his feet was the head of a man who had come, like many men before him, and treated his family like they have treated the entire country. They came as conquerors abusing the country's welcoming traditions. They have violated the innocence and beauty of this land and usurped its resources. This man had taken away from Jacques' family its symbol of pride. And even when his ancestors thought they had freed themselves from the white man's predatory grip, he remained behind cursing Jacques's family, controlling his every move, thwarting his most valiant efforts. Imagine the mean and stern face of a master waiting at the top of a ladder letting you climb but knowing that he will send you right back to the bottom. "Start over. You do not belong here. That is not good enough." Meanwhile, people of his clan are allowed to proceed. For centuries, a small group of expatriates from the Middle East have come to this country and have dominated the political and economic scene of the poor island nation. They have chosen presidents, senators, and congressmen, and dictated policies. They have monopolized every aspect of commerce, the gas, and the production of electricity. They destroyed local production by flooding the market with second-quality products from abroad, bribing politicians, and controlling customs. They control the flow of currency and weapons into the country, striving for political instability and insecurity. The citizenry is forced to flee the country and seek opportunities elsewhere. When they are sick, they would rather fly to the nearest country instead of building local hospitals. The white man has been vanquished on this land. Yet they are always on the prowl, seeking a way to come back in search of new adventures. Like many others, Claude O'Connor has returned, with promises of golden street and infinite wealth. Like many others, O'Connor has come here, consumed our liquor, depraved our youth, and stolen our souls. Some of them have gone back home, with an inventory of our resources to plan their next move, all the while calling us refugees if we dare show up on their shores.

Right here at Jacques' feet, the skull of a white man whose evil deeds have caused it to turn the color of ashes. Right here at his feet, the skull of a man, remnants of his physical being, a man whose soul had departed on an everlasting trip. The soul of a man tormented, looking for Nirvana. The soul of a man who needed Jacques to put an end to his misery. Jacques would oblige. He seized his dagger. He raised it to the gods. It was a moment that he seemed to have been waiting for all his life. Jacques finally had the opportunity to let out years of frustration and pent-up anger. He could get even once and for all. He felt that just like him, his country had been carrying a curse. He felt that his country had been held hostage for a very long time. With this dagger in his hand, he had the power to put an end to the bondage.

O Haiti, O my country, after tonight, you will be free.

No longer will you be fooled by long and empty promises!

No longer will you be so naive as to believe that every white man that comes to your rescue is another Christ!

Were you fooled too by the idea that your Savior and Redeemer would be white?

How many times will you let your children fool you?

When they conspire with the white man to rape you and take away your innocence, is it any less painful?

May this dagger free you!

May this dagger break the patch off your eyes!

May you finally see and recognize who your true enemies are!

Your enemies are also your sons who mortgage your future, and sign contracts with the white man to build roads that will not last.

Your enemies are those politicians who seize power with guns and transform the country into a killing field to hold on to power.

Those who rule by the power of Uzi, AK 47, and AR-15,

transform your youths into gang members and are your real enemies.

The light on Jacques' face was projecting his shadow on the wall. He stood almost twelve feet tall. In his eyes, was the determination of a man who was at the finishing line of a long and exhausting marathon. He looked like Abraham ready to offer his only son Isaac in immolation to a demanding and testing God. It did not matter. The moment was too grave, the winning prize much too immense for anything to matter. Jacques would proceed. At this point, he could have easily been annihilated by the forces at play in his room. Jacques could have easily vanished by some process of instant combustion. But he was not alone. With him that night, Jacques had the power emanating from the soul of all fellow Haitians fallen victims to injustice everywhere, from the bateys of the Dominican Republic to the detention camps in Guantanamo, or Krome Detention Center in Miami, those chased by horse-riding officers in Texas. They were here to express their discontent at all of those who meet in the smoke-filled board rooms and whisper amongst themselves, "Those dammed Haitians, why don't they go away?"

How could Haiti ever rise if leaders are transformed into brokers or mercenaries in their own country, ready to sell out the resources of the country for a hefty sum of money or for the promise that international law enforcement agencies will look the other way when such leaders engage in illicit activities like drug dealing or arms trafficking. Such agencies maintain a detailed dossier on the leaders to be used against them later if they renegade on the agreement and dare get in the way of the powerful nations' interests. Leaders who take a more nationalistic stance from the start, try to open the eyes of the nation and demand reparations for past treatment of the citizenry and the resources looted by the colonialists are overthrown in rather a theatrical manner using infiltrators portrayed as revolutionaries. Such montages are reminding of the old episodes of Mission Impossible in the 80s. You could always hear the recording: "The current president of Haiti has been raising hell and want reparations for all the gold and other resources that now ornate the Champs Elysée and the ransom money paid to France and used to build la Tour Eiffel after their independence. We cannot allow that to happen, lest we want all the past colonies of Africa to come with a similar claim. It would be very destabilizing for the world economy including the US. Your mission, should you choose to accept it is to manufacture a coup d'état. Make it look real. Should you be caught or killed, we will not acknowledge any of your actions. This tape will self-destruct. Pshuuuu!

"Not at all implausible. The examples in the history of my country are many." Thought Jacques.

Had this leader been allowed to finish his term, maybe and only maybe the Haitians would have coalesced in a true nation where the institutions would be strong and respected, where the interest of the nation would be above that of any one individual.

Take America for example. You might not totally agree with their ideology and their boastful claim of exceptionality because every nation has a unique history and can make that claim. You might say that they only think about their own interest. That is the way it should be. Poor nations have not learned that countries have interests, not friends. You can never say, however, that they do not have very strong institutions. It is because of the institutions that they have been able to survive and stand against all enemies domestic and foreign. Some might say that America is a nation in flux where many issues remain to be resolved before they become a true democracy. But they are ahead of many countries and people around the world that look at them with envy like a shining city on the hill.

Tonight, Jacques will leave out all these considerations. It is his moment. It is his time. He shall prevail. He would avenge all the prejudice and discrimination that Haitians have endured all over the world. A country that once was the Pearl of the Caribbean, la "Perle des Antilles," had slipped into chaos. Its only crime was to stand up to the white man and say "Libete ou la mo!" Freedom or Death! Because the Haitian people had dared to say no to slavery and declared themselves independent, the white man conspired to keep him at the bottom of the pit. Haiti might have freed herself from the chains of slavery, but Haiti is still in bondage. Haiti still wears the chains of economic dependence and mental slavery as Bob Marley describes it. All Haiti has received was empty and hypocritical words of encouragement. The white man has conspired with dictators and crooks to keep the Haitian people in abject poverty. Tonight, was Jacques' night. With all his strength and all the energy that his body could carry, he would raise his dagger and put an end to his curse and the curse of his battered homeland. Jacques felt as if all the energy from the Caribbean sun was going through his body. He was possessed. His was not recognizable. Sweat was pouring down his cheek. He went into a long diatribe as he repeatedly and forcefully drove his magical dagger into the skull:

"Go, go, departed shade Claude O'Connor
By Omgroma Epin Sayoc, Satony, Degony, Eparigon.
Die again, Claude O'Connor, die.
And with the dead, you must stay.
Into thy proper place, you must go.
This world belongs to the living.
Let there be no link whatsoever between you and me
So mote it be!
So mote it be!
So mote it be!"

Jacques repeated his commands three times, just to make

sure. And on the third time, as he was completing the magical words, a bolt of fire came out of the breaking skull as it turned into ashes. The small house was fully illuminated, as if giant projector lights had been rushed in for the occasion. At the spot where a few moments ago the skull stood, frightful, there was just a little heap of ashes. This was one of those moments that happen once in a lifetime. To the title Jacques acquired back at Ge-klere's residence, another one could be added: Jacques the Slayer. Jacques was amazed at his own accomplishment. The ashes from the skull were handled very carefully. Jacques could not take any chances. He had come from too far to let things get out of hand. He only had a few minutes to prevent the force of evil to reclaim the soul of their disciple Claude O'Connor. He was down now but not necessarily out. If the story was to be believed, Claude O'Connor was not an ordinary man. He was endowed with indestructible powers. He had an irrevocable and eternal pact with the devil. At that very moment, however, Jacques and his gods had the upper hand. He needed to make it a cinch. Jacques mixed the ashes with the dirt he had collected from the cemetery while mumbling the following words:

"Tonight, Claude O'Connor, by the power of Osiris and Baron Samedi and all the gods who are with us tonight, I order you to go away forever. When I return you to the place where this dirt came from, be gone, forever and ever! Amen! Amen! Amen!"

Now Claude O'Connor was one with the rest of the dead where he belongs. The world was a much better world without him. His soul was no longer wandering. For Claude O'Connor, the Lord's prophecy had finally come true:

"All your life you will sweat for food,
until your dying day.
Then, you will return to the ground.
from which you came
For you were made from dust,
and to dust you will return."
Genesis: 3, 19

Jacques concluded the seance by sending off all the spirits he had earlier conjured to this place. He added even more garlic, myrrh, and Sulphur to the incense burner. The mixture burned in a yellow flame. Jacques so far was happy with his progress. He recited the following verses:

"O great and holy *Vassago*
You were here, but now you must go.
Let there be peace between us evermore,
So mote it be!
So mote it be!
So mote it be!"

The agitation and chaos that prevailed in the room seemed to have instantly stopped. No more cracking of the walls. There were no broken walls. No broken mirrors. The place was as quiet as a deserted church. Evil was gone. Peace was hovering over the house. The forces of good could now fill up every square inch of the old wooden home.

Let there be peace!

Let there be harmony!

Let there be love!

Jacques cleaned up the place. He carefully collected the ashes into a little bottle, scooping every bit with an improvised shovel made of paper. Jacques would need to return the small bottle to the cemetery. He needed to make the trip this time before the strike of noon. He would make a symbolic offering of rum to *Baron Samedi,* the spirit who guards the cemetery, and to *Papa Guede*, the spirit of the dead. For good measure, he would distribute bread and pennies to all the beggars who hang around the gates of the cemetery. This should be a very easy task. Significant danger could still loom for anyone who would retrieve the red bag that contained the little container with the ashes, a small flat bottle of liquor, and thirty-three dollars and thirty-three cents. Jacques would perform this important task the next day. It could happen at any time before noon. The house was filled with different scents. Jacques was no longer in danger of being troubled by the ghosts. They had just lost

Claude O'Connor, their commander-in-chief. His long contract with the devil with all its powers was broken.

The king is dead! Long live the king!

Everything was so peaceful. Jacques even added some jasmine and some ilang-ilang for good measure. The aroma filled the air. Only good could come out of this wonderful feeling. Jacques was cheerful and his heart was full of gratitude:

"Oh, let all living creatures proclaim the glory of God.

For tonight he has shown His might and made me a free man.

Make way for the Lord, for today he has liberated me.

Evil has returned to trenches of the dead forever and ever!"

His mission accomplished, Jacques could now live and think as all free men do. In the process, he had rid his family of the shame brought by Claude O'Connor.

Requiescat in pace, Claude O'Connor!

May you rest in peace, Claude O'Connor!

Requiescat in pace, Giraud Gaetan!

May you rest in peace, Giraud Gaetan!

This world belongs to the living.

Let bygones be bygones!

O'Connor was out of commission. Hors d'état de nuire... Unless someone would inadvertently go and interfere with his newly found peace. Jacques could now find himself forever grateful. His gods had given him a new outlook on life. He drank a glass of Manischewitz wine and offered the following prayer borrowed from an old communion hymn:

"Sun, who all my life dost brighten.
Light, who dost my soul enlighten.
Joy, the sweetest man e'er knoweth;
Fount, whence all my being floweth.
At thy feet, I cry, my Maker,
Let me be a fit partaker!
Of this blessed food from heaven,
For our good, thy glory, given."

Let us bring the laurels. Let the orchestra play a victory march.

"Thou shalt break them with a rod of iron. Thou shall dash them in pieces like a potter's vessel."

Psalm 2,9

What would the future hold for Jacques? He did not know. But he was sure that he no longer would leave it up to somebody else to decide. A new day had dawned over the land. For Jacques, life would never be the same again. He had taken a long journey back home in search of a part of himself left behind. He had to overcome many perils, but victory came to him...

"A vaincre sans perils, on triomphe sans gloire!

"To vanquish without risk is to triumph without glory!"

Le Cid, Pierre Corneille.

Jacques could now keep his head straight and face the world. Life was his for him to take on.....

PART III

A

PIECE

OF

THE PIE

So, it's home again, and home again, America for me!
My heart is turning home again, and there I long to be,
In the land of youth and freedom beyond the ocean bars,
where the air is full of sunlight and the flag is full of stars.

America for me, Henry Van Dyke

Chapter 27

"Emancipate yourselves from mental slavery

None but ourselves can free our minds

Have no fear of atomic energy

Cause None A dem can stop the time

How long shall they kill our prophets

While we stand aside and look

Some say it's just a part of it"

We've got to fulfill the book

Redemption Song, Bob Marley

Jacques had made a mature decision to return to America. He was quite a different man who went through the usual formality as he was asked the ready-made questions by the immigration officer.

"How long were you out of the country, Mr. Gaetan?"

"About three weeks, twenty-four days to be exact," Jacques responded.

What a different interaction. Jacques remembered how nervous he was when he entered the country over fifteen years ago. He never could understand why there was a need for passports and immigration officers anyway. If the leaders of the superpowers can buy into the concept of the global economy and global security, why not global citizenship? Jacques envisions a world sans frontiers, where the only proof of citizenship one would need is to be born on this planet. People would have a computer chip implanted on their deltoid. This chip would carry all necessary biographical, medical, criminal, and other information about the individual. Jacques would then be considered a citizen of the world, born and raised in Haiti. All the immigration officers would be retrained to become data entry and information upgrading officers. People living in a certain area would abide by the rules of the region. They would be made responsible for the preservation, and the protection of the environment. Everyone would live under the general rule: You can use but do not abuse. Pay as you go! Just imagine, no need for extradition. You violate the rules, and you pay. War criminals and people who commit crimes against humanity, politicians and dictators who violate a whole country would have no place to hide, nowhere to go. Jacques could rightfully claim what he has always felt: I am a citizen of the world by birth. Can you think of anyone who cannot make that claim? Jacques was still lost in his thought when the whiny voice of the officer caught his attention:

"Welcome back home, Mr. Gaetan!" the immigration officer concluded, as he handed Jacques his passport.

"Thank you!" Jacques said.

Madi gras m' pa pe-ou, Ce moun ou ye.
(Masked man, you don't scare me, you are human).

That was the statement of a man full of self-confidence. Jacques had come a long way. He left the country in a state of emotional distress, on the verge of a psychotic break. He had returned as strong as ever. He had freed himself from a curse that originated from the outside and that he had internalized under the weight of cultural ties that he could not dissimulate. However, in his relentless pursuit of happiness, Jacques still had to contend with some other conflicts that were gnawing him inside and still had the potential to destroy his newly found equilibrium, his internal harmony. He needed to deal with his pent-up anger about the racism that was so rampant around him. Every day he would come across evidence of this cancer that was eating at his humanity and that of his fellow black men and women. Jacques also felt that he was now free to rediscover that little twinkling light inside of him, the arrow of Cupid, he once experienced when he met Suzanne. Jacques would like to fall in love again, and lastly, Jacques believes strongly that in the final analysis, one is defined by the role that you are willing and able to play in the community. Jacques wanted to pursue another dream. He wanted to establish a professional identity. A profession might give you some credibility and a voice. It is not a guarantee, but you must start from there. Jacques might find out that often people from minority groups need to be overqualified to compete with the next guy for the same job. The racist in our midst does not necessarily belongs to a racist organization. He does not go around in a white hood or participate in meetings in some remote exclusive ranch. The racist in our midst is probably a devout Christian who swears by the bible and can be seen in the pew on Sundays singing his heart out with unquestionable piety.

On a hill far away stood an old rugged cross,
the emblem of suffering and shame;
and I love that old cross where the dearest and best
for a world of lost sinners was slain.

The racist in our midst might even belong to some charitable organization and often contributes to feeding the poor. Never put into question his privileged position. The racist in or must never questions anything that is the way it has always been. The racist in our mist never wonders why Black youths four times are as likely to be detained in juvenile facilities as their white peers. He never questions why Blacks are six times more likely to be imprisoned than white people in the US and why Blacks are more likely to be in jail during pre-trial on minor offenses, causing the detainee to accept a guilty plea with all the negative impact on the detainee's future. The racist in our midst never questions why Blacks are least likely to receive a life-changing kidney or cardiac transplant than their white counterparts. The racist in our midst will not acknowledge how despite the federal laws on the book, housing discrimination is still rampant and how gentrification has chased away Blacks from their neighborhoods and destroyed their families. The racist in our midst is blissfully unaware. He is not totally to blame. After all, such topics are not a menu item on the 24/7 news network that only cares about viewership and Nielsen Report. Politicians on the campaign trail will not pick that up as an issue because it will not get them the votes that they need to get elected. In fact, it is exactly the opposite. Some politicians want to revert the gain of the Civil Rights movement. Racism is like a cyst that could lay dormant in the soil for hundreds of years until it finds the proper environment to come alive and flourish again. They are promoting an "anti-wokeness" movement that is anti-everything, a movement that does not want Black history to be taught in the classroom. They claim that such programs are only designed to make "white people feel bad about their own white heritage." As a recent article in The Guardian puts it the wokeness ideology is nothing else than the rebranding of bigotry as a resistance movement". Another recent racist theory is the so-called "replacement theory" according to which Black immigration only purpose is to replace white European populations, a colonization in reverse of sort. Such theories fortunately have been rejected by more moderate conservatives.

This theory is making a comeback, finding support from authors such as Jean Raspil and Renaud Camus in Le Camp des Saints and The Great Replacement ironically from no other than France, the cradle of the French Revolution of 1789, the precursor to America's struggle and democratic ideals. The danger of such extremist views is that they are being promoted under the guise of patriotism. Some believe that everything is fine and that nothing needs to change. For these groups, the notion of a society where different groups could make contributions to create a much richer environment is out of the question. The multiculturalism movement of the '80s is dead. The idea of a post-racial society was short-lived and had no other effects than to push the black youths toward complacency because the struggles of the civil rights leaders were before they were born. How would Jacques live in such environment?

The issue is much too complex for Jacques to even consider taking it on. He could promise to remain aware of the issues but trying to engage in a struggle against something so big, would be like suicide. Jacques promised he would concentrate on his own problems and try to secure a piece of the pie. Besides, Jacques rationalized, one cannot overgeneralize. Not everyone in the community is racist. Some genuinely believe in the words of MLK that 'one should be judged not by color their skin but by the content of their character" However, Jacques needed to learn how not to take everything personally. Jacques saw his problem as essentially the same as that of his African American brothers. He had carried within him a lot of anger and resentment and the white people know it. Every Black man, in their mind, is angry and resentful. Jacques promised himself that he would avoid falling into their traps. Now that he had come back from his emotional journey, now that he had recaptured his soul, a much tedious and painstaking kind of work needed to be accomplished... They were born in a world that placed them at the top of the ladder. It has protected their interest. Why would they want it changed? It has nothing to do with being a good or a bad person. Racism, the mayor of a large metropolitan city once said, "is as American as apple pie and the fourth of July."

First Jacques needed to take a realistic inventory of his ability. He could not afford to invest his energy and get into a field to find out soon thereafter that his heart was not in it. He needed to choose carefully. He thought about seeking some help from a vocational advisor. He decided against it, as he felt that he would be facing the same problem that he had when he sought help from culturally inept professionals. How would Jacques make his life experiences play in his favor? Becoming a neurosurgeon was out of the question. Medical school was much too demanding and admission too competitive, whatever field he decided to get into, he would have to contend with the age difference between him and the other students. He decided to take the first step. He would register for English classes in the local community college. I would get a chance to experience how it feels to be back in school. He needed to show better mastery of the English language anyway. He was determined to make this re-entry into America a real new beginning, a successful one.

The transition to college life went smoothly. Jacques's apprehension about being around younger students was unfounded... There were many students in the same situation. Some of the classes were offered online. Besides, Jacques had a few things working for him like his passion for reading, his maturity, and above all his determination to find his place under the sun. He wanted to create a professional identity. He learned that an accelerated nursing program was being offered at Florida International University. The requirements for admission were straightforward. Among other things, he needed to write an essay stipulating his reasons for wanting to join the program. It was the opportunity that Jacques was waiting for. He was able to display his maturity and emphasized multiculturalism and the need for cultural competency and empathy toward the patient. The caregiver, he wrote needed to be attuned to his patient and have the capacity to listen. It was music to the ears of the admission committee composed of individuals from different ethnic backgrounds. He was accepted. It was all up to Jacques now. Financial assistance and various grants were readily available because of the highly publicized shortage of nurses. Things according to most analyses would only get worse.

Jacques quickly realized that he had much stronger affinities for studying than he thought. He was encouraged by the positive feedback from his professors. He stayed on top of his class for the duration of the program. His familiarity with the hospital environment having been a patient on several occasions served him well. He rotated through various specialties. He saw up close and personal what it was like being in the hospital not as a patient but as a caregiver albeit as a student. He progressed well and quickly acquired the skills needed to join the vast body of people dedicated to alleviating the suffering of fellow human beings. His self-confidence was growing every day. His longtime dream of becoming a neurosurgeon was long gone, but somehow Jacques was carving a place for himself among the privileged group entrusted to the care of suffering individuals. Jacques was hopeful his dream would soon become reality. Jacques was able to clear the different state-required exams with ease. He knew that soon he would have to abandon his job at the library for the hospital units where life dramas were on display every single day.

Jacques needed to deal with many issues.

Jacques decided that he should move out of his studio and started to look for a more comfortable apartment. He made an appointment to meet with the manager of The Breeze, a magnificent apartment tower by Oleta Beach in North Miami. He was surprised that the manager was ready to see him the same afternoon. He got to the office twenty minutes ahead of schedule. A Caucasian man in his early thirties who looked like a car salesman was engaged in a very lively discussion with a young white couple. The salesman was extolling the lifestyle at The Breeze. Jacques gathered that the complex was under new management and that a new security system had just been installed and that the management reviewed the background of new tenants very carefully to keep the undesirables out.

"You know what I mean," he continued.

The couple was given a choice between a sea view and an interior garden view.

"I would like to show you a couple of two bedrooms that would meet your needs." Why did he have to speak so loud, Jacques did not know, but he was certainly revealing an awful lot of information in this lively exchange. The manager walked by Jacques who was slouching in the rattan chair and did not even seem to notice him.

"Mr. Jones," Jacques said, "we have a four o'clock ...."

"Not now, we only interview for the groundskeeper positions in the morning...." Mr. Jones interrupted.

"Mr. Jones, I am not here for a job...I spoke to you earlier about an apartment."

Mr. Jones was speechless; his face became as red as a Mexican tomato. What an inopportune time for such an encounter! He was just telling his customers how some people were screened out of the apartment complex, and Jacques was confronting him with prejudice. Mr. Jones had assumed that since Jacques was black, he was responding to an ad for a groundskeeper. No, Jacques could not possibly be expecting to be offered an apartment at The Breeze. The reaction from the young couple was even more revealing.

"Mr. Jones," said the man looking at his watch as if he had just remembered an appointment with his tax man on April 15, "I really must go, I will come back for the tour another time. I have your card; I will give you a call."

Mr. Jones was mad. This very loquacious man had suddenly lost his tongue.

"Mr. Gaetan, I misunderstood you. We do not have any apartments for rent currently, we are only accepting people who are interested in buying. Is this what you want?"

At any other time, Jacques would have confronted the apparent expression of prejudice head-on. But Jacques was a different man. He decided to wait for a better opportunity.

"Mr. Jones, I am not interested in buying currently. You did a good job with that couple. If I were them, I would choose the apartment with the garden view. Looking at the sea can become boring after a while. Wouldn't you say, Mr. Jones?"

Idiot! Jacques thought, he probably did not even get the point. *America had not changed!*

The next incident would cause Jacques a lot of pain because of its implications for his state of health. He had always promised himself that when his turmoil was over, he would attend a tennis tournament at Biscayne Grove. After all, he had dropped many travelers who had made the trip just to watch their favorite player participate. Jacques had good reason to want to attend. A young Haitian tennis player, Clitandre, had made it to the quarter-finals. Jacques felt out of place. Very few African Americans had made the trip. He decided to get a shirt from the gift shop. He paid thirty-seven dollars for the jersey. He figured that a Lipton jersey would look much better than the denim shirt he was wearing. Jacques changed into his new top. He decided to get a second one. He went back into the store and picked out another shirt. A young Caucasian woman was at the cash register. Her hair was bleached as if she wanted to turn herself into a blonde. She was staring continuously at Jacques, visibly puzzled by his presence in the store. Or so Jacques thought until she made the following comments.

“I hope you will pay for both shirts, the one you have on and the one in your hand.”

"Excuse me, lady, can you repeat that?" Jacques inquired.

“I said,” continued the young cashier, “I hope you will pay for both shirts.”

Jacques looked around, visibly shaken by the audacity of this woman. At least five other customers were wearing brand-new shirts. The only difference was that they were all white.

"Miss!" Jacques said in a loud voice, "Is there any reason why you chose to make those remarks to me? Are you going to ask those other customers to pay for the shirts they are wearing too? If not, I would like you to apologize because I should not have to pay twice for the same item."

The cashier did not expect such a display of assertiveness. The activities in the small gift shop had come to a halt. Nobody knew who called the police, but an officer who looked like a character out of LA in flawless uniform was already there. Order was to be kept at all costs. He went straight to Jacques since he was the one who did not seem to belong. Jacques pulled his receipt out of his pocket and went on to explain how he felt the cashier had made some racist comments. The officer did not want to take sides but attempted to diffuse the situation. "This is a civil matter; it is not within my purview. It is up to you to pursue this matter if you feel that your rights were violated."

"You are dammed right they were", Jacques thought.

He was willing to accept an apology, move on, and enjoy his outing. He was also surprised by the conciliatory position of the police officer. That was a change. An almighty white officer who was not ready to erect himself as judge and jury, dish out the blame, and issue summons. Disturbing the peace. Violation of civil rights. False accusation. How would the police officer have handled the case if there were any evidence that Jacques was the violator? This time, Mr. Cop was not willing to jump and crack the case. Maybe he was moonlighting on these premises, or he had some financial interest in the business.

"Officer," Jacques continued, "All I am asking is for this woman to offer an apology. She could do it now, or maybe she would rather do it through my attorney."

By that time, the young woman's supervisor had replaced her at the cash register. No apologies were offered. The small crowd of shoppers had abandoned the scene. They did not say a word. They did not seem to understand what the big commotion was about anyway. They had a tennis tournament to watch. The crowd would probably have been more sympathetic if the incident was about a lost puppy. The afternoon was ruined. There would not be any more fun in watching two grown men chasing a small ball. So, Jacques rationalized, visibly upset. He decided to go back home, full of rage. There was a message in all of this for him somewhere. Maybe, in the early twenty-first century, as a black person, he could not be a spectator of a tennis tournament in Biscayne Grove. Or maybe, this girl was much too young to know about Martin Luther King, Andrew Young, and Malcolm X or maybe she was out on Crystal K and acid when Black History was being taught in the shortest month of the year.

America had not changed!

There were many more incidents of racism. Jacques did not believe that America had suddenly become more racist, but for some reason, he could no longer ignore what was going on around him. He could see the good and the bad. What was he going to do with this rage that was boiling inside of him? At the root of Jacques's anger, was the relation that maybe his lifetime and that of many generations would be wasted if he were to wait for some kind of acknowledgment and reparation from those who have done injustice to him and the people of his race. America would not suddenly have a moment of epiphany. Jacques' troubles were not over. It was not enough for him to accept his roots, his cultural heritage. It was not enough for him to free himself of the curse placed on him by a white man. There was another curse, much more discreet, but a hundred times more powerful, the imprints left on his psyche by generation after generation of racism. Jacques needed to free himself from "mental slavery". The whole country needed to extirpate from its mind the scars of racism or else it was bound to develop a new form of seizure, a real incurable one. Or worse of all, the type of collective seizure that could make America and communities like Watts, South Central, Los Angeles, and Overtown explode with rage any time the chalice of racist America has been filled up started to overflow. Be it the treatment that Jacques receives when he goes to a ritzy department store. No attendants are rushing to help, because the assumption is that he is not there to buy, he cannot afford anything in this store. Be it how he is treated when he attends an official function. The assumption is that he is there to serve the hors d'oeuvres not to consume them. Excuse me, would the old white ladies say in the isles of the department store, what is the price of this item? You should see the look on their faces when the inquiry is met with complete silence from Jacques.

"Dodo bird, I am a consumer just like you." Jacques would feel like screaming.

There will be more trigger-happy white police officers shooting black law-abiding citizens. More police brutality was caught on videotape. There will also be more all-white juries to find no evidence of wrongdoing. The black communities will continue to show signs of "incurable seizure." At the root of the problems are the scars left on the black collective brain by institutionalized racism.

America has not changed!

Like Jacques, it seemed like the entire community needed to take a journey in quest of its soul. The white community needed freedom from the world wide web of racism. The black community needed total freedom, not just from the heavy physical shackles of slavery, but from the enduring atrocities of his unmanaged anger.

The first step for both communities is the decision to do something about the problem. Jacques realized that he still needed a lot of help. He was no longer haunted by the recurring dreams about a black skull, but he was confronted daily with the reality of a racist society. Jacques needed to make the final leap. A leap of faith in the abilities of trained professionals from his own background. There probably are not enough Black or Haitian psychiatrists for the large proportion of blacks in the community, but with some ingenuity, Jacques should be able to find one.

What does Jacques want from a good psychiatrist anyway? The ideal psychiatrist would be a real person who is comfortable with his view of the world. Someone humble enough to realize that the solutions would not come from a textbook checklist, but from Jacques' daily life experiences. Someone who could listen with his eyes and see with his ears. Someone who is willing to stay in for the duration until the finish line is crossed. A tall order, one might say. However, how could Jacques expect any less? He has put himself through gruesome experiences and now stands ready to push the envelope until total recovery is achieved. There cannot be any compromise.
Can the Dr. Dickensons of the world foot that bill? Probably, but unlikely. It would take a different mindset. The Dr. Dickensons of the world would have to be willing to give up some of their own worlds to incorporate some of Jacques' world in order to

create a new environment where both could live comfortably as equals. Can you imagine the Dr. Dickensons of the world accepting Jacques' Voodoo beliefs as a bona fide religious system designed for the survival of its adepts in the same way as the Jewish faith or Christianity? Very unlikely.

Now that Jacques has accepted his Voodoo beliefs as part of his cultural heritage, he would not compromise on this pre-requisite. One would not think about trusting a young surgeon with a scalpel and other surgical instruments in the operating room before he is fully proficient in handwashing techniques. Therefore, one cannot trust the Dr. Dickensons of the world with treating Jacques before they show cultural competency.

Will Jacques make a leap of faith, put aside his own bias, and seek help from a psychiatrist of his own background, from a Haitian professional? This choice would not necessarily guarantee success, but it offers a good starting point. The dominant culture would have the minority professionals believe that because they have achieved a certain status, they are different from the commoners. They have even made comments like, "But you are not like them...." referring to the uneducated Haitians. As if there were two Haitis, two cultures, two Haitian peoples. The truth of the matter is, in America, there is one large group of immigrants who come from that place called Haiti, the poorest of the hemisphere, as the media often remind everyone. The blood donor's policy did not apply any differently to the Haitian professionals and the Haitians with low socioeconomic status. This trick is probably as old as the world:" Diviser pour regner", Divide to Conquer! When a Haitian becomes famous, his Haitian origin is quickly dropped. Alexandre Dumas, the author of "Les Trois Mousquetaires" was born in Jeremie, Haiti. He is known worldwide as a Frenchman. Jean-Baptiste, the founder of the great city of Chicago, was an immigrant from Haiti. Audubon, the founder of the now renowned Audubon Society is from Les Cayes, Haiti. Jacques realized that and was going to live and act according to his newly accepted beliefs. Tomorrow, he would find a Haitian psychiatrist.

Chapter 28

Jacques has been able to secure an appointment with Carl Dubuisson, M.D., a Haitian-born psychiatrist who was trained at McLean Hospital in Boston, the same hospital where Dr. Dickenson received his postgraduate training. He had worked in major university centers and had established a flourishing private practice in the southern end of Palm Beach County. He was highly recommended by the local chapter of the American Psychiatric Association.

The first meeting was very informal.

"Good morning, Mr. Gaetan, I understand that you have seen a psychiatrist at the University of Miami before...."

Those were the only words spoken in English during that meeting that day. Dr. Dubuisson was probably a couple of years younger than Jacques. He had a very warm personality and had no trouble putting Jacques at ease. By the end of the hour, Jacques knew probably as much about him, his passion for world history and painting collections as he knew about Jacques. How did he manage to become such a successful man in front of so many adversities? Jacques was dying to find out. Jacques would have plenty of opportunity to find out. During the first few sessions, they became very acquainted with each other. It was almost as if this doctor was waiting for the right person to tell someone about his own encounters with racist America. Jacques heard many stories during his treatment with Dr. Dubuisson. As the doctor was going through a divorce early in his career, the divorce lawyer, Mr. Taylor, suggested that he settled early and move to another state and that it was unlikely that he could be found. The doctor responded that all any smart investigator would need to do was to consult Marquis' Who is Who? The lawyer responded with anger on his face, "Ha, you will never make it to Who is Who?" The doctor has lived with the determination to prove Mr. Taylor wrong and has been placed in the famous directory in several places. Every time a racist comment was directed at him, he would become more determined to succeed. When he informed the chairman of the department about his plan to go into the field of psychiatry: "You will be analyzing your patients in Creole," he said. The older doctor had no faith that Dr. Dubuisson could master the English language. Dr. Dubuisson shared with Jacques, comments once made by a white colleague: "I cannot imagine going to your country and becoming so successful, therefore, you should count your blessings and be happy with things the way they are." Dr. Dubuisson had to face what most black professionals are confronting every day. The black professional is not allowed to display a bit of ethnicity like his Caucasian colleagues. Should he speak with authority like sometimes experts do, he is quickly branded as having a "Hollier Than thou" attitude. Should he, during a debate express his view forcefully, he is described as aggressive while his white colleague is seen as assertive. The educated black man is often seen as an aberration, a phenomenon to be displayed when auditors are visiting, and a token to be polished and showcased when some large philanthropic corporation with a fat checkbook is in town. Dr. Dubuisson has been in this situation many times. He is expected to show up, not say much, lest he say the wrong things. At another time, Dr. Dubuisson would be expected to stay out of sight like the black man in Langton Hughes' poem who is sent to eat in the kitchen when strangers come. The racist does not necessarily look like the devil with horns coming out of his head... Dr. Dubuisson remembers how flabbergasted his boss at the university was when he initiated the first contact with a newspaper to arrange a talk about a topic, he was fully familiar with. Dr. Dubuisson's supervisor was afraid that the limelight would be taken away from him. He was once invited to visit a program, and his supervisor flatly objected making the following statement in front of the whole clinical team made up of psychologists, social workers, and therapists.

"We have to be careful how our program is portrayed and who represents us."

What could that statement possibly mean if not that Dr. Dubuisson was of the wrong color, as he had already established his credibility as a clinician? Dr. Dubuisson did not respond to every provocation, he did not fight every battle. He had developed an armor as thick and as tough as the hide of a rhinoceros in an African safari park. When you swim with sharks, you are bound to get some cuts, but if you are going to get eaten up, do not swim. He has remained indomitable. He took his inspiration from the words of Jesse Jackson, "Keep your eyes on the prize." He did not display overt anger. Dr. Dubuisson had a secret and effective weapon, his French humor. It is not clear whether his white colleagues always got the joke, but who cares? It was even better. This technique goes way back to slavery time. The slaves would often communicate their meeting sites or *mots d'ordre* (marching orders) about their plan to escape, right under the nose of their masters using double entendre, patois, and other encoded language. Dr. Dubuisson will quickly admit that his defense mechanisms did not always work. He often developed increased blood pressure. How much can one man take? How many times could he endure seeing his suggestions being discarded as pure nonsense, to see the same ideas being embraced as genial because it is now being put forth by a white student? Dr. Dubuisson often went home, feeling that his interaction with his colleagues was a pure exercise in futility. They often say that unless the athlete visualizes himself going over the bar in a jumping competition, it is unlikely to happen. Well, Dr. Dubuisson visualized himself on a battle filed at the end of a long day. The clash of the spears and armors has ceased. The surviving warriors have returned home to have biscuits and gravy. All his enemies are on the ground, defeated. There he stands, victorious. Such a victory, however, is only possible if the black man has the wisdom and the patience to pick his own fights. He should not be lured into the battlefield to only realize that he was outgunned, outmanned. The man with the most staying power and the strongest backbone will come out on top. Guaranteed! All of those who have discarded him as irrelevant if they could only see him now. It has been a long day indeed! Battles that the black man thought were fought and won are back on the field. Inequality? What inequality? Injustice? What injustice? What do the black professionals want anyway? Isn't it enough that we make exceptions for them and let them live in our midst? We look the other way when they marry our daughters. As they say, it is their nickel. What do they want, then? How about breaking the glass ceiling? How about equal recognition for equal performance? Why do black professionals have to be ten times more qualified than their white counterparts before they are even considered for a position?

Dr. Dubuisson knew that it was a dangerous proposition to reveal so much about his own struggle to his patient. He felt, however, that it was worth taking the risk. How else would he convey to that man that he understood his pain and that he too was feeling the same anguish? Showing empathy towards

Jacques was neither forced nor fake. It was a natural outcome of a therapeutic relationship based on compassion and the realization that both doctor and patient had a common problem. Daily, they were being slapped in the face with flagrant manifestations of institutionalized racism. They also realized that the racists of the world often had human and likable face. Racism is a learned behavior that needs to be unlearned through a long and tedious process of de-conditioning. Have you ever noticed black and white children spontaneously start playing with each other in the park until they are given the look or pulled by a wary mother? When do children lose this sense of innocence? Dr. Dubuisson had come a long way. He had all the outward signs of success. He had become comfortable in different circles. However, like many black professionals, he felt very isolated. He was often accused by people of his own ethnic group of betrayal because he did not necessarily condone the outlandish hairdos, the excessive display of gold, and the hoochee-mama look. To the white members of the community, he is often seen as an over-educated man who wants to be white. Jacques took heart that if Dr. Dubuisson could survive that much adversity, maybe he too could survive.

Now that the common threads of their problems had been identified, Jacques and his doctor needed to find a solution. They practiced role-playing. They perfected the techniques of relaxation. Jacques was now able to use imagery to get away from stressful situations. If Jacques could not change the behavior of people around him, he could at least learn how to cope better with the stress they can cause him. Over several sessions, Jacques and Dr. Dubuisson replayed different moments they have been involved in and attempted to find better coping strategies. Some of the sessions were very intense and at times it seemed that the good doctor was losing control of the situation. Dr. Dubuisson did not give up. He just knew that he was serious about helping his fellow man. He wanted to have a lot of faith in the therapeutic process. Maybe, the most memorable session of psychodrama they had was the one described below.

The year: 2001

The Protagonists:

BLACK MEN AND WOMEN

VS.

OLD MASTERS OF THE BLACK RACE

The Place: The Supreme Court of the United States of America. In view of the magnitude of the case and the interest manifested in this unprecedented case, it was decided to hold court in a giant stadium as big as Pro Player Stadium, Giant Stadium, and Fenway Park put together.

Case Number: 1800ENDTHE PAIN-2001

ATTORNEYS FOR THE DEFENDANTS:

Jim Crow: Only a case of this magnitude would get him to step down from his seat as Senator of North Carolina, a seat he has held for umpteen years. The cold war is over, but he still sees every emerging black world leader as a crazed communist to be psychologically assassinated. There would be more harmony in the world were it not for the venom that he spits out constantly. He is close to one hundred years old.

Newton Gangrenit: One of the best orators this country has produced. An extremely talented and crafty individual. He could put his foot in his mouth, take it out and have you believe that it was meant to be that way. He might even get you to give him a $300,000 loan with no interest. He has mastered the art of lying, the art of wheeling and dealing A man to watch, he might become President one day...

Harvey Star: Has a well-established record in witch hunting. He might need it, given the historical nature of this case and considering that one party has had the exclusive right to keep all the records.

These were the lead attorneys for the defendants. There were many, many more with all different areas of expertise in asset disposal and statistics, etc. etc.

ATTORNEYS FOR THE PLAINTIFFS:

Anousar Moses Mubarak: He is originally from Egypt, the land of the Pharaoh, Tutankhamen, Cleopatra, and the Pyramids. The land where civilization started.

Josef Kefale: Has a doctorate in history and anthropology. He is from Ethiopia, the land of Emperor Haile Selassie, seen by many blacks as the Black Messiah.

Lloyd Garvey: Great-grandson of Marcus Garvey born and raised on the island of Jamaica, the land where Bob Marley once tried to tell the struggle of the Black people with a rhythm of his own.

Anita Haynes: Born in Longbranch, New Jersey, the first African American woman to graduate from Harvard Law School. In judicial circles, she carries the nickname of "The Black Zapper." Specializes in Civil Rights cases. She is running a winning streak of twenty-seven cases.

Jacques Stephen Alexis, Jr.: Born in Haiti, the western part of the island of Hispaniola where in 1791, the first rally for freedom was held under the leadership of Boukman.14 He is an expert in African History and could establish family trees all the way back to the western coast of Africa.

Jacques had carried within him a lot of anger. At the root of Jacques' anger was the realization that maybe his lifetime, and that many generations, would be wasted if he were to wait for some kind of acknowledgment and reparation from those who have done injustice to him and the people of his race. Jacques often imagined himself taking the old masters to court on one thousand and one counts. Oh, what a case it would be? This would be the trial of all trials. This would be the trial of the millennium. In the era of satellite and the internet, this event would have worldwide coverage. Oh, what a trial it would be for Ailey and the Dance Theatre of Harlem as backup, just in case our best orators like Johnny Cochran, Jessie Jackson, Louis Farrakhan, and Jean-Bertrand Aristide get thrown out of court or get struck by stage fright. The show must go on. The case must be made. Because we need all the intelligentsia, we can garner to figure out why after so long, we have not yet overcome. The court would be as large as three football fields put together.

Outside every stadium, not inside, just like in the old Roman Empire, there will be one million men, women, and children. And if the court does not hear our case, we will do what we do best. We will sing, we will dance, and we will rap. We will dress up in the most shocking colors. We will show the judges moves that they will not believe. Maybe, we will get the officers of the court to loosen up a bit. Every single culture on this planet will be represented at that event of epic proportions. The Bell Curve Theory15 would be dissected, confronted, debunked, and put to rest once and for all. The affidavit would read something like this:

Black men and women

vs

Old masters of the black race

The counts would be listed as follows:

Count one: Destruction of families - fathers were separated from their wives and children. Newborns were pulled away from their nursing mothers to be sold on the slave markets. Men were packed like sardines and shipped to America.

Count two: Kidnapping and unlawful imprisonment: The black man was uprooted manu militari from his hometown and sent to unfamiliar places to work until he dropped dead, when not beaten to death for daring to resist.

Exhibit #1:

Listen to the poetic words of William Cullen Bryant as "The African Chief" after giving a fierce battle to his captors, finally succumbs. He begs to be released:

"Look, feast thy greedy eyes with gold
 Long kept for sorest need;
Take it-thou askest sums untold,
 And say that I am freed.
 Take it -my wife, the long, long day,

Weeps by the cocoa tree,
And my young children leave their play,
And ask in vain for me."
The African Chief's captor shows no mercy:
I take thy gold-but I have made
Thy fetters fast and strong,
And ween by the cocoa shade
Thy wife will wait thee long."

The black man's wife has been waiting since for the return of her man. Since then, it has been generation after generation of fatherless children, of single mothers trying to raise their children alone. New versions of slavery have taken hold of the land. The black man is now a slave to drug addiction, gun violence, and epidemic after epidemic. The black man does not own gun manufacturing companies or large drug cartels. Who are the masters? Same victims, same masters. No, the world has not changed. All the black men and women marching in Selma ever wanted was the right to be counted. Instead, they received dog bites, bullets, and water cannons. Today they want a drug-free neighborhood where their children can play. They want a world without guns. They want a fair share of the American pie. They want to benefit from the tremendous progress of American medicine. They want their life expectancy at birth to be closer to their white fellow man. Most of the black children are still waiting for their fathers just like the children described in the "African Chief." They want their fathers to tell them bedtime stories. I could just hear the clamor of the gargantuan crowd.

Can't you hear the clamor?

I hear children crying at the kitchen table, alone they sit, and their fathers' seat has long been empty.

I hear mothers lamenting

Tonight will be another sleepless night once again,

They will long for moments that could have been.

The children wish they would take a ride to the park with their father,

The mothers wish they would have some help raising the children.

Alas! Fathers, and husbands, will not be at the rendezvous.

They are filling the jailhouse or lifeless they lay in the ground, victims of AIDS, drugs, and violence.

Why can't you hear the clamor?

Same masters, same victims!

Different form of slavery…

The black man still yearns to be totally free.

Count three: Working without pay: How much do you

figure the black man is owed in back pay for centuries of work with no remuneration? Not that the business they have worked for has gone bankrupt. Not at all! America has done very well for itself. America is the most vibrant economy on earth. American ingenuity and technology are second to none. However, do you ever wonder why the American soil is so fertile?

Do you ever wonder why the oranges from the American plantations are so sweet?

Do you ever wonder why the Kansas wheat fields produce more than any other?

Do you ever wonder why the Everglades sugarcane field is so green?

Do you ever wonder why America has remained the land of plenty?

Wonder no more, my friends!

It is because the blood and the sweat of the black man have nourished and fertilized this land.

It is because the ashes of the black man have fertilized the soil.

It's because the soul and spirit of the black man are still wandering those fields...

Count four: For treating the black man as sub-human, second-class being with unequal access, unequal pay, and unequal opportunity.

On September 15, 1963, in that Baptist church on Sixteenth Street in Birmingham, Alabama, four little girls died. Their names were Denise McNair, 11; Carole Robertson, 14; Cynthia Wesley, 14; and Addie Mae Collins 14. They were American children. They were God's children. There must be something wrong with any ideology that would make one believe that these innocent children needed to die. There is something wrong with racism. All the families ever wanted that Sunday, was to tell God their sorrow. And to make matters worse, not one white person from the town was present at the funerals. Were the real culprits even brought to justice?

Count five, six, seven, one thousand and one etcetera. , etcetera. Yadee, Yadee, yada.

The Judges:

Thurgood Marshall?

No Jacques, haven't you heard? He is gone.

Tip O'Neal?

Come on Jacques! You know that the old man from Capitol Hill has gone to better things.

Clarence Thomas?

Nah! I cannot be sure where he stands. Just cannot trust him. Only his skin is black. He looks like one of those people Frantz Fanon describes in Black Skin, White Mask as a black man who insists on portraying himself as white. Let us not take any chances. We will wait and see on that one. Won't we, Jacques? Is there anyone left on the bench that could be sympathetic enough to even hear the case? Jacques wondered.

But who would be the judge? Can the magistrate rise above his own bias and be as blind as Lady Justice? Let the person who feels that he could render justice come forward! No one! Jacques did not think so.

Who would serve on the jury?

Is there someone on this planet that can show some objectivity and listen to the merit of the case?

How long would the jury have to be secluded from the media?

Mission Impossible!

Is there someone that has not been influenced by emotions on either side of the issue?

May that person please rise and be the first juror!

This matter before the court needs to be laid to rest once and for all. Who would Jacques call a witness?

Res non judicata

Affaire non jugee

Cause not heard

The Witnesses:

Who would Jacques call as a witness?

Will Jacques and all the Ge-kleres of this world raise the ghosts of the fallen fathers, the young men beaten to death for daring to keep their heads high and say no? How about the many men who never made it across the Atlantic, whose bodies were fed to shark-infested waters? How about these men with their heads shaved, covered with honey, and left to die in the Caribbean sun?

Would Jacques and the Ge-kleres of the world also raise the ghosts of the black man fallen victim to gang warfare and drive-by shootings in the ghettos of South Chicago, Los Angeles or Overtown, Miami, or East New York?

If Jacques would be allowed to bring ghosts as witnesses, he would have no trouble calling well over one thousand and one witnesses.

Could Jacques trust the authorities of the church to hear the case? It would be highly suspect since the church has for the most part sided with the slave owners.

Enough hatred! Enough anguish! Enough grudges! When will it finally be time for closure?

Won't the old master find within himself the courage to apologize?

If not, will Jacques as a black man find within himself the magnanimity to forgive? In the words of Rudyard Kipling from his masterpiece: "If:"

"If you can wait and not be tired by waiting,
Or, being lied about, don't deal in lies,
Or being hated don't give way to hating. . . .
Yours is the Earth and everything that's in it,
And- which is more - you'll be a Man, my son!"
Something must change.
Let bygones be bygones
Fellow black men and women may the Earth be ours!
Will Jacques and his former master take a solemn vow together:
Let the barriers of inequality fall forever.
Let the white man live without fear of the black man's revenge!
Let bygones be bygones!
Let the black man live without fear of the white man changing the rules in the middle of the race.
Let bygones be bygones!

Let competition for jobs and college entry be based on merits, not on color.
Let every contest be like the Olympics
Let bygones be bygones!
Let the black man not just be seen on track and field
Let the black find a seat at the corporate conference table and on Capitol Hill
Let bygones be bygones!
Let the black man and the white man not fear to be together after

five pm.
Let it be no more integration at the workplace, apartheid at the residential place.
Let bygones be bygones!
Let the black man accused not fear the white jury.
Let the white man trust that the black juror too can render justice
Let bygones be bygones!
Let the white woman not go into panic and increase her steps when a black youth is coming by on the sidewalk.
Let bygones be bygones!
Let Black history be taught in every school of the land year-round including the contributions of non-African American Blacks
Let bygones be bygones!
Let it be no more white men and black men, just men
Let it be no more black children, white children, just children
Let it be no more black doctors, white doctors, just doctors
Let bygones be bygones.

So much creative energy has been wasted on both sides, the black man to fight injustice and lick his wounds, the white man to hold the black man back and inflict those wounds. Just imagine what the world would be like if all the men and women of this land would always display the same solidarity and care they do after disaster strikes. Jacques remained amazed at the will of America and could have easily written the following words:

Like a Commander-in-chief reviewing his troops after a long battle, you stand in America, contemplating the horizon. Full of pride and rightfully you proclaim:

Mission accomplished! The enemy has been vanquished. The war has been won. America, your might is second to none!

How about your enemy from within?

How about your public enemy number one?

How about racism?

That enemy too, shall fall!

Whenever you declare war on that enemy, whenever racism is seen as a clear and present danger to your greatness, that enemy too shall fall.

That enemy too, shall fall!

What better time than now?

The history of the world is full of those moments when leaders come out and say the right words to write the rest of history. Remember the words of JFK, "I'm a Berliner." The words of Ronald Reagan in his Russian homologue, "Take down that wall."(Referring to the Berlin Wall). Remember the words of Charles de Gaulle in Quebec in 1967, "Vive le Quebec libre." This simple phrase still echoes in Canadian history. Pope John Paul did not shy away from his historical duty when at Port-au-Prince airport, looking at the Haitian people's anguish and the results of three decades of dictatorship, he declared, "Fok sa change," Something must change. Three simple words which would serve as a catalyst to move the struggle of the Haitian people along. The events that followed the statements above at different eras have been written forever in the annals of history. Someone needed to take the risk. Jacques believes that the world is at such a crossroads and is awaiting a leader to shout the rallying cry, "Racism must end." The world is waiting for America to fulfill one more time its destiny as leader of the free world. . . . Because. ... If not America? Who will? If not now? When?

This is where Jacques's therapy sessions with Dr. Dubuisson took him. It was a very unorthodox approach, considering that Dr. Dubuisson was trained to keep his boundaries from his patients and avoid immersing himself too much in the patient's personal problem. Well, if his unusual and bold method was going to ease the anguish of his patients, so be it.

It had been over three months now since Jacques started to see Dr. Dubuisson. He knew that he needed to move on and leave his anger behind him. He wished that others would go with him on the arduous journey of recovery, but it would be unrealistic to expect that. Having rediscovered and accepted who he is, he is ready to make that commitment. The question is, will every black man and white man, correction. . . Will every man of this beautiful land accompany Jacques on the unprecedented journey? Jacques had already made his choice. No longer will he let the anger and resentment he has harbored until now direct the rest of his life. Today is as good as any other day to start. Today is the first day of the rest of Jacques' life. He felt alive. He felt as if he had found the fountain of youth. He developed a completely new attitude about his position as an immigrant in America. Having found his soul and his identity as a well-integrated person, he no longer had any fear. Gone was his fear of being engulfed. He was not just another black individual from the poorest country in the hemisphere. He was Jacques Gaetan. He understood and accepted the fact that the weaving that made up his fabric was like an iridescent piece of material that could take many shades. African, he is and will remain. He inherited the richness of a culture where civilization started many thousands of years ago. He bears the pride of his royal ancestors and will not bow in defeat. His more immediate forefathers' physical beings were enslaved but not their spirits. He knows that the biggest lie of all was that his ancestors were savages that needed to be civilized. How deceitful when the white man landed on Hispaniola's shores with chains in one hand and the cross in the other. In good faith, Jacques' ancestors have accepted the God of their masters as their own. They did not, however, give up their own gods. How could they? The gods have been there in times of calamity and in times of joy. They have been there in times of famine and in times of abundance. You see, Jacques' ancestors and their gods go a long way. When the black man was living in slavery and the white man's god and its church seemed to be looking the other way, Jacques' ancestors' gods were there to console him.

In Jacques' and every black man's heart, there is an immense affinity for spirituality. Call him Jehovah, Buddha, Mohammed, Christ, or Erzili Freda, Jacques, and his fellow black men will make room for him. Didn't the philosopher write "If God did not exist, man would have to invent him?" Jacques understood that his people had to invent a lot of gods because they had a tremendous need for them.

Jacques also accepted the influence of his European mentors. Poetry, Greek Mythology, classical music, and gospel music are all very much part of Jacques' life and he will have to make room for all of that.

Jacques is in tune with his natural environment and has learned to appreciate the beauty around him. He could see the hands of his creator in the serenity of a sunset by the sea. He could pay attention to the songs of nightingales, greeting the new day, and go into ecstasy and veneration while watching the pristine clarity of the river as the morning is rising.

Jacques can no longer ignore the voice within him along with his third eye, always guiding him through difficult moments. Jacques carries within him a guiding light, the stabilizing force that keeps it all together and creates for him, a state of bliss and internal harmony. No longer can he feel tormented by the chaos and tumult that surround him. He now can filter in as much as he can handle at any one time.

Jacques is now aware of his own creativity. He will now be able to describe and accept the world as he sees it and does not have to consume the cliches and stereotypes forced down his throat by the media.

Jacques is now more aware of the continuity between the worlds as seen, heard, and felt by his senses, and the world beyond. Jacques feels he potentially has the power to connect these two worlds.

He is very much aware of his finality and understands that someday he will pass from this tangible and physical world to another one, where the limitation of the senses is very evident and is transcended.

Jacques' blackness and" Haitianness" can no longer be made into a liability, but an asset. No longer will he let people he meets tell him who he should be, because:

"It matters not how strait the gate,
How charged with punishments the scroll,
I am the master of my fate
I am the captain of my soul. "

Invictus, William Ernest Henley

Chapter 29

Since his return to Miami, Jacques has been keeping a journal. Some days there would be no entry. On a Sunday morning, he wrote the following:

O belle Suzanne.
Oh beautiful Suzanne, where are you?
Life has been so empty without you.
For so many years you have haunted my dreams
I have searched for your irresistible look in every woman's eyes.
No woman can ever match the softness of your ebony skin.
Like Calypso did Ulysses on her remote island, you have kept me captive.
My nights have been sleepless, as I long for the warmth of your body.
I have dreamed that you would just return and sweep me off my feet.
Alas! It has been many years.

Jacques obviously had not given up hope of meeting Suzanne again, although he knew it was unlikely. Maybe what Jacques was longing for was part of his youth that he had kept alive through the memory of Suzanne.

How could Jacques put the matter to rest? Jacques decided to do what most people in his situation would have done, were not for the state he was in prior to his trip back home. The last time Jacques ever heard anything about Suzanne, was about five years before. The name Suzanne Chevalier was mentioned over the radio as part of an obituary announcement. Suzanne's grandmother had just passed away and a notice was read a few times. Jacques thought about sending a sympathy card to her but could not gather the courage to do so. Jacques was not ready to deal with what he might discover. He started to ask around. He was about to give up on the idea, but his persistence paid off. After a couple of months, Jacques learned that Suzanne was living in Longueuil, a suburb of Montreal. Jacques' luck was turning around. He was even able to secure a telephone number. He was extremely excited. He had the telephone number for a few days now, but he could not decide what he would do. He found himself pondering the different scenarios. What if Suzanne had changed into a completely different person? Would she even remember a relationship that lasted close to a year over fifteen years ago? Even worse, what if she was married with children? What if she had grown into some religious fanatic who spent her time away from society? Jacques imagined all the above possibilities and did not like any of them. It would mean the end of a long dream, maybe the end of a phase of his life. Jacques has lived in the past all this time, and he was about to face reality. He nervously dialed the number. . 1-514- 621... He misdialed several times and finally he was connected. His heart was pounding... What would he say if Suzanne was suddenly at the other end of the line? This is exactly what happened. From miles and miles, a woman's voice answered.

"Hello, this is Suzanne!"

The timbre of the voice had not changed a bit. Suzanne still had that well-articulate and somewhat dragging kind of voice.

Jacques hesitantly answered, "Hi, this is Jacques!"

"Jacques? Jacques Gaetan?" Suzanne exclaimed, almost screaming.

"Yes, Suzanne, Jacques Gaetan, the one and only."

She inquired first, "Where are you calling from? Last time I heard, you were moving to Miami." Jacques was surprised that Suzanne had been informed.

"You are right, I am still living in Miami, and it has been almost four years now. How about you?"

The questioning went on for some time. They both avoided talking about the good old times. Instead, Suzanne chose to talk about her current life. Jacques learned that Suzanne was in her second marriage. She had a total of four children, the oldest being a thirteen-year-old boy, Timothy, who is attending Middle School. She was now happily married to a chemical engineer and has traveled all over the world. She had become an Intensive Care Nurse. She has had her difficulties juggling the role of a mother and that of a career woman. One could not be any more settled than that. The conversation was very cordial. It ended with mutual promises that they would keep in touch. Well, they probably would not. They were now in two different worlds. Suzanne had a family. Jacques was like a campfire waiting to be lit. As to that feeling that Jacques has carried in his heart all of these years, it felt like a lamp that had just been turned off. The thrill was gone. It was over. Jacques knew it. Jacques somewhat felt relieved that this long odyssey has been brought to closure. Jacques was free now.

At age forty-four, Jacques was still a young man, but he no longer carried the athletic vigor that he once had. Those years with the love and emotion they carried, were gone, and would never come back. For Jacques, it was a very painful conclusion. These feelings found him completely unprepared. However, Jacques was hopeful. Until now, holding on to his imaginary love for a person which whom he had no contact in over fifteen years, had both soothing and isolating effects. Jacques had kept away from any unwanted interactions. He could hardly consider himself a virgin. He has had his share of sexual encounters. Some of them, he would rather forget. But it was all behind him for now. Such an approach left Jacques with little experience in dating and initiating relationships. All of this has left Jacques ripe for a brand-new set of experiences.

Jacques would like to meet that one person that would sweep him off his feet and become his soulmate. He would like to find this person that would bring him so much comfort that he would have no second thoughts about letting himself go. Jacques had a clear idea of the kind of women he would like to meet. He had never been the type of person to hang out in clubs or parties. Jacques decided to join a fitness club and build on his newly found energy. He would also go to the library and the bookstore more often. Jacques needed to start exploring the possibility of pursuing his academic studies. Why not? Why stop at a Bachelor's degree in nursing? Jacques started to go into the reading room of Barnes and Noble very frequently. To Jacques, it was like a reader's paradise. He would spend hours there going through different sections. He found out that most of the books that he once read in French had an English version. It would have been very difficult to go and ask about a specific book because the translation of the titles was often completely different. He rediscovered the work of authors like Albert Camus. He was able to read an English version of "Ainsi parla Zarathustra " (Thus spoke Zarathustra). Jacques was able to immerse himself in poetry and drama. He became acquainted with the work of Charles Dickens and Edgar Allan Poe. He discovered the power of Lang Hughes and Maya Angelou and the heart-pounding action novels of Tom Clancy. If one would visit that Barnes and Noble store on a weekend, one would see

Jacques moving about like a hyperactive child in a toy store. He would be caught talking to himself, exclaiming his surprise as if he had just come across a long-lost treasure. Jacques would become very engrossed in his reading, unmindful of the time. Maybe, it was only fitting that an event would happen at Barnes and Noble that would mark Jacques' life forever. Jacques was feeling very good that day. He had just mailed his application and his tuition back to Florida International University. He would be taking more credits per semester toward a Master's degree in nursing. He wanted to build on his prior success with nursing school. Jacques now had a much brighter outlook on the future. He has not been bothered by any of his old symptoms. He has had no seizures since that night at Ge-klere's place. He has been exercising three times a week. For some reason, he did not want to go on the scale, but he felt much stronger than he had in a long time.

Chapter 30

A soul that knows it is loved but does not itself love betrays its sediment: what is at the bottom comes up.

Beyond Good and Evil, Friedrich Nietzsche

It was just another beautiful Florida day. The sky was cobalt blue. A drizzly rain had started to remind everyone that the gods in the heavens were still in charge and that no days on this earth should be so perfect. To confuse us mortals even more, a rainbow was ornamenting the sky. Everything was so beautiful. Jacques knew this was going to be his day. His face was cleanly shaved. He was wearing a khaki Dockers pair of slacks with a navy-blue golf shirt. He got to Barnes and Noble relatively early that day. He had always wanted to have a cup of that gourmet mocha coffee at the bar inside the store. Right in the middle of the store, there was a coffee bar elegantly decorated with a 50's style. Well-varnished chairs with forest green seats were placed around four good-sized coffee tables. Surrounding the bar is a gold-trimmed glass fence. The whole atmosphere was very serene and relaxing. This would turn out to be the luckiest cup of coffee in his life. As he approached the counter, he could not help but notice an attractive woman who was sitting at a coffee table reading a gold-trimmed book. The whole room seemed filled with the presence of this woman. She was wearing a colorful silk blouse with a pair of Calvin Klein jeans. Her shoulder-length hair was neatly held together with a large brown clip. She hardly wore any makeup. Her palpebral fissures seemed perfectly cut. She looked as if she was left behind by the other goddesses, as they were being rushed back to the heavens. She was exquisitely beautiful. Jacques was moonstruck. He must have been staring at this woman for a good while until she took notice and commented:

"Must you always stare at a woman having an innocent morning cup of coffee?"

Jacques could not believe his ears. Jacques was melting with emotions, to the point of looking completely silly. There he was, dumbfounded, unable to utter a single word. If only he could find the right words, he would tell this lady that she was as pretty as the first day of spring. He would say that her very presence in this place made it like a studio fit for a queen. He would say that she seemed like she was in transit on her way back to the other goddesses, but Jacques could not find a single word. It took him what seemed to be like an eternity before he could respond:

"Oh not at all, I just could not help but admire your irresistible beauty."

She responded, "That is very kind of you, I'll take it as a compliment. Thank you."

As she hesitated, Jacques came to the rescue:

"Jacques! My name is Jacques Gaetan. What is yours?" Jacques was getting bolder.

The girl seemed to hesitate, then said, "My name is Florence Benoit."

"Do you come here often?" Jacques asked.

"Yes, I do. This has become one of my favorite places. It is so peaceful," Florence answered.

"Really? Me too. I must come here at least twice a week."

By that time, Jacques had come closer to the coffee table, and timidly asked Florence's permission to join her. She did not mind. The conversation continued in a very animated manner. Jacques learned that Florence was born to a Jamaican mother and a Haitian father and that Florence had been living in this country from the age of seven. Jacques estimated that Florence was probably in her early thirties but thought it would be improper to ask. They shared their common interest in English literature and poetry. Jacques felt as if she had known this woman for a long time. The conversation went so smoothly and so naturally. To Jacques, it was so refreshing to know that there were still people around that could hold an intelligent conversation without feeling threatened. There was no attempt by either one to impress or to outsmart the other. Just two individuals having a friendly chat. The vibes between them seemed to be positive ones. Florence did not seem a bit nervous about the apparent intrusion on what were her simple pleasures of life. The book she was reading turned out to be an anthology of poems by Maya Angelou. The book was opened with the poem "And Still I Rise," one of Jacques's favorites. Jacques sat at the table, extended his open hands, and placed them over the page. He closed his eyes and started to recite extracts from the famous poem:

"You may write me down in history.

With your bitter, twisted lies.

You may tread me in the very dirt
But still, like dust, I'll rise. . . . .
Leaving behind nights of terror and fear
I rise.
Bringing the gifts that my ancestors gave,
I am the dream and the hope of the slave.
I rise
I rise
I rise."

Florence was lost in wonder at Jacques' ability. He could not believe it himself. He knew that he had read those verses over and over, but he had no idea that he could retrieve them so spontaneously and deliver them in such dramatic fashion.

Jacques made it look so easy. Hopefully, Jacques was not going to be put to the test again any time soon.

Jacques was quite amazed at his own ease talking to this woman that he has just met. He saw this as an ominous sign of better days to come. Jacques' angels were still with him at every step of the way. He felt confident that this was going to be the beginning of a meaningful relationship. No, Jacques did not believe it was just coincidental that they both would just happen to be there on that beautiful morning. It had to be a message from above. Jacques, at the risk of sounding weird to the goddess sitting across the small coffee table, asked:

"Do you believe in karma?"

"Absolutely," Florence responded convincingly.

"Wow!" Jacques murmured in amazement. That was the only word that Jacques could find to describe the magic of the moments he was living.

Jacques wished that those moments would stay unchanged forever. Maybe they will. It was up to Jacques now to create new memories to compensate for the lost moments that were gone and would never come back. Having searched the past with a fine-tooth comb and having not succeeded in bringing any of it back, Jacques needed to create tomorrow's past today. Poets and philosophers alike have begged the time to stop so they could savor the present. Remember the famous cry of Alfred de

Vigny:

"O temps, suspends ton vol." This desperate call is still waiting to be heeded. Jacques needed to enjoy this very moment with all the senses that he possessed. Jacques was doing just that, but he decided against showing too much eagerness. Florence was probably thinking the same.

Jacques apologized for disturbing the girl's moment of peace:

"Your Highness," Jacques said jokingly, "I hope you won't find me guilty of disturbing your morning reading. Men sometimes do foolish things. I beg for mercy from the court."

Florence was catching on.

"What if I did find you guilty?" she asked, "what then would your sentence be?"

"Well, maybe I could get your telephone number so I could run all your errands including car wash, and oil change. I will even do windows."

Jacques could not believe what happened next. Florence tore up a page from a small telephone book and wrote:

"You are hereby sentenced to keep this phone number, 431-3939."

"Certainly, your highness," Jacques stated, visibly pleased with his sentence.

"I have to go now, it was a real pleasure talking to you," Florence said.

"Thank you," Jacques retorted, "the pleasure was really mine."

"Sure!" Florence answered.

They left each other, timidly waving goodbye. Jacques was aglow with joy. He could not get Nat King Cole's song out of his head:

"You stepped out of a dream. . .

Could there be eyes like yours?

Could there be lips like yours?

Could there be smiles like yours?" . . "

What is that ticklish feeling that Jacques had in his heart? It was like his heart was just given a jolt of electricity. What is that little fire that was burning inside of him? Is it love that he was feeling? If only Jacques could sing. Nothing could render better Jacques' feelings than the simple but beautiful words of the immortal Reggae master Bob Marley:

"I wanna love you, and treat you right

I wanna love you, every day and every night. . .

Is this love, is this love, is this love, and is this love that I'm feeling?

Is this love, is this love, is this love, and is this love that I am feeling?

I wanna know, I wanna know now

I gotta know, I gotta know now. . ."

Sing along and rejoice, you mortals. Take a real good bite. Love is here. Jacques felt as if he had ants in his pants. He was even walking funny. Behave yourself, Jacques, he said to himself, Florence might still be watching.

Enough to make Jacques want to jump and sing his joy and happiness. Yes! She is the one! She must be the one! How do you spell L O V E? Give me an F. Give me an L. Give me an O, an R, an E, and an N. The streets outside no longer looked the same. The sounds of traffic were like an orchestra to Jacques' ear. The world had just taken a surreal quality. It would never be the same. Jacques was thrilled with the anticipation of things to come. Was it just another one of Jacques' dreams? Not this time, he had the page from the telephone book to prove it. R. . ight here! He said pointing to his shirt pocket as if he was talking to an imaginary friend. Even more, Jacques could still smell the cologne that Florence was wearing Champs-Elysees by Guerlain. Most definitely French.

Chapter 31

The same night Jacques decided to build on his good fortune and called Florence. He was still apprehensive that the number might not have been, real and the whole thing was a joke. No, said Jacques. This is impossible. Why would she want to play games like this? Jacques caught himself. Come on Jacques, there is no room for this negative thinking. His anxiety came to a quick end. The voice on the phone was real, very real. Awesomely sweet and comforting.

"Hello," Jacques started, "I am reporting for my first assignment. How are you doing?"

Jacques felt very awkward. He could not get his cues from the expression on Florence's face and did not know how to proceed.

Florence answered with a question, "And what would that first assignment be, may I ask?"

"Well, maybe I could take you out to the movies. I hope you like movies," Jacques inquired. Jacques struck a chord there. Florence went on and on raving about the different genres of movies and why she does not like the ending of certain detective and mystery movies. By the time the conversation was over they had agreed that Jacques would pick her up at six o'clock the next day.

Jacques went to sleep that night, his heart was full of anticipation for the day to come. He was not tormented by nightmares, but he still had very little sleep. Just like a little boy who was promised a trip to the fair the next day, Jacques tossed and turned the whole night. He woke up bright and early and went on to plan his day. First, he would take a trip to the barber to get a haircut. He needed a fresher and neater look. He shaved himself very closely, put some lotion on his chin, and looked carefully at himself in the mirror. His exercise was paying off. His cheek no longer looked as round and full as they did, not too long ago. He has been sleeping well and was no longer preoccupied. His new classes at Florida International University would start next week. He has a few interviews scheduled in the area hospitals. He was ready to start he could start working again at least on a part-time basis. Jacques' plans were coming together beautifully. He opted for a casual and relaxed look. He did not want to scare the girl away. Jacques looked very sporty in his linen beige shirt well tucked into his pants. He took extra care of himself that evening, for he had a date with a queen. His appearance was impeccable. Finding Florence's address was not difficult at all. Her residence was in a new development in Miramar. Most of the houses were painted in soft peach pastel colors. The streets were relatively quiet. Here and there, father and son were washing the family car, or throwing balls. Jacques pulled into the driveway and went to the bell at the entrance door. He anxiously waited for a response. A teenage boy wearing Tommy Hilfiger baggy shirt answered the door.

Good evening," he said, "may I help you?"

"Good evening, is Florence here?"

He did not have to respond. There she was, coming down the small staircase dressed in a light-yellow dress. Her hair was gently pulled to one side and barely touched her shoulder. A yellow barrette matching her dress completed the outfit. The contour of her eyes was accentuated by a very discreet layer of coloring. Her lip's fullness was made more evident by a touch of low-tone lipstick. She walked towards him gracefully. The smell of her cologne filled the room. Elegantissima! Very elegant, were the only words that Jacques could think about. Jacques was gaga over such a display of grace and beauty.

"Hello," she said simply, "did you have trouble finding the place?"

"Not at all," Jacques said, "You look very nice, Florence."

"Thank you, you look quite handsome yourself," she quickly responded.

Jacques? Handsome. Jacques has never been told that he was handsome before.

She introduced the teenager.

"Jacques, this is Ronald my nephew from New York. Ronald this is Jacques."

"Hi Ronald," Jacques said.

"Are you ready?"

They went through the door as Ronald closed the door behind them. "See you later, Ronald."

"See you later," Ronald responded.

Jacques let Florence into the Maxima, opening the door for her. The car had been washed and vacuumed for the occasion. Jacques had an assortment of CDs including Fausto Pappeti, instrumental music, and love songs from Whitney Houston and Barry White. He was ready to please Florence's taste.

They decided to go to the Sawgrass Mills cinema complex where Evita was playing. What a choice, considering that the movie was about overcoming adversities, and the triumph of love over negativity. Evita had been raised over her own life circumstances to influence the destiny of a whole country at very a difficult time. They probably would have to watch the movie again to catch all the nuances. It was not because the movie was extremely complex but because the young couple was too busy chatting and learning about each other. Florence was a very analytical person who paid attention to every detail. Jacques learned that Florence was the youngest of three sisters. Her sisters lived in New York. Florence came down to attend college at the University of Miami. She fell in love with the yearlong tropical climate of South Florida and decided to stay. She was able to convince her parents to join her. They all lived in a large three-bedroom house in Miramar. Her parents often went away on trips to Port Antonio, Jamaica, where they are starting up a bed and breakfast business. She was a graduate of the University of Miami, where she received a degree in Veterinary Arts. Her other interests were in languages and foreign literature. She believed that men and women are equal and should be treated as such but does not see herself as a feminist. Florence and Jacques felt very comfortable with each other. As they were sitting in the theater sipping on Coke and munching on Raisinets, they came into proximity a few times. They looked at each other very intensely. Whoever said that eyes could not talk? Whoever said that lovers needed words to communicate? Their lips were searing. There were quite a few moments that night when no words were spoken and a whole lot was said. And then, as Evita was making her plea to her crowd, as the crowd was standing in attention eating every word out of Evita's lips, Florence leaned forward and kissed Jacques on the lips. The contact lasted only a few seconds. A jolt of electricity traveled through Jacques' body. It was very strange. His body was suddenly awakened. Jacques was alive. If only Jacques could describe it. Suffice it to say that it felt very good, exquisitely good. Jacques returned the favor. He gently kissed Florence on the lips while brushing against her neck with his fingers. Their tongues met. She held on to his for a while, and he held on to hers. They wanted each other very much. Magic in the air. Jacques and Florence were awakened from the dreamy moments by the last scene of the movie. The musical score went louder and louder. The credits started to race up the screen. The movie was over. They were saved from their burning desire.

On their way back, Jacques invited Florence for ice cream. The parlor was almost empty as the attendants were getting ready to close for the day.

“What flavor?” the girl asked.

Florence looked at Jacques, and after some hesitation said,

"Vanilla with a cherry on top."

Jacques played it safe.

“Same,” he said.

“Will it be a cup or a cone?”

“ A cup,” they both responded in unison.

The girl handed them their portion and said,

“It will be six dollars and forty-five cents.”

Jacques gave her the money and left the parlor following Florence's steps. As they got on the sidewalk. Jacques stopped for a moment and scooped the cherry from his cup and attempted to feed Florence with it. The cherry fell on the floor. They both busted laughing. They laughed and laughed to their heart's content. Jacques could not remember when he last had such a burst of spontaneous laughter. This scene could certainly have made it to the “America’s Funniest Videos” contest. This moment would go straight to the memory book. This woman was definitively sending positive vibrations in Jacques' direction. Maybe the feeling was mutual because there was a certain brightness on Florence's face. She was visibly pleased with the first evening out. So was Jacques. The drive back to Florence's residence was surprisingly silent. It was one of those evenings that both wished would never come to an end. With and without words, it seemed that everything had been said. What did the evening all mean, both Jacques and Florence were probably wondering. Maybe neither one of them wanted to say one word too many. Neither one of them wanted to break the charm of the moment. But the evening had to come to an end, Jacques realized as he made the final turn to Florence's residence. Florence broke the silence first:

"Jacques, I must thank you for a wonderful evening."

"Thank you, Florence, I had a very good time."

Jacques pulled into the driveway, went around to Florence's side, and opened the door. They stood there, looking at each other, suddenly short of words. The only language they could speak was the one only their hearts could read. Their eyes were very eloquent in these late moments of that memorable evening. As if to confirm and sealed the understanding, they kissed each other passionately.

"We had better go," Florence said.

"I think you're right; I think you're right," Jacques responded.

Chapter 32

Jacques had many dreams that night. They were all very sweet. He was visited by a beautiful princess. He was dressed like a prince himself, wearing a white tunic with a golden design around the square-shaped neck and the oversized sleeve. He was sitting by a fall in the middle of a garden with gigantic trees. Everything was so perfect and blissful. Jacques' good angels were very clearly sending him an omen, a very good one this time. What a difference a few months could make in his life. He needed to give thanks. The next morning, he pulled out his incense burner and his lamp. He lit up his lamp rogatoire and prayed as he was burning some incense to his gods. They were with him. Jacques just knew it and was never going to forget it. His gods will continue to guide him and show him the way. He had a few things to do the next morning. He wanted to express his hope to Florence about the relationship they were about to start. He went to the flower shop and ordered a dozen red roses. He included a card that contained the following words:

"I know I feel something inside that is very pure and awesomely beautiful. I do not claim that I know what it is. I just hope that you will help me discover it and make it grow every day. All I know is that you have stepped right into the middle of my life and suddenly everything seems full of sunshine. "

Signed, Jacques.

Jacques' first interview at Coral Gables Hospital was scheduled in a couple of weeks. In the meantime, he wanted to respond to an advertisement for a job as a part-time librarian. The interview with Mr. Ryan went very well. Jacques was promised a response within three days. He had to decide what kind of job would be more convenient since he wanted to concentrate on his college courses. The library job would keep him near the books and a nursing job would help him build his clinical experience. Nursing jobs, however, can be very demanding.

Jacques received a telephone call from Florence that evening. She sounded overjoyed almost on the verge of tears. She got home late that day but wanted to thank Jacques for the flowers. She acknowledged that her life was also different. She too, was hesitant to name whatever she was feeling. She could not deny that the indescribable feeling was making her heart go tick.

Let there be love!

Let there be joy and happiness!

Let's seize the day.

Carpe diem!

Let us invite all the nightingales to a concert.

Let them sing the most beautiful love songs from around the world. Love is a universal feeling, isn't it?

The next day, Jacques received a call from Mr. Ryan. The job at the library was his. He could start whenever he was ready. Jacques was well on his way to becoming a productive citizen again.

Chapter 33

The relationship between Florence and Jacques took off like a rocket. Pretty soon, they became inseparable. If you went around town, you would catch them riding the Metro Rail together, walking at the Bayside shopping mall, and holding hands. You might see them strolling down the aisles of the Historical Museum. They have been to auto shows and boat shows. They even went to the Copa Latina Soccer Cup finals together. They felt very proud when the Haitian soccer team won the championship for the third time in the Cup's short history. They have been to jazz festivals and arts and crafts exhibits. Jacques had even observed Florence taking care of her animals at the "Filou Animal Hospital." There, it was a different story. Florence seemed to be totally in her element. She seemed to be so passionate about her work. She was an animal lover and showed total dedication to the puppies placed under her care. Jacques had been in South Florida for many years now and never knew that the places where he has dropped loads of tourists time after time could be so magnificent. This time it was his turn to go around and enjoy it in style, as he was accompanied by a woman of tremendous grace and beauty. This time, Jacques was not alone.

Jacques and Florence had grown very fond of each other.

It had been over two months now since that meeting at the bookstore, but it seemed so far away. They had spent so much time together, although Jacques was now keeping a very busy schedule between his class at Florida International University and his new job. They felt ready now for more intimate commitment. They decided to go to Hawks Cay in Marathon, Florida for a long weekend. It was halfway between Miami and Key West. The decor was as close as one could get to the Caribbean. If not careful, one could easily miss the entrance to the resort which was obstructed by large vine trees. They made it to the complex in good time, as they decided to leave early to beat the Friday afternoon rush hour traffic. A long-twisted brick-covered road led to the main building of the hotel. The outside walls were painted with a very light pink pastel color with white borders. A porter greeted them at the door. He was dressed in a white uniform consisting of shorts, a Chinese-style shirt with gold buttons, and a pith helmet. Huge Monet-style paintings depicting nature scenes decorated the walls. The early evening light was reflecting softly on the guests at the registration desk. Exotic birds were roaming about the place paying little attention to the commotion in the busy lobby. It was not planned, but both Jacques and Florence were wearing white shorts and tops. They retrieved their plastic access card to their room and walked away. They went across a large terrace where a buffet was being set up for the evening event. An ice sculptor was putting the last touch to his masterpiece representing a mermaid. The theme for tonight's event is "A Stroll with the Gods in Eden." At the poolside, a Reggae band was interpreting one of Rita Marley's songs, "One Draw." The small group of tourists were experimenting with their latest steps. They were out of rhythm. They could not keep up with the beats. Nobody seemed to care. They were having a lot of fun.

The room was very clean. It did not seem to hold the smell of mildew so characteristic of hotel rooms. Everything was tidy, including the proverbial ice bucket, water pitcher, and glasses. The bed seemed comfortable. The large flowery covers were meticulously pulled on the king-size bed. Jacques inspected the bathroom. Everything seemed in order. Florence pulled the drapes and discovered a sliding door with a view of the marina where a farm for dolphins was maintained. To Florence, it was like paradise. She promised she would teach Jacques how to listen to the sounds transmitted by the dolphins at night. Florence suggested that they go to the bar for a Piña colada. Excellent idea, Jacques responded. They sat at the counter and waited for their drink. They toasted the future of their relationship. They left the bar and decided to take a walk on the beach. They tossed their shoes by a bench and raced each other to the water. Jacques was about to win the race when he fell, his mouth wide open, with sand all over his face. The couple could not stop laughing. Florence helped Jacques wipe the sand off his face. They walked a couple of hundred yards on the wet part of the beach, leaving their ephemeral footprints on the sand. The sound of the wave breaking on the beach was very soothing. Jacques and Florence could forget all their daily stress. Should things get bad in the future, Jacques and Florence could always count on their memory bank to fill the void. Jacques would not trade this moment for anything. The couple realized that they were alone on the beach. The night has descended upon the land. The incandescent lamps from the tall poles were shedding their light over the water that had suddenly gone very still. It seemed that the whole world was waiting for another moment of adoration. Distantly on the water, one could see the moving light of a cruise ship, carrying around a shipload of lovers who, like Florence and Jacques, were admiring the beauty of the world when one no longer feels alone. The young couple had not exchanged a word for a few minutes now. What words could describe the magnificence of the moment? What words could describe the communion that existed between Florence and Jacques and the elements of nature around them? No words could ever catch the essence of the moment. The night went on from discovery to discovery. The couple went back to the room and dressed more appropriately for a candlelight dinner. They feasted on red snapper and heart of palm and drank white Chablis. Jacques and Florence were pampered by the waiters and had an exquisite time. On that famous night, with the party outside still going on, with the mixtures of man-made sounds and the songs of the birds, it all happened. Florence and Jacques just succumbed to the magic of the moment. They went through a long series of gestures and motions. It was all very spontaneous. There was no pressure, no hesitation. Both lovers were committed to providing each other the most pleasure. They surrendered totally to each other. None of the inhibition or the prudery that usually characterizes such encounters was noticeable. Jacques and Florence were as exposed as they could ever be both figuratively and literally. In love, they were making a powerful statement about reclaimed innocence. In their nakedness, there acted naturally. There could never be any question about the sanctity of the act they were about to perform. Jacques gently caressed Florence's neck with his lips and followed the design of every muscle of her body. Florence manifested her pleasure by letting out some indescribable moaning sounds. Her body was on fire. Florence's nipples were erect. Jacques moved his head towards her breasts and took her nipples between his lips barely touching them. He moved his hands down her flanks and softly stimulated her inner thighs with his fingers like a virtuoso performing a difficult piece from Chopin. Florence had the most gorgeous mount of Venus that one will ever see. Florence was holding onto Jacques's legs, exploring every square inch with her lips. Jacques was growing bigger by the minute. Their touch was as light as a feather. They stroke each other for a while and then they locked into each other in an ultimate communion of body and soul. There was a perfect harmony of movements and sounds. The night had descended upon the resort. The seagulls had retired from the deserted beach. The candles had given up their last glimmer of light. Florence and Jacques were totally oblivious to their surroundings. Every single one of their senses was put to the test. Their intercourse reached orgasmic intensity several times that evening. It took all the creativity of an artist and a believer to render that masterpiece. But was it music? Was it painting? Was it sculpture? Was it poetry? It was all the art forms in one gigantic masterpiece, created as a testimony to the creator of all things, dedicated to Buddha, Jehovah, Mohammed, Erzili, and all of the gods. Jacques and Florence that night were graciously allowed to be one with nature, and the music continued throughout the night, changing from Calypso to Reggae. There was even some Salsa and Meringue. The tempo changed to the sexy voice of Whitney Houston. The vibrant and incredibly beautiful voice of Gloria Estefan joined the concert. Jacques and Florence expressed it all in perfect harmony. Jacques discovered that when guided by love, there were no doors that could not be opened, there were no obstacles that could not be surmounted.

Jacques found out that night that he had no demons left to vanquish. He was whole. Jacques had passed the ultimate test, the one that sooner or later a man had to face, the test of manhood, the test of virility. Jacques passed with flying colors. He could just imagine a certificate being printed in his name with the following words:

OYE! OYE!

LET IT BE KNOWN THAT, IN THE YEAR OF GOD TWO THOUSAND AND FIVE, JACQUES GAETAN. . . .

It was as if Jacques has just been re-born. He is a Homo Novus. The beauty of the world had been rediscovered. Congratulations, Jacques! The world is now yours to love, share and appreciate, along with your fellow human beings and everything else within it. Handle it with care! Once destroyed, it is gone forever! There is no second chance. As if to heed the warning, the young couple woke up the next morning at the applause of a small crowd watching a dolphin show, just across their room. They decided to join the audience. What a majestic sight. The morning sky was perfectly blue. The seawater was still, reverberating the rays of light from the sun. Everything seemed to attention. The dolphins were performing, and what a show it was! They could flip. They could sing and they could dance. Florence was ecstatic.

The romance between Jacques and Florence grew with every sunrise. They guided each other and leaned on each other's shoulders as they continued to read through the many signs around them. Together they could see beauty when no one could see it. They could hear the pain of their fellow men when no one else would dare listen. Together they could dare to demand that the suffering stop. Together they could suffer and accept that people can be different. Together they could hope that one day this world, this country would live up to its destiny.

They saw beauty in the smile of the mother who delivers her first child.

In the joy on the face of the toddler who rides his first bike,

They saw beauty everywhere!

They saw beauty in the pride that shines through the eyes of the father who watches his daughter receive her High School diploma.

They saw beauty everywhere!

Will you too, open your eyes and see...

"And if you wake up one morning, look up at the skies.

and see no rainbow,

do not panic my friends!

It is because God is back in his lab mixing up the colors.

And if you wake up one morning, look up at the skies

and see a long black streak,

still do not panic!

It is because that is the result that God has gotten!

So go ahead my friends, do not be afraid!

Mix up the colors of the rainbow.
And please tell me, tell the world what you have got!"

"Si tu te reveilles un beau matin, regardes le ciel
et ne vois pas l'arc-en-ciel
N'aie pas peur!
C'est parce que le Bon Dieu est retourne dans son laboratoire
Pour melanger les couleurs.
Si tu reveilles un beau matin, regardes le ciel
Et vois une longue bande noire
N'aie pas peur!
C'est parce que c'est le resultat que le Bon Dieu a obtenu.
Alors, vas-y mon ami, n'aie pas peur , melange les couleurs de l'arc-en-ciel
Et reviens me dire, et dire au monde entier, ce que tu as trouve! "

"Si ou leve gnou matin ou gade an le, ou pa we Lakansiel
Pinga ou pe
Ce paske Pe Letenel tounin nan laboratwa-l lal melanje koule-yo
Si ou leve gnou matin ou gade an le , ou we gnou bande tou nwa
Pinga ou pe
Ce paske se rezilta sa Pe Letenel trouve
Ki donk, lamitie, pinga ou pe melanje koule lakansiel yo
Epi tounen vi-n di-m, vi-n di tout moun ki sa ou trouve!."

"Si despiertas una manana, miras al cielo
Y no ves el arco iris
No tenga miedo amigo!
Es porque Dios esta en el laboratorio mezclando los colores.
Y si despiertas una manana, miras al cielo
Y ves una linea larga y negra
De todas maneras no tenga miedo,
Es porque es el resultado que Dios ha obtenido!
De manera que sigan, adelante amigo mio
No tenga miedo
Mescla los colores del arco iris
Y por favor dime, y dile al mundo lo que ha obtenido!

Und wenn lhr eines Morgens aufwacht, im dem Himme! schaut un keinen Regenbogen seht, habt keine Angst meine Freunde! Es is so, weil Gott Zureuck in seinem Labor die Farben neu mischt.
Und wenn lhr eines Morgens aufwacht, in dem Himme! Schaut und einen langen schwarzen Streifen seht, habt trotzdem keine Angst!
Weil es das ist, das Gott erreicht hat!
Matcht weiter meine Freunde, habt keine Angst!
Mischt die Regenbogenfarben und sagt mir bitte und der Werlt, was herausgekommen ist!

Chapter 34

Eighteen months later...

Jacques is a couple of weeks away from graduating. He has managed to keep a very hectic schedule. He has a lot of fun studying a subject related to the medical field, where his heart is. Despite his part-time job at the library, he has maintained a 3.8 average in his courses. He will receive a degree as a registered nurse. He has been promised a job in a major South Florida hospital. Florence is still enjoying her work at Filou Animal Hospital. The couple has developed a relationship based on mutual respect, generosity, and love.

Jacques has taken a trip to New York to officially introduce Florence to Madam Maurice. They seem to have hit it off right from the start. One Friday evening, Jacques seemed particularly excited. The couple seemed to have some difficulty deciding between a play at the Broward Performing Arts and a cruise around Ft. Lauderdale. Jacques insisted on the cruise. Something was afoot.

The couple boarded a water taxi at the Double Tree Hotel in Sunrise. They went up and down the intercostal admiring the beauty of the Atlantic Ocean, watched the rich and famous in their cigarette sport boats, and appeared aghast at the majesty of the mansions with their well-manicured landscape. They held hands and exchanged furtive kisses. The moment was perfect. Jacques nervously pulled a little box out of his pocket. He then went on one knee, placed one hand on his heart, and looked Florence straight in the eyes. He pulled a diamond ring out of the box, and offered it to Florence while saying, "Florence, will you marry me?"

On the deck of the ship, for a short instant, it was complete silence. The onlookers were caught by surprise, and so was Florence. The passengers started to chant, "Say yes, say yes!." The crowd was anxiously waiting for a response from a completely shocked Florence. The words came crystal clear from her.

"Of course, Jacques, I will marry you. I thought you would never ask! Now get off the floor, you silly man!"

Jacques jumped on his feet. The couple embraced and kissed. The small audience broke into applause. And as if to bless the covenant, it started to drizzle. Once again, the gods had spoken.

Madam Maurice was thrilled at the news. Likewise, Jacques had met Mr. And Mrs. Benoit and in the traditional chivalrous manner, asked for their blessings to marry their daughter. His request was granted. The wedding is being planned for next spring. The official engagement took place a couple of weeks ago...

The love that sealed Florence and Jacques' destiny has

grown even stronger. There is so much affinity between them.

They have become lovers, friends, and soul mates. They have traveled around the country. They have discovered the beauty of their new country. They have revisited both Jamaica and Haiti. They have discovered the common threads and nuances between the different Caribbean islands. They have vowed to continue to affirm the uniqueness of their culture while promoting universal understanding among everyone. They envisioned the world as a giant iridescent quilt where every piece can contribute to the beauty of the whole...

AFTERWORD

And so, the story was told. The story of Jacques Gaetan, the Haitian American who migrated to America. In the beginning, we find our hero completely deracinate (uprooted). He is tormented by his phantasms, his unfulfilled dreams, and his cultural heritage left behind. Jacques was like an unfinished art piece. He was missing that final touch by the artist. He needed that masterful stroke of the brush, "ce coup de pinceau magique" that would turn a common work into a masterpiece. Voila!...

Now, I would like you to take a mental trip with me.

Close your eyes! Relax! Imagine yourself sitting on your keyboard in front of a computer screen. You are now the author.

Let us rewrite the story!

Our hero is Alachua, an American-Indian who left his reservation and finds himself thrust into an urban civilization that often ignores the power of man when he remains a respectful and mindful partner of the forces of nature…

Keep your eyes closed!

Let us rewrite the story!

Our hero this time is Matthew, an Irish-American who was the victim of much derision in this country as he was redefining himself in the earlier years of American History…

Let us rewrite the story!

Our hero is Felipe Gonzalez, a Mexican-American, a Chicano, who left behind his ancient, multifaceted, and vibrant Hispanic heritage to embrace a new way of life in America. . .

Let us rewrite the story!

Our hero is Aixiang Hashimoto, a Japanese-American who. . .

Let us rewrite the story about the Italian-American, the Jewish-American, the Arab-American, the Gays and Lesbians, the non-binary and transgender rejected and outcast by their own elected officials, the female executives, the Muslims, and every ethnic and cultural group of this nation, of this globe...

As you can see, Dear Reader/writer, the story is more than just about Jacques the Haitian- American. It is about every American. It is an American story. It is a human story. It happens every day in America and around the world. It occurred in the nation built by Nelson Mandela and the people of South Africa. It is taking place today in Bosnia and the new European Union......

Open your eyes now! Admire the beauty of this blessed planet and all of its people. . .

GLOSSARY

Assoto - Large drum, part of a set of three sacred drums.

Ayida Wedo - Lwa is often represented by the rainbow.

Ayibobo! - War cry or salutation used often by the Voodoo priest to arouse the audience during ceremonies.

Ayizan - lwa of the marketplace

Ason - A well-decorated sacred rattle used in rituals by the houngan or the mambo to lead the ceremony.

"Bon die Bon" - (Haitian Proverb) - The Lord is great. (He will provide).

Baron Samdi - lwa, guardian of the cemetery, is usually represented by a cross.

Calabash - A gourde, used to carry beverages.

Cha Cha Cha - old dance of the mid-century. Has disappeared over the years. Damballa Wedo: Lwa or spirit represented by the serpent, the partner of Aida

Erzili Freda - Lwa or spirit of love

Fwet cash - Long whip from slavery time. Used now to lead the cattle and to lead zombies and in Voodoo ceremonies. It is usually made of sisal.

"Gade foute!" or "Gade foute tone": Watch it! Swearing exclamation, expressing one's anger.

Gede - The Lwa of the dead

Grimele:Light skin mulatto girl

Hougan: Voodoo priest

Hounsi: Woman or transvestite member of the Hougan entourage. They serve as ushers during the ritual.

Hounfor: Place where the ceremony takes place (see also peristyle)

Hougenikon: Woman leading the chorus.

Ibo Lele: Lwa or spirit represented with a seven-mouthed pot.

Laplace: An assistant to the Hougan. He plays the role of master of ceremony.

Legba: (Papa Legba), the spirit of the gates and crossroads.

Lwa: Spirit or god.

Manje Marasa: Food offerings to Lwa marassa.

Marasa: Sacred twins.

"Madi gra m' pa pe-ou, se moun ou ye" (Haitian proverb): Masked man, I am not scared, you are human (like me). Taunting words by children during mardi gras when confronted with scary masked characters.

Mambo: Voodoo priestess.

Manje Lwa: Food offerings to the spirit or Lwa.

Matinet: Old homemade whip, consisting of a stick with a few lashes attached to it. It is still used for corporeal punishment.

Ogoun: Spirit of fire.

"Oue pa oue anteman pou kat tre" (Haitian Proverb): "There is no getting around it, the funeral is set for 4 o'clock". The expression conveys a sense of urgency and inevitability.

Petro: One of two groups of lwas. This group includes the more violent, tormenting. The lwas in this group include Legba, Erzili, Baron Samedi, and Guede.

Peristyle: Voodoo temple.

Poto mitan: The sacred center pole of the temple. Lwas are supposed to arrive through it during the ceremony.

"Pwen fe pa, mo red":(Haitian proverb) There shall be no mercy, sudden death! (Take no prisoners!). The expression is also used as game rules when playing marble or hopscotch.

Rada: One of two groups of lwas. The lwas in this group are more of the benevolent, gentler, kinder types. They include Damballah Wedo, Aida wed, Ogoun, and Loco Atison.

Shanpwel: Terms used to refer to secret societies.

Seconde: The second largest of three sacred drums of the Voodoo ritual.

Tafia: Over proofed alcohol consumed heavily among farmers while working in the fields. Same as Clairin.

Tablet Lakol: Very sticky candy made out of sugar cane syrup, ginger, cinnamon, and other spices.

Veve: Symbolic drawing representing the attributes of a spirit or god. It is traced on the ground with flour and cornmeal to welcome the spirit.

Chwal: "horse" An individual designated as a medium by the lwa to manifest itself. Gro Bon Zanj: One of two kinds of angels who are supposed to protect the subject.

Pie Mapou: The sacred tree of the Voodoo religion. (Ceiba pentandra of the botanical family Bombacaceae).

Ti Bon Zanj: Part of the spirit that leaves the body after death. The hougan

Pwin: Same as Wanga

"Tro presse pa Fe job Louvri" (Haitian Proverb): Rushing will not make dawn come any sooner.

Kata: The third and smallest of the set of three sacred drums used in Voodoo.

Zotolan: Meadowlarks, small singing birds.

BIBLIOGRAPHY

Angelou, Maya: And Still I Rise.

Antoine, L.B. et al.: Exclusion of Blood Doners by Country of Origin and Discrimination Against Black Foreigners in the USA, AIDS, 1990, Vol 4 No. 7.

Aristotle, On Dreams, Library of the Future, World Library Inc. 1990-1994.

Bryant, William Cullen, The African Chief, Library of the Future, World Library, Inc. 1990-1994.

Budge, E.A. Wallis, Osiris & The Egyptian Resurrection, Dover Publications Inc.

Corneille, Pierre.: Le Cid, Anchor Book of French Quotations, Anchor Books Doubleday

Cosentino, Donald J., Sacred Arts of Haitian Vodou, 1995 Regents of the University of California.

Davis, Wade, The Serpent and the Rainbow, Warner Books, 1987.

Depestre, Rene, Hadriana dans tous mes reves, Editions Gallimard,1988.

Du Bellay, Joachim: Id., XXXI, Anchor Book of French Quotations, English Translations by Norbert Guterman, Anchor Books, Double Day, 1963.

Goethe, Johann Wolfgan Von, Faust, Library of the Future, World Library, Inc.

Fanion Franz: Black Skin, White Masks, Grove Press, Inc. 1982.

Flack, Roberta: Killing Me Softly.

Homer, Odyssey, Library of the Future, World Library, Inc. 1990-1994.

Hudson, Paul, Mastering Witchcraft, Perigee Books, 1970.

Kipling, Rudyard, If: One Hundred and One Famous Poems, Barnes and Nobles.

La Fontaine Jean De: Fables, Maxi-Poche Classiques Francais.

Leek, Sybil, The complete Frt of Witchcraft, Penguin Books, 1971.

Lucretius, On the Nature of the Universe, Frederick Ungar Publishing Co, Inc. 1972.

Madhere, Serge, Piti Piti Plen Kay, KAPAB, Inc., 1987.

Marley, Bob, Redemption Song.

Marley, Bob, Is this love?

Nat King Cole, You Stepped Into My Dreams.

Nietzsche, Friedrich, Beyond Good and Evil, Vintage Books, 1966.

Paracelsus, Paragnum.

Poe, Edgar Allan, A Dream, Library of the Future, World Library, Inc.! 990-1994.

Schroeder, Willy, A Rosicruscian Notebook, Samuel Weiser, Inc., 1992.

Tunneshende, Merilyn: Medicine Dream, Hampton Roads Publishing Co, Inc., 1996.

Van Dyke, Henry, America for Me: One Hundred and One Famous Poems, Barnes and Nobles, 1993.

Final Judgement

That day will creep on me, I know,
Drawing futile and wimpy protests from loved ones.
Alas! There shall be no 2-minute warning,
Nor shall there be any trumpet-blowing angels.
Ready or not, I shall proceed through the giant gate of light
And face your solemn and inevitable question:
How do you plea?
In all my nakedness, having shed my cloak of false pretense
For the first time ever, I shall remain speechless.
No longer will I find comfort in fine repartee;
Words will have lost all their earthly meanings.
No debate. No double meaning. No double entendre.
How do you plea?
Oh yes! Rebellious and defiant I have not ceased to be:
I have demanded equality; I was offered emancipation.

I have wished for soulmates, I had to accept companions.
I have pursued happiness; I have met the pain of solitude.
I have yearned for knowledge; I have found more mysteries.
I have searched for power, fame, and fortune; they have all escaped me.

How do you plea?

Here I am, at the end of my sojourn,

My quest still unfinished,

My thirst still unquenched...

How do you plea?

How do you plea?

How do you plea?

Guilty, my Lord...

Guilty of wanting to be in your image...

Printed in the USA
CPSIA information can be obtained
at www.ICGtesting.com
LVHW090539220624
783727LV00039B/157

9 781088 214336